SEARCH
FOR THE
BURIED
BOMBER

SEARCH
FOR THE
BURIED
BOMBER

Dark Prospects Series Volume 1

XU LEI

Translated by Gabriel Ascher

amazon crossing

Text copyright © 2011 by Xu Lei.
English translation copyright © 2011 by Beijing Guomi Digital Technology Co., Ltd.

Search for the Buried Bomber was first published in 2010 by Beijing Guomi Digital Technology Co., Ltd. as 大漠苍狼:绝地勘探. Translated from Chinese by Gabriel Ascher. Edited by Gabriel Ascher, Michael Armstrong, and Verbena C.W. Published in English by AmazonCrossing in 2013.

Published by AmazonCrossing
PO Box 400818
Las Vegas, NV 89140

ISBN-13: 9781611097948
ISBN-10: 1611097940

This book is dedicated to the older generation of prospectors, who toiled mightily and endured great hardships in the vast mountains of the motherland.

The following is a work of fiction. Any resemblance to persons living or dead is entirely coincidental.

PREFACE

I had to think this story through for a long time before writing it. So much of what happened remains a mystery, even to me. Other parts were simply absurd. They failed to conform even to our most fundamental ideas of the world at that time. Perhaps such things should not be passed on, I thought, but rather left buried and forgotten for all eternity.

Still, I have decided to record my story. To not do so, I realized, would be a terrible pity and a great disservice, not only to those who lived through the events with me, but also to the very history of our nation itself.

I am a retired geological prospector formerly attached to the Geological Prospecting Unit of the People's Liberation Army. In the red madness of those years, we were blessed to escape the storm of the Cultural Revolution. Instead, it was our fate to wander the great mountains and rivers of China in search of untold riches hidden deep beneath the earth's surface. For two decades we journeyed across China's no-man's-land, alternately facing extreme suffering and numbing boredom. And then the things we encountered...the nameless terrors, things far beyond the scope of the imagination. Such things were never supposed to be real. Not one word about them will ever be seen in the official records. Any trace of their existence has been sealed away forever. Some of what follows comes from my personal experiences, and some of it was told to me by my older comrades. We swore to never reveal what we saw to the wider world. I will not break that oath. So remember, what follows is merely fiction and nothing more.

CHAPTER 1

The 723 Project

I was a prospector for twenty years. It was dangerous work, but more perilous than any raging rapid was the indescribable boredom. During one long stretch in my early years, I looked out upon the endless wilderness that surrounded us and felt a suffocating tightness descend upon me. To know that one must remain in such a place for many more years…only one who has experienced it could understand that sort of torment. But that feeling vanished completely after what happened in 1962. I learned then that hidden deep within those dreary mountains were terrifying mysteries. I finally understood that the fearful stories the older prospectors told about the mountains were more than just idle talk.

Most older prospectors will have already heard of the 1962 incident. As for you younger readers, if your mother or father was a prospector, ask them. Back then there was a well-known prospecting initiative called the Inner Mongolia 723 Project—"23" being the assigned number for coal-focused prospecting work in the mountains of Inner Mongolia that year. Three large groups of prospectors entered the primeval Inner Mongolian forests in quick succession, prospecting the area in small blocks. Then, only two

1

months after it began, the 723 Project suddenly ended. The project headquarters began quickly pulling technical personnel from other prospecting teams. These specialists were subjected to rounds of thorough questioning, made to fill out endless forms, and had their personal records carefully scrutinized. Not one of them was ever told where the information was being sent.

At last, a large group of prospecting specialists was selected to join the new 723 Project. The 1962 incident was causing a great deal of excitement. Rumors flew back and forth about the incredible thing the 723 Project was said to have discovered. But despite all the stories, no one really knew for sure what had been dug up. For those not directly involved, this is generally where the story ends. The Cultural Revolution began, and in those dark times no one paid any more attention to the mystery of the 723 Project. After being escorted by military trucks into the mountains, those specialists were quickly forgotten.

I was among the forgotten. There were twenty-four of us— selected and, by military order, put on trains to either Jiamusi or Qiqihar. There we were packed into military vehicles, which rocked and bounced down the long road from Heilongjiang to Inner Mongolia. We began our journey on paved roads and highways, but the farther we drove, the more hazardous the terrain became. By the last few days, we were driving along steeply winding mountain passes far from any sort of civilization. I didn't have the slightest idea what was going on, but listening to my fellow passengers, I could tell that whatever had taken place within those mountains was far from ordinary.

At the time, we all guessed it had to be something industry related. Most of us thought it was a large oil field. Some of the older guys who'd been part of the huge Daqing oil-field exploration spoke vividly of its discovery. It had been a similar situation, they said: After Daqing was first located, a select group of experts from all across China was transferred to the area. It was only after several months of discussion and verification that the oil field's existence was confirmed. We couldn't help but feel a sense of pride upon hearing this. After all, we'd been chosen.

When we arrived at the lower base, we suddenly realized things weren't so simple. The first thing we saw was an unbroken line of army tents, large and small, stretched out along the basin, like a chain of grave mounds running infinitely into the horizon. It looked nothing like the base of an engineering brigade, but rather like the field station of an army preparing for battle. We stared dumbfounded at the bustling camp and all the engineering corpsmen running back and forth. For a moment we thought our leaders had simply gone mad and were preparing to attack the Soviet Union. We soon discovered, though, they weren't all troop tents. Most were filled with supplies. A few veterans went off to take a peek and came back raving that the tents were bursting with Soviet equipment.

In those days, our prospecting equipment was terribly out-of-date, and our methods had changed little since the time of liberation. Our country had only a small amount of so-called modern equipment, most of it bought from the Soviet Union at extremely high prices. As on-the-ground specialists, we'd never had the opportunity to see gear like this. The problem was, this Soviet equipment was used only for deep excavation—at a range of three thousand to forty-five hundred feet underground. Until then no one in China had mined to a depth of more than about fifteen hundred feet. Our country simply lacked the strength and ability to exploit those deep deposits. Even if we had wanted to, it would still have taken five to seven years to set up the proper infrastructure before the mine would be operational. China needed resources to grow, but as the saying goes, distant water cannot quench present thirst. It was the government's policy to keep the discovery of deep deposits a secret, saving them for the next generation to use, rather than fruitlessly attempting to extract them. So to find this seemingly useless equipment here was puzzling. Our hearts were troubled by a strange unease.

Nothing would be made clear that night. We new arrivals were assigned sleeping quarters, three men to a tent. Nighttime on the mountain was deadly cold. There was a stove inside the tent, but it was impossible to sleep. Even if you managed to doze off, the attendant would come to add wood, the wind would rush in, and the cold immediately awoke anyone still sleeping. There was nothing to do but sit up and wait for the light of dawn to break across the sky.

There were two other guys in my tent. One was older. He was born in the late twenties, in Inner Mongolia, and seemed to be rather well known. Everyone called him "Old Cat," but his real name was Mao Wuyue. I told him it was a good name because he had the same surname as Chairman Mao. The other guy was a sturdy Mongolian from Heilongjiang named Wang Sichuan. He was about my age and dark as coal. Everyone just called him "Bear." Old Cat never said much. Bear and I would be chatting away while he just sat there puffing on a cigarette and chuckling at us. Who knew what he was thinking about?

Bear was your typical northerner, jovial and outgoing. We soon became as close as brothers. He told me his grandfather's generation had intermarried with Han Chinese, and the whole family had moved to inner Shanhaiguan to become horse traders during the great westward migration. When the War of Resistance against the Japanese broke out, his father joined the logistical squadron of the Northern Chinese field army, serving as a horse trainer for Luo Ruiqing. After liberation, his father moved back to his hometown in Heilongjiang province and became the manager of a coal mine.

It was because of his father that Wang Sichuan became a prospector, though it wasn't what he set out to do. When Wang Sichuan was young, China's key industries were in dire need of resources, making coal a valuable commodity and coal mining an occupation of great importance. Wang Sichuan's father spent the second half of his life buried deep within the coal mines, emerging only occasionally to return home. It was all he thought about, all he spoke about. Even when he talked in his sleep, he talked about coal. Wang Sichuan's mother would rail against this obsession, and his parents got into horrible fights, so from an early age Wang Sichuan hated coal. When he grew up, his father wanted him to enter the coal industry. Wang Sichuan firmly refused. His dream was to be a driver in the military, but he lacked the connections. In the end, after living at home for half a year with no job or source of income, he was forced to compromise. He would work for his father so long as his responsibilities had as little to do with coal as possible. That's how he became a prospector. To his surprise, he found he had a talent for the work and was soon able to attend university thanks to a pro-minority university admissions policy.

Hearing Wang Sichuan's hatred of coal, I had to laugh. What he said was true. Even though our work was the foundation of the industry, we rarely came into contact with any actual coal mines. Probably no other mining-related job had so little—physically, at least—to do with the mines as ours.

After he'd finished talking about his life and family, Wang Sichuan asked me about my own. In those days, my family's class was nothing to be proud of, so I just told him we were common farmers and left it at that.

Actually, my grandfather's generation really could be considered farmers. My ancestors were poor peasants from Hongdong in Shanxi province. People say that, for a short period of time, my grandfather was a bandit and amassed a small amount of property.

Because of these holdings, he was reported during the land-reform movement and labeled a counterrevolutionary rich peasant. But my grandfather was stubborn. He took my grandmother, father, and uncle and fled to the South. There, my grandfather made his two sons take a Buddhist monk for a second uncle. Because this monk was considered a poor peasant, my father and uncle were now also ranked as poor peasants. But even though I was considered a poor peasant, my grandfather remained a counterrevolutionary, and that could be dangerous.

Wang Sichuan and I talked about what we thought was going on here, and about the local customs and our hometowns. Wang Sichuan was a northerner and I was a southerner. He was ethnically Mongolian and I was Han Chinese. There were an endless number of things for us to talk about. Both of us had endured our share of hardships, and so a single cold, sleepless night was no great ordeal.

That morning, brigade headquarters dispatched someone to give us a tour of the camp. I think his name was Rong Aiguo. He looked about thirty or forty, but with prospectors it's always difficult to tell someone's true age. The harsh elements take a toll on one's features. And there was something not quite right about this man. Though he escorted us all around the camp, he seemed to be merely going through the motions. He would answer no questions and remained silent whenever one was raised. He told us, for example, that the 723 Project was actually initiated three years ago, that work hadn't started until this year due to inadequate personnel, but he never said anything about what work was being done here. Everything that left his mouth was mundane day-to-day information like "The canteen is located over here," or "This is the procedure for going to the bathroom."

A month passed with no developments whatsoever. We continued to idle away our time at base camp, doing nothing, knowing nothing. No one seemed to be paying any attention to us. After a while, some of the veterans were unable to stand the boredom. They goaded some workers into tracking down Rong Aiguo—several times, in fact—but he always had one excuse or another to avoid us. Slowly, an awareness of the strangeness of our situation crept over us. A contagious anxiety spread throughout the group. A few even began to suspect we'd all been found guilty of some terrible offense and were soon to be executed. Public executions were all too common in those days. I could feel my heart pound in my chest as I listened to these rumors.

It was already fall in Inner Mongolia, and the temperature was dropping fast. As soon as we stepped outside, chill gusts penetrated our bones. We southerners found it particularly hard, but it was tough for everyone. Many began to suffer from nosebleeds. I remember us passing a whole month barely ever leaving the warmth of our stovetop kang beds: chatting, nibbling on steamed corn bread, and using raggedy old socks to wipe the blood from our nostrils.

Then, early one Wednesday morning, semiconscious, we were once again stuffed into a truck and, along with two other vehicles packed full of engineering corpsmen, driven farther into the mountains. By now, the mix of excitement and uncertainty that I had felt at the start of this assignment had changed to full-on fear. Through a gap in the tarp that covered our People's Liberation Army truck, I stared out at the cliffside plank road we seemed to be driving toward. Beyond, the expanse of mountains and ancient forest extended unbroken into the distance. I looked at the faces of the engineering corpsmen sitting around me. They were expressionless. The atmosphere within the truck had turned deadly serious. None of us spoke. We simply braced ourselves against the vehicle's interior as it rocked and jolted along, silently awaiting the end of our journey.

CHAPTER 2

Arrival

We wound our way along the saddle ridges twisting through the chain of mountains. In many places the path was just a small gap between trees. The tracks we followed had been built with planks cut from the trees around us. The difference between such temporary measures and real roads, you could feel it in the rattling of your bones. Hours of twisting roads and constant jolts slowly shocked us senseless.

As we drove along, we each tried to figure out where we were. We'd been told the 723 Project was in the Greater Khingan range, but the area we were passing through bore little resemblance to it. Some of my fellow passengers said that though the deep forest here was similar to the Greater Khingan, the terrain and topography were entirely different. Plus, the Greater Khingan would have been even more unbearably cold this time of year. They figured we'd entered the Langshan ("Wolf Mountain") range instead, and that we were being driven directly into the depths of the forest.

These, of course, were only guesses. We really had no idea where we were. Judging from the size of the mountain range around us, Old Cat told me later, he'd thought we might have already crossed the Chinese-Mongolian border and were now in Outer Mongolia.

The road went on forever. The saddle ridge coiled itself back and forth through the range. As our driver threaded his way along the twisting mountain passes, we soon lost all sense of direction. We could only resign ourselves to going wherever it was we were being taken. We drove along at a terribly slow pace, and the truck broke down frequently. Our tires kept sinking into the black morass of fallen leaves that littered the path. I can't remember how many times I was awoken to get out and help push. By the time we finally reached our destination, four days and five nights had passed.

I remember our arrival as if it were yesterday. A sweeping valley appeared before our exhausted eyes. Amid the thick brush, we could see rusted chain-link fencing crawling with green vines. Looking closely, we could just make out the faint trace of Japanese characters written on the wooden fence posts. Inner Mongolia had been part of Manchukuo, a puppet regime the Japanese had established in the Northeast. They had carried out all kinds of secret activities throughout the region. While prospecting, we would often come across hidden Japanese bunkers built into the mountains. Most had been doused in gasoline and set alight when the Japanese withdrew, but some still contained strange installations. I remember once finding a three-story building in which each story was only half the height of an average human. There were no stairs and you had to climb a chain to reach the next floor. To this day I still have no idea what that building could possibly have been used for.

After we drove past the fence and the trees that stood behind it, there appeared to us a number of simple wooden cabins, all of them in advanced states of disrepair. Long, tendriled vines climbed the walls. The roofs seemed to have collapsed beneath the weight of fallen leaves. They looked to have been abandoned for thirty to forty years. Several PLA trucks were parked alongside the cabins, and more than ten military tents had been set up. Seeing our truck arrive, a number of engineering corpsmen hurried over to help us unload our belongings.

Rong Aiguo was here as well, but he didn't come greet us. He just stood at a distance and watched, his expression serious as ever. I later realized this was the last time I ever saw the man. I don't even know whether Rong Aiguo was his real name. After the project was over, I ran into most of the men who served beside me at 723, but I never saw Rong Aiguo again or heard even a single mention of his name. I asked many veteran officers—men with vast numbers of contacts—as well as the numerous high-ranking military commissars with whom I sometimes worked. None of them had ever heard of a Rong Aiguo. I have to believe that whatever Rong Aiguo's true identity was, it was something remarkable. He wasn't just some common official within the engineering corps. Of course, all this was after the fact and has nothing to do with the events that were about to unfold.

After exiting the truck, we were led to our rooms in the broken-down log cabins and helped to settle in. These had previously housed Japanese soldiers, and the furniture they'd used was still there, all of it neatly arranged but ruined to such a degree that the wood flaked off like butter when rubbed between one's fingers. The rooms had been quickly straightened up for our arrival and lime powder sprinkled about to kill any insects, but one shake of the bed's wooden baseboard and a whole pile of unidentifiable dead insects came pouring out. The baseboard itself was soaking wet. There was no way to sleep on it. The only thing to do was unroll our sleeping bags and sleep on the floor. I detested those cabins. The atmosphere inside them gave me a strange, uncomfortable feeling. People from my generation are all similar in this respect: as soon as we enter a place somehow connected to Japan, a heavy, difficult-to-express feeling comes over us. Still, I had no choice but to stay there.

After we finished unpacking, a young private took us to get something to eat. Some of the other guys and I stuck by Old Cat. Of all of us, he seemed the most at home. I'd watched him when we first rolled in. As soon as he saw all the tents already laid out, he began to smirk, as if he knew what was about to happen. There was a certain gravity to Old Cat, and you could tell he had a handle on things. I breathed easier at his side.

It was a quiet afternoon. As night fell the twenty or so of us were led to a large tent. A curtain had been drawn at the front of the room and a projector set up at the back. The man conducting the meeting was a colonel. I felt that I'd seen him before, but couldn't remember where or when. He began by very formally welcoming us to the 723 Project and apologizing for the inconvenience we had suffered due to its secrecy. Of course, his face didn't betray a hint of regret, and as he spoke he wasted few words.

"Today's meeting will contain national secrets of the highest order," he said, "and so I must request that you all raise your right hands and swear that, for the rest of your lives, you will never divulge what you are about to learn, not to your wives, your parents, your fellow soldiers, or your children."

We were all accustomed to taking oaths. Our work as prospectors often involved national secrets. We were frequently required to swear that we would keep our work confidential before beginning a project. In those days, taking an oath was a serious thing, seen as representing our revolutionary sentiments. These days taking an oath is about as meaningful as having lunch.

At the time, national secrets were divided into three levels: confidential, secret, and top secret. For the most part, prospecting projects—like the Daqing oil field, for example—were considered secret, even though photographs of them were still sometimes published in newspapers. None of us had ever worked on a top-secret-level project before. We really had no idea what sort of extraordinary information we were about to be privy to, nor could we have ever imagined.

A number of us glanced around the room from one face to another. We'd been held in suspense for such a long time. I admit having been a little excited. Of course, there were many who remained unimpressed. It was common in those days to make a big hubbub about insignificant events. We'd often be told with great seriousness that we were about to be informed of an issue of extreme national secrecy, and it would turn out to be some ridiculous trifle—the recent whereabouts and mundane behavior of some Party leader, for example.

Someone later explained national secrets to me in this way: if a secret involves the livelihood of the people, it's confidential; if it involves the economy or military affairs, it's secret; and if it involves Party leaders or some impossible-to-explain subversion of the current worldview, only then is it considered top secret.

Of course, in all plans there exist a few snags. As I watched Old Cat swear himself to secrecy, I saw him use his other hand to draw an X on his thigh, meaning the oath wouldn't count. This was a pretty grade-school maneuver, but I could understand being fed up with the absurdity of it all. I mean, the older generations of my family had been involved in some illicit dealings, activities much worse than violating an oath, and none of it had seemed to leave the least sort of negative impression on my father's character. Besides, most people probably wouldn't believe me anyway.

As the oath ended, each of us was filled with his own thoughts. Then the colonel extinguished the lantern and someone at the back of the room started the projector. As it began running, I realized how ignorant I really was—this would be no slide show. That little machine was a film projector. We'd only watched movies on huge screens with correspondingly large projectors. We were all very curious about this miniature version. The colonel, however, gestured sternly for us to stop jabbering.

Ten minutes into the film, I felt my whole body stiffen. I understood that the severity with which we had been instructed to conceal this information was far from just talk. The movie we were being shown was one whose contents should absolutely never be revealed—a "Zero Film."

CHAPTER 3

The Zero Film

Zero Film was a code name born in the winter of 1959 at the Harbin Film Studio. They were producing a movie documenting the early exploration of the Daqing oil field: its location, development, the infrastructure and manpower assembled for the project. The film was shown only to the highest echelon of Chinese Communist Party Central Committee members. From then on, the term Zero Film came to denote a movie that could be shown only to the top brass. No one knows what happened to all the Zero Films. An old prospector once told me the films were most likely destroyed. Just one more of the countless incomprehensible acts committed during the Cultural Revolution.

The clip we watched appeared to be a portion of a longer movie. The events unfolded slowly—government movies of the time were always preoccupied with every minute bureaucratic step—but as the grainy images flickered against the curtains, the purpose of our transfer to this remote place became clear.

In the winter of 1959, while fighting a forest fire in the southern foothills of the Greater Khingan range, a lumberjack discovered the wreckage of a Japanese transport plane sunk in a muddy bog.

The heat from the fire had already evaporated much of the water. As the bog shriveled, the snapped wing of an aircraft was revealed. The lumberjacks on the scene climbed into the wreckage and began pulling out spare parts and components. The parts passed through many hands, from the cadre leader at the local lumber mill, to an associate of his at the county level, until finally, they were seen by a retired military officer. He immediately reported up the chain of command and news of the incident reached the highest levels.

In those days, Party leaders took discoveries of leftover weapons and military equipment very seriously. They were useful for research, and a plane like that would probably still contain some antipersonnel bombs. The Central Committee immediately dispatched a team to investigate the wreck. After digging the plane out of the pit, the team searched the still-intact cabin. They were shocked to discover the plane had been transporting only one thing: Japanese army documents regarding the geological exploration of Manchuria and Mongolia.

It's common knowledge that after occupying the Northeast, Japan expended a great deal of effort searching for mineral deposits, the most pressing being oil. However—and it's not clear why exactly this was—the Japanese did not drill very deeply. So no matter how much they searched, they failed to find even the hint of a deposit. Japanese prospecting teams even explored just above the ore beds in Daqing. Japan thus decided that China was an oil-poor country, and it wasn't until Huang Jiqing discovered the oil reserves at Daqing that this opinion was reversed. (In fact, prior to the Japanese occupation, prospectors from the United States also searched for and failed to find oil in China. That so many capable countries were unable to find China's oil, one can't help but find a little strange.)

Nonetheless, the foundational prospecting work that Japan did in the Northeast was exceedingly precise. When the Soviet Union's

Red Army attacked the Japanese, our spies went to any lengths to locate the information the Japanese had compiled. We failed. The documents had vanished without a trace. We Chinese believed they'd been seized by the Soviet Union. The Soviet Union believed the Japanese had burned them. The Japanese believed surrendered Japanese soldiers had disclosed the information to their Chinese captors. No one could have guessed that they'd been lying at the bottom of a swamp for almost twenty years.

This was precious data and was later used as essential reference material for large-scale, low-depth mineral-prospecting work at several locations across Inner Mongolia. The documents showed how scrupulously the Japanese had handled their affairs: all the materials were immaculate—hand copied with no errors—and divided into various leather chests, with different types of information placed into different-colored containers. Later, after being delivered to the classified-information branch of the Beijing Archives, the documents were rigorously analyzed and sorted. Because all the documents were in Japanese and included a great deal of numerical data, teasing out their secrets required translators and prospectors to work together. The process of arranging this information was slow and arduous, but in the middle of it, a peculiar outlier was uncovered. An archivist discovered a locked black steel case at the bottom of one of the leather chests.

This little steel case was totally inconspicuous—seemingly left by accident at the bottom of the chest—but it was sealed with a code lock of great precision. Obviously it had been designed for military secrets. What could be inside? Its existence aroused great interest in the Party leaders. Experts were consulted and tremendous effort was expended before locksmiths finally broke through the lock. Inside was what appeared to be another geological-exploration document, but one written entirely in code.

Those present at the time were all bewildered by this discovery. Why had this document in particular been specially coded and concealed? The Central Committee suspected it contained clues to the oil fields the Japanese had been searching for, but the Japanese were highly skilled code writers and, at the time, there was no way to decipher the document's meaning. The United States had information on Japanese codes, but the Korean War had only ended a few years previously. You couldn't just call up the Americans and ask to borrow their books for a quick look-see. All we could figure out was the location and scope of the prospecting area that the document seemed to refer to.

The 723 Project and the special organization in charge here were created on the basis of this information. Three prospecting teams were selected and sent into the thick forests of Inner Mongolia to hunt for clues to the document's meaning. The discovery of this temporary Japanese base hidden deep among the trees confirmed everyone's suspicions, but the camp was already long abandoned and everything burned away. Not even a single scrap of paper remained. It was only through locating traces of former activity in the surrounding area that we could tell the Japanese did in fact have a prospecting team here, and that they had engaged in comprehensive carpet-style prospecting on 80 percent of the nearby forest and mountain regions. Our teams began a general survey of the vicinity, but to no effect—nothing could be discerned from looking at the earth's surface. Shallow excavations were then made, but again there was nothing to find. The area was completely lacking in any of the characteristics that normally merit geological exploration.

The extreme importance attached to this area by the Japanese and the total lack of any discovery by our troops confounded us, but our leaders had faith in the accuracy of the Japanese data and knew that oil reserves are often found deep underground. They commissioned the use of seismic exploration equipment obtained from the Soviet Union. Seismic prospecting was fairly advanced for the time. Basically you fire a seismic wave from the surface into the ground. If it encounters rock layers with different physical qualities, the wave will be reflected and refracted. This reaction is then identified by a wave-detecting device located on the surface or in a well. By recording and analyzing these seismic waves, the quality and form of underground rock layers can be inferred. Detailed seismic exploration of the layers of stratification, together with precise prospecting work, is superior to all other methods of geophysical investigation. The depth of seismic exploration can range from dozens to tens of thousands of feet underground.

China began importing this kind of equipment in 1951, and by the time of the 723 Project it had already been successfully operated in a number of real-world trials. Such equipment was generally used in the exploration of very deep mineral beds, and the technology had developed to the point where the feedback data could be presented three-dimensionally. This was a pretty damn spectacular development, but to the average person the data was just a terribly confusing mass of jumbled lines and shapes. Even ground-level tech specialists in the military like us have trouble with such abstract data. Through the use of geological-data-imaging equipment, however, this jumbled mess can be converted into a fairly comprehensible black-and-white filmstrip.

The seismic exploration work continued for about five months, and when the contents of the find were revealed, it was enough to leave people speechless. According to the data, an abnormal seismic reflection had been recorded thirty-six hundred feet below the surface of the region. On the filmstrip, this reflection appeared as an extremely prominent, irregular white shadow. It was shaped like a cross and shocking in its precision and exactitude: 147 feet long and 102 feet wide, it seemed to be a great piece of metal embedded in the shell rock thirty-six hundred feet underground. Seeing this image projected onto the curtain, we all began to talk excitedly. It just seemed too inconceivable to be real, but when the technical personnel enlarged the shot the whole tent went silent. The geometrical contours of its exterior were clearly visible and all of us immediately recognized it: a plane! Somehow, embedded in the shell rock thirty-six hundred feet below the surface, our team had discovered a bomber!

CHAPTER 4

The Shinzan

At this point, a lot of you probably think this is all nonsense. I mean, really, this was just strange beyond measure. We'd received thoroughly practical educations, and materialism was the dominant philosophy of the time. Anything extraordinary had to be explained on the basis of what we could see and touch, no matter how forced and far-fetched the explanations sometimes became. This seemed unexplainable. My first reaction was to call it bullshit. It just wasn't plausible. But when you know something is true, when it's staring you in the face, all that remains is explaining how it happened.

The Zero Film ended here. I was in shock and barely noticed the movie was over. Later I learned that there was a lot more that wasn't shown to us. At the time I was indignant and wanted to know why this content had been kept from us, but when I was older and had been put in charge of my own unit, I finally understood what our leaders had been thinking. Maturity always comes at a price. I realize now that every time I have reached a new level of understanding, it has almost without exception been accompanied by lies and sacrifice. There's no way of avoiding this.

The colonel asked if we had any questions. Many believed the cross was purely coincidental, that during some natural catastrophe underground iron had coagulated into this shape by chance. But the colonel told us that based on a detailed analysis of the object's exterior it fit the description of a Shinzan, a highly uncommon Japanese bomber. Used mainly as a troop-transport plane, it was introduced at the end of World War II and there were very few in number. The likelihood that this was all just a coincidence was extremely slim.

Since it wasn't a coincidence, there had to be some fact-based explanation. For this sort of occurrence, there could be only one explanation: so long as the plane hadn't traveled through some sci-fi space-time warp to appear deep underground, then the Japanese must have moved it there. There had to be some sort of passageway for the plane to get to where it was. It was obvious, however, that no tunnel would be large enough to accommodate the thing if it were moved in its entirety. It must have been dismantled and transported piece by piece. In this very spot and through methods unclear, the Japanese either dug or located a tunnel that led deep underground. They then disassembled a Shinzan bomber, transported it down the passageway, and at the tunnel's end, thirty-six hundred feet below ground, they rebuilt the entire plane. This all seemed pretty crazy, but it was the only rational possibility.

Still, we needed to find evidence to verify the hypothesis. We had to locate the underground tunnel and uncover some trace of the extensive equipment that must have been previously amassed here. The colonel said they'd already found large amounts of anti-freeze residue nearby. That seemed to satisfy the second prerequisite. As for the first, the engineering corps was now conducting a wide-ranging search of the area. A group would be organized once the tunnel was located. They would then make their way underground to find out just what was down there. At last, this was the reason we were here.

The meeting ended. The colonel repeated our oath of secrecy and told us we were free to wander about the camp. As soon as he left, the entire tent erupted like a pot boiling over. It wasn't that we were afraid—when it came to cave exploration, we were all experienced and fear was out of the question. No, we were excited. As I've said before, prospecting can be a dull line of work. This opportunity was more than a little enticing.

Later, after returning to our tents, we were still too keyed up to sleep. Only Old Cat went to bed. The rest of us, even though we were exhausted, stayed up all night, soaking in the excitement, discussing the job, and letting off steam. Looking back, though, it seems a little strange that in all our discussions no one ever asked why the Japanese would expend so much effort to move an entire plane deep underground. The Japanese obviously considered the prospecting records regarding this location exceptionally important—locked as they were within a coded steel box. Judging from the remains left at this camp, though, it was clear the Japanese had only engaged in common geological exploration work before they suddenly decided to carry out this seemingly impossible act. What had they found? What made them do it? I suspect this question was on everyone's mind, but we knew that there was no sense in discussing it. So we chose to let it go.

CHAPTER 5

The Cave

The entirety of the engineering corps was dispatched to carpet the area. We asked to be included in the search, but the colonel firmly refused without any explanation. We became rather spoiled at camp, sitting around all day, excitedly or nervously guessing at what was to come, waiting for news from the forest. A discovery was made on the twelfth day. A unit of engineering corpsmen located a long-abandoned roadway on a mountain five kilometers from camp. After following it another three kilometers, they uncovered a large tectonic cave covered in cracks and fissures. The mouth of the cave had been concealed beneath a canvas sheet hidden under a layer of fallen leaves. The soldiers had only found the cave when they stepped on top of the canvas. The opening yawned ninety feet wide and appeared to be a vertical drop for at least the initial eighty to ninety feet, though the engineering corpsmen weren't carrying the right equipment to explore too deeply.

At noon the colonel made an announcement: we would set out the day after next. He asked us to make the appropriate preparations. This pushed most of us to the peak of anticipation, but our nervousness intensified as well. Caves are some of the world's most hazardous locations. We were used to exploring them, but that made us only more aware of their danger. The chatter that had filled our days screeched to a halt. With each of us attending to his own responsibilities, the whole camp soon took on an orderly, professional atmosphere.

As the days passed, I felt an increasing admiration for Old Cat. Although I seemed to notice a trace of anger in his eyes, despite the excitement all around, he just carried on in the same brazen and rather shameless way, with that slight smirk playing across his lips, as if he didn't care about anything at all. While everyone else was bustling about in preparation for the expedition, he stood apart, watching us from the cabin steps and barely lifting a finger. He always seemed to know something that I didn't, and there was nothing favorable in his expression as he watched us.

Every generation is typified by a certain kind of person, and so it was with Old Cat: he characterized the times that he lived in. In the early days of the war, this old guard was privy to many things no one should ever have to see. They learned the truths that lie below the surface of our world, truths that they found themselves powerless to change. Perceptive and clever, a guy like Old Cat took pleasure in being aware while everyone else went around in a daze. He delighted in his hard-won knowledge and would never deign to rouse you from your stupor. Of course, all of these reflections were made many years later. At the time I was curious about Old Cat, like an adolescent around some rock star. I wanted only to get closer, hoping to somehow become just like him.

That night I made up my mind to ask Old Cat what he was thinking. At first he just laughed at me and said nothing, but after I handed over some cigarettes, he softened. He smoked a few, then told me that this thing we were doing, there was something wrong about it. First of all, he said, that cave had definitely been discovered before we arrived, otherwise they would never have transferred so many people here so urgently. After being in the area for such a long time, could they really have only discovered it just now? Second, he was sure that there were branching paths in the depths of the cave, otherwise they wouldn't need so many men. He didn't know what sort of tricks the leaders of the 723 Project were playing, but whatever they were, they weren't telling us. It was all extremely strange, he said, especially the plane hidden underground—that was simply too much. The situation gave him a bad feeling. After he finished he gave me a pat on the back and, looking right at me, told me that whatever came next, I'd better be extremely careful.

I didn't say anything, but his suspicion made me think less of him. He was overthinking the situation, I told myself. Of course there was nothing simple about what was happening, otherwise they wouldn't have needed so many men and so much equipment. Even if they didn't tell us everything, I figured those in charge had reasons for concealing this information. I didn't think too much about it. We took the next day to rest, reorganize, and hold target practice. Then, on the third day, we joined up with a large contingent of engineering corpsmen and set off for the saddle ridge, me with a smile on my face.

We didn't have any pack animals—just one dog—so we had to proceed on foot, each man with a heavy load on his back. The cave was supposed to be a full day's hike from camp. At some point along the way, I realized Old Cat wasn't with us. Some of my comrades told me the old bandit had claimed to be running a high fever. I could feel my stomach drop into my boots. He hadn't been joking. Knowing he'd intentionally avoided going, the air around me suddenly seemed darker.

Still, it was better marching along than bouncing around in the back of a truck. Each of us had a rifle strapped to his back. Wang Sichuan told me this meant we were near the Mongolian border and not near the Soviets. The Soviet snipers might pick you off long-range if they saw that you had a gun. Our forces rarely carried arms near their border. But there were lots of roving bandits near Mongolia. You needed a gun for self-protection.

I dearly wanted to get a better idea of where exactly we were, but we stuck to the lower ridges that straddled the gaps between mountains and there was never a view. The built-up layers of fallen leaves beneath us turned the ground to fetid swamp. With each step our feet came up covered in swollen masses of muck that belched black water. And with so many people, someone was always falling over and making us stop. We labored onward, our conversations dead and left behind. My thoughts of scenery withered. By the end, I had only the strength to keep my eyes on the back of the man in front of me.

We finally reached the cave on the afternoon of the second day. Immediately I realized Old Cat had been right: there was no way this cave had been found just two days before. Several tents had been erected and piles of knotted rope were strewn all about—two weeks wouldn't have been enough time to transport this much equipment. The others didn't seem to notice anything wrong. Honestly, had I not spoken with Old Cat, I wouldn't have paid attention to these details either.

Great trees blocked out the sun, and the ground was covered in bushes. The mouth of the cave opened to the sky just behind the massive, horizontal trunk of a dead tree. From some unknown source, long roots extended into the opening and climbed down its throat. This was a textbook example of a tectonic cave—a giant tear in the mountainside—not some common mountain cavern. Standing next to the opening, all we could see was a steep drop-off into pitch-black. The wind came whistling softly out of the pit. It was impossible to tell how deep it went. Where the sunlight fell upon the steep cave walls, it illuminated a host of ferns and lichen clinging to the rock. The opening chute seemed to be horn shaped, the emptiness below appearing even larger than the cave mouth. Engineering corpsmen had already placed a net over the opening. At its side was a system of pulleys hooked to a diesel engine that was now lowering basket after basket of army-green cloth bags into the hole. Evidently people were already inside.

The colonel told us the engineering corps had completed an initial exploration of the cave: The vertical drop continued for 642 feet. At its bottom ran an underground river. We would navigate it in inflated oxskin rafts. About two hundred feet down the river, the path branched in four directions. We'd have to divide into groups.

I could feel the sweat running down my brow and Old Cat's words tugging at my heart—everything that son of a bitch had said was coming true.

CHAPTER 6

Splitting Up

So it went like this: There were twenty-three of us prospectors in total. We were going to be split into four groups of four, with the remaining seven acting as reserve and support. A few engineering corpsmen would also join each group for protection and to help carry equipment. There's a big difference between prospectors and engineering corpsmen. Prospectors are special-technician troops attached to the wider geo-prospecting/engineering brigade, while engineering corpsmen are much more like standard troops with a little extra training. We had it much easier than they: far fewer military rules and regulations and a respectable military rank. We were the brains and they were the necessary brute force. Of course, we'd once been fit like them, but as our volume of work increased over the years, we let our conditioning slip. Now we needed the engineering corpsmen, especially during cave exploration. The ropes were extremely heavy, and we needed a great deal of them to get past the steep cliffs and wide crevasses we were likely to encounter. The more people available, the easier it was to travel great distances during exploration. The new enlistees could march thirty kilometers with twenty kilograms on their backs. I don't know what exactly they were carrying, but they didn't seem too distressed.

Remembering what Old Cat told me, I tried to stay toward the back of the group, hoping to be kept in reserve. The groups, however, were divided based on age. Being relatively young, I was placed in the second group with Wang Sichuan and two men from Shaanxi, Pei Qing and Chen Luohu. I'd worked with these men before at the massive oil-extraction project in Karamay, off in the Northwest. Later, we'd often run into each other when one of us was leaving a project and the other was going in. I'd never really gotten to know them before, but I guess we'd have the chance now.

Pei Qing was going prematurely gray. Although his pure white face made him look quite young, that silver hair gave him a fierce and imposing aspect. He had a bit of arrogance about him. It was said he was highly educated and the technical backbone of his unit. He didn't talk much, but I heard he was a real lady-killer. Chen Luohu was Pei Qing's polar opposite: he'd risen from the very bottom through hard work, but he still didn't even speak proper Mandarin. He'd laugh like a donkey whenever anyone told a joke, no matter what it was about. "Aw, you don't say! Isn't that hilarious!" he'd guffaw. He could laugh all day about any little thing— which was quite entertaining for us—but there was also something treacherous about him, a sense of caution in how he approached everything, like an ambitious low-level bureaucrat. None of us relished having to deal with him.

Five men from the fourth squad of the sixth company of the Inner Mongolian engineering corps were coming with us. Their deputy squad leader's name was something like "Kangmei," but I'd never heard of the other four. We made no formal introductions at the time, just saluted, noted the fresh faces, and left it at that.

The deputy squad leader carried a Type 56 assault rifle (a Chinese copy of the Kalashnikov). The other four soldiers had Type

54 submachine guns, and they loaded us all down with ammo. Wang Sichuan told them they were being more than a little excessive: wild animals might be lurking in the caves of the South, but the most we'd find here were bats. The temperature in the cave was too low to support cold-blooded animals, and there was no way a larger animal, like a bear, would be able to negotiate the vertical descent. The only problems we needed to worry about were staying warm and having enough oxygen, though the engineering corpsmen didn't seem to be preparing for that. Soldiers never listen to our advice.

We prospectors refused to carry guns and merely strapped on Sam Browne belts (wide leather belts with a shoulder strap). We were each assigned different pieces of equipment. I was given a geologist's shovel and hammer, for which I felt fortunate, as each could be used for self-defense and neither was particularly heavy. Wang Sichuan was made to carry the cutlery. It clattered and jingled as he walked, and he made his dissatisfaction very clear to us.

After finishing our preparations, we were hooked to the towrope and lowered one by one into the mouth of the cave. I can still remember swinging back and forth, trying to keep my balance, for what seemed like hours. I prefer to swing down on my own. It's much smoother than being lowered in by pulley. Honestly, scaling cliff faces has become fairly routine for me, and I wouldn't consider a six-hundred-something-foot descent to be all that deep. I once climbed a cliff in Shandong far more formidable than this one. Sunlight illuminated the first stretch of the descent, but after ninety feet the cave began to twist and the sky disappeared. Fifteen or so feet below that, I entered into total darkness. I could see beams of light glimmering from the bottom. I glanced about at the cliff rock. It was clearly limestone from the Cambrian and Ordovician periods, meaning this was a complex cave—in possession of the features of both limestone and tectonic caves. The cave bottom was as big as a soccer field and, as I neared the ground, I could see it was mostly covered by slow-moving water. An underground river—a common feature of limestone karst caves.

Many provisional steel shelves had been erected on the cave floor. I wasn't sure whether the Japanese had left them or if we'd set them up. The shelves were packed with large gas lamps and the army-green bags that had been lowered earlier. Engineering corpsmen were busy unpacking the oxskin rafts from inside the bags. Several had already been blown up and were calmly floating atop the dark river. The water itself didn't appear very deep. Many soldiers were standing in the river with rubber galoshes. Wang Sichuan had descended before me and was off to one side, shining his flashlight across the cave walls. He'd even lit up a cigarette.

As soon as I touched down, my professional habits took over. I flipped on my flashlight and joined those around me in scanning about the dark cave. Years ago, when I first became a prospector, caves held a strong sense of enchantment for me. I loved standing amid those dark walls, running my fingers across the earth's secrets. I always felt as if I'd come to a place that did not belong to the human world. We prospectors often considered caves the blood vessels of the mountains. While exploring their deep tunnels, we sometimes felt a strange sort of air, almost like breath, pass over us. How natural it would seem—the mountains were alive. Now, though, I look at caves like a gynecologist searching for illness—I only pay attention to what I have to.

I'd been in a cave like this in Shanxi. We call them "Pits of Heaven," because they seem to appear out of nowhere as if some god had smashed them into the earth. Pits of Heaven are often terribly deep. This one, though, was significantly more complex than the others I'd been in. Something about it felt different. Part of it had to be that this was a complex cave, one with both limestone and tectonic features. Caves like this are formed by tectonic activity and water erosion occurring simultaneously. They are dotted with thousands of watery trenches and ravines, crisscrossed by jagged rocks of grotesque shape. They have extremely complicated tunnel systems. Normal watery limestone caves tend to be relatively easy to explore. You can navigate the length of their underground rivers by oxskin raft, rarely encountering more than a few obstacles. The dark rivers of tectonic caves, however, often conceal extremely irregular faults. You could be floating along, smoking a cigarette, and suddenly come upon a three-hundred-foot waterfall crashing into the blackness. Run into one of those and you're dead for sure. We try not to go too deep in tectonic caves.

This time there was no escaping it. I turned to tell some corpsmen they'd better tie some rocks to the raft anchors to weigh them down, but Chen Luohu was already instructing them. I jumped down into the water. It didn't reach my knees, but the cold struck at my heart and seeped into my bones. I took in my surroundings: the walls were all limestone. Seeing Wang Sichuan, I walked up behind him. He was concentrating intently on one of the cliff walls. He noticed me as I walked over and motioned for me to take a look at something. I shined my flashlight on a portion of rock. The wall seemed polished, as if it were covered in a layer of wax. He then used his flashlight to point out several other spots that all bore similar markings. I stared at it for a moment, then glanced up at him, that "Now what do you think that means?" look in my eye.

"What you're looking at is glazing," he said quietly. "Meaning that, at some point, there was most likely a violent explosion somewhere in this cave."

CHAPTER 7

A Few Clues

Rock glazing most commonly occurs during a volcanic eruption when rivers of lava hit masses of rock. There can be violent explosions and fires. Wang Sichuan's inference was basically correct, but whether it was in fact an explosion or a severe fire that caused the glazing still remained to be seen. He figured it was an explosion because he knew that, as the Japanese were departing, they would have wanted to seal off the cave. The most common way armies did so was by demolishing the mountain around it. I personally believed that a prolonged fire had left the damage. With an explosion of that size, there was no way the mountain could have maintained its current form. But if it was a fire, then this cave must have been continuously scorched for over forty hours to leave such an impression. Who knows what they were burning?

We waded twice around the length of the cavern. The river didn't keep to a consistent depth—one step might be deep and the next shallow. The bottom was covered in pebbles. Shining my flashlight in the water, I could see many small fish swimming about. Had this been in the South, it would have made an excellent place to visit during summer vacation. A pity that the North is simply too cold. Even wearing galoshes, the chill pierced my bones.

The rest of our party continued to descend one by one. Some of these were guys I knew. We exchanged cigarettes and talked about the situation in the cave. It was the corpsmen's job to make the final preparations. There was no reason for us to interfere. We talked about the Japanese troops that had been stationed here. Back in those days, everybody had heard the rumor that Japanese soldiers who'd never withdrawn had been captured in the mountains, some of them already little more than savages. They had no idea World War II had ended. Who knew if any lived in this cave, but if some did, our situation would get a lot more interesting.

Two hours later everyone had descended into the cavern and all eight rafts—two per group—were fully inflated and ready to go. We were all feeling a little anxious. A few people kept up a nervous chatter, and the whole cave echoed with noise. Then the colonel descended into the cave. He had switched into battle garb and, seeing him like this, I realized who he was. He had been my boot-camp instructor, though he clearly no longer recognized me. He gave us a pep talk, the main point being to take care and be safe, then shouted, "Do you have what it takes to complete the mission?" We were well trained. We responded as one: "Yes!" We took a deep breath, slipped on our waterproof gear, climbed into the rafts, and with that our adventure officially began.

According to our analysis of the geological-imaging film, following this river would lead us to the plane. Of course, the river didn't go straight down. It meandered this way and that as it flowed underground. Though its total length was impossible to pin down, it was certainly going to be more than thirty-six hundred feet.

We waited a minute after the first group's two rafts launched before pushing off ourselves. The corpsmen rode the raft in front, their light switched on to help lead the way. We propped the oars out on either side to keep the raft from running into the cave walls. The cavern shrank and the sounds around us hushed. The light dimmed until only the boat and our most immediate surroundings were visible. Sweeping the water with our flashlights, we discovered it had already become quite deep. These changes were characteristic of tectonic caves, but here it was both sudden and very pronounced. The cave was far from wide—perhaps only thirty feet across—but it was quite tall. Though we craned our necks upward, we couldn't make out the ceiling. It felt like floating through a deep and narrow gorge. Shining our flashlights above us, we could see the roots of plants climbing down the walls. It was a magnificent sight and we paused for a moment to take it all in. Chen Luohu even pulled out a camera and snapped two pictures using a magnesium flash.

Having floated not ninety feet farther, we reached a fork in the cave. We waited here for the last two groups, then we all went our respective ways. At last we'd entered the truly fearful portion of our journey. When it came to cave exploration, working on a fifty-person team and a five-person team are different matters entirely.

Both rafts floated a few radio buoys beside them. If the raft ahead hit something unexpected, we'd see the movement of the light and the buoy signal would change. At least we'd know in advance that something wasn't right. The current was still slow. As we watched the lighted buoys and the corpsmen's raft slowly drift ahead, we relaxed and followed in the wake. The dangers of cave exploration have often been exaggerated in novels. Really, as long as you stick to the correct procedures and remain cautious and alert, it's actually relatively safe. The greatest danger comes from the instability of the rock itself. If the cave collapses with you inside, then you're dead. Simple as that. To see all the corpsmen up ahead—tense as could be, knuckles white, gripping their rifles— made us laugh to ourselves.

Everything went smoothly for the first four hours, and soon we'd floated over two kilometers. Then the current began to pick up. We were rushed around bends and down short staircase waterfalls.

Stones had been piled below the surface, and various objects, pre-sumably left by the Japanese, were wedged into cracks in the walls. Indistinct Japanese characters were painted on the sides of these wooden crates and rusted barrels. None of us had any idea what they were trying to tell us.

Just as our attention was being drawn by these old signs, the raft in front of us suddenly skidded to a halt. We knocked into it and one of the men perched on its side nearly fell out. Our raft spun head to tail, pressing up against the raft ahead. We couldn't see anything from the surface. Why had we stopped? Was something hidden underwater? We swept about with our paddles, hit something, and with a good, forceful yank, pulled a sheet of wire netting from underwater.

"Damned Japs left a trap for us," the deputy squad leader cursed. He commanded two corpsmen to hop in and cut away the rest of the netting.

The two soldiers immediately stripped off their clothing, clenched their flashlights between their teeth, and dove in, splash-ing us with water so cold it made us shiver. You had to admire their nerve—told to jump, they did so without a second thought.

The two men were back up not three seconds later. "Squad leader," said one of the men, shivering with each word, "there's a dead man down there, caught on the river bottom."

CHAPTER 8

The Dead Man

The deputy squad leader removed his clothing, jumped in, and the three of them dove to the bottom once more, the force of their exertions stirring up the surface. Wang Sichuan is an impetuous man. He stripped off his clothing and was about to jump in, too, when I pulled him back. Three people was enough.

All the movement underwater caused the wire netting to jerk our raft back and forth. I lay flat across the bottom and did my best to keep it from flipping. The deputy squad leader soon emerged, towing some blue-green object. The other two soldiers broke the surface after him. With a great tug followed by a spray of water, the three of them pulled the thing up from the depths, splashing it directly onto our raft.

We all leaped in surprise. At first glance it really did seem to be a dead person, but on closer inspection it became clear it was no such thing. It was a decomposing green-black gunnysack with holes torn all along its length by the netting and filled completely with rusted iron wire. Propped up, it did bear a remarkable resemblance to a rigid corpse. The gunnysack was disgusting. It covered our hands in watery rust. It was also extremely heavy. As soon as they set it down, the tail of the raft pulled up out of the water. Chen Luohu immediately shrank to the back of the raft. Any farther and he would have cowered right off the side. Luckily, Wang Sichuan stepped over and grabbed hold of him. The three corpsmen climbed, huffing and puffing, back onto the raft. The deputy squad leader stared for a moment at the gunnysack, his brows wrinkling. Then he turned to his two subordinates, rapped them once each atop the head, and cursed, "What the hell is this? A corpse? Is this what the corpses of your family members look like?"

The two soldiers hung their heads in embarrassment, then quickly jumped back in to finish cutting the wire. The deputy squad leader felt he'd lost a little face. "Those two new-recruit knuckleheads," he explained, "they're a pair of cowards." In fact, we'd all been given an awful fright. Seeing the thing thump down on the raft was terrifying. Thinking back on it, I'm pretty sure the corpsmen thought us a little soft and were trying to thicken our skins a bit.

Wang Sichuan shined his flashlight on the bag. "You think this thing was left behind by the Japanese?"

I was sure it was. This kind of gunnysack was called a buffer bag, I told the group, and was used as a provisional form of cover during explosions. I was sure it had once been filled with sand. The thing had probably been lost over the side at some point back when the Japanese were transporting equipment along the river. Indeed, it had begun to look as if the Japs really had set off a large explosion down here.

Wang Sichuan suddenly cut me off. He yanked on the rotting bag. "Wrong, Old Wu," he said. "This really is a corpse."

He tore open the soft, rotting bag, and we could see the remains of a human wrapped in the iron wire. The wire was wound around the bones and desiccated skin. The person had struggled violently before dying, tearing holes in the gunnysack's exterior. The corpse was already partially decayed, though the person had been so thin there wasn't much to decompose. Seeing his face distorted in suffering, we all shuddered involuntarily.

What I'm telling you is the truth, real as could be. I haven't exaggerated it at all. Indeed, once I saw that corpse laid out on the raft in the dark of the cave, my hair stood on end, and there was no way I would ever forget it. Not having witnessed it with your own eyes, it would be impossible to fully understand the gravity of such a sight: that the Japanese, in their frenzy, were capable of lining buffer bags with the bodies of still-living Chinese people, for use as protection against explosions. For a long time we stood in silence, Wang Sichuan the most obviously affected, his expression dark as night. When the two young soldiers finished cutting the wire and clambered back aboard the raft, they didn't know what to make of us—the looks on our faces must have been baffling. We pushed the corpse back into the water and continued downriver.

We didn't speak the rest of the way. To joke about anything seemed inappropriate. To divert our attention from what we'd seen, we watched the stone walls pass silently by. As the tunnel descended, the structure of the cave began to change, and our surroundings became increasingly bizarre. Features typical of a watery limestone cave began to replace those of a tectonic one, with waterfalls running down the rock walls and spouts seeping through the stone. We all put on our waterproof gear.

It was difficult to say if the limestone cave system had formed earlier than the tectonic features or the other way around. Tectonic caves are usually at least 100 million years old, while limestone cave systems can vary from 100,000 to 200 million years old. Perhaps 100 million years ago a mountain rose swiftly from the ocean and the geological activity stemming from this occurrence first resulted in a tectonic cave. Then, once an underground river had formed, it eroded the limestone around it, after which the characteristics of a limestone cave began to manifest. Generally speaking, the systems of large river caves that exist within karst terrain are netlike, with one layer on top of another and stringlike tunnels extending in all directions. With no prescribed rules or routes to follow, navigating such caves is not some sightseeing cruise where you just follow a river directly to its bottom.

Because of the water seeping through the walls, the surface layer of limestone was carried deeper into the cave, and the level of erosion should become increasingly severe as we proceeded downstream. Nonetheless, we estimated that once we reached a certain depth, our surroundings would become tectonic again. The pressure at that point would be too great for a karst-formed limestone cave to bear. We discussed each of these guesses, but what really captured our interest was, where did the river end? Was there an underground lake somewhere far downriver? It would be hard to imagine all of this water somehow dissipating through cracks in the rock and becoming groundwater.

Calculating approximately how much time we'd need to reach our destination, we accounted for the river's gentle slope, and estimated we were about sixteen kilometers from a thirty-six-hundred-foot depth. So long as nothing unforeseen occurred and we made camp that night on schedule, we figured we should arrive by ten the next morning. Of course, the prerequisite was the assumption that we had taken the correct branch in the river and that there were no more forks up ahead. Otherwise the map was blank, and the devil only knew where we would end up.

We soon found one of our guesses about the cave structure borne out perfectly: the erosion really was getting more severe. After we reached a depth of approximately 960 feet, the characteristics of a limestone cave burst into view. On both sides of the river the walls were transformed into a scrolling mural of complex and terrifying shapes. Falling all around were waterfalls with bases like plates of bone. Thin strands of rock interlaced crookedly like sharp teeth in a dog's mouth. Above the river there stretched a high stone bridge, seemingly suspended out of nowhere. From the roof of the cave, several waterfalls fell straight down, their force great enough that when we passed beneath them we had to curl into the raft for protection. Besides the Japanese, no one had seen this place for a million years. Now all of its secrets were being exposed to us. I felt as if we were drifting through the skeleton of some giant animal, and I didn't know whether to be frightened or excited.

Soon enough our theories encountered a serious challenge. After we'd passed beneath a giant waterfall, huge boulders appeared before us, blocking our path and encircled by rapids. We were sucked through the whitewater right into one of the rocks, our raft wedging itself into a crack.

"Fallen rocks," said Pei Qing, motioning with his flashlight. "They must have ripped from the ceiling during some cave-in."

"Anyone can see that," Wang Sichuan shouted. "Goddamn it, who's going to help me climb up and take a look?"

We climbed onto the rock to survey our predicament. We were shocked. A rocky shoal spread out before us, the river flowing on beneath the stones. The shoal was made of irregularly shaped rocks, the largest as big as the hood of a truck, the smallest the size of a fist, the ground extremely uneven. Black gunnysacks, just like the one we'd dredged from underwater, filled the gaps between the rocky chaos. The sight flooded our eyes. Many of the bags had almost rotted away and the twisted corpses within them jutted out in every horrid pose imaginable, still bound tightly in wire. We were looking into hell.

CHAPTER 9

The Underground Shoal

The gunnysacks were piled five or six layers high. Many of those trapped within had struggled to free themselves, their arms and legs now protruding. In the end their iron fetters had simply been too strong. The corpses were desiccated, their expressions frozen in torment and pain. To examine them in detail was too much to bear.

As soon as we tried to move some of the bags, the wires would twist together and hold tight. Chen Luohu was terrified, utterly scared out of his wits. If he hadn't taken a piss when we first arrived, I suspect his pants would have been wet through. Pei Qing said nothing, his expression very composed. We dropped anchor. The deputy squad leader clambered up some rocks to have a look at our surroundings. The body-filled shoal continued for a long way. If there weren't a thousand corpses, then there were at least seven or eight hundred. It was a mass grave. As a prospector, a dead body is something you rarely come across. To see that many, suddenly and all at once, was chilling.

After discussing it as a group, we decided that these had to be workers captured by the Japanese. Moving a bomber deep underground piece by piece would require a huge amount of labor. When it came to negotiating this sort of terrain, there was no more nimble a transportation tool than a human being. Because these activities were strictly confidential, the workers had to be silenced once the job was done. This was the method they had used. Still, there was something strange about it: Why had they stacked the bodies in this specific location? No way could these "corpse bags" have been used as anything other than buffer bags. Was this the site of an explosion? What if the cave-in that caused these boulders to drop and shatter was actually manmade?

But after taking a look around, we couldn't find the slightest evidence of such a blast. Pei Qing said that deep in the crevices between the rocks you could see where the boulders had been made glossy and smooth by running water. Stones required tens of thousands of years to be scoured to that level of polish. The cave-in must have occurred long, long ago. Moreover, this location wasn't suitable for demolition work. It would be far too easy to cause a chain reaction across the layers of rock. And the buffer bags had been heaped in a very careless manner. It seemed likely they'd simply been abandoned here. What if these bags were merely extras?

It was now no longer possible to use the oxskin rafts. Our orderly plans were thrown into disarray. The deputy squad leader ordered his corpsmen to begin packing up the equipment. We were responsible for carrying a large portion of it as well. The deflated rafts were extremely heavy. Once we were ready and I shouldered my bag, the weight nearly pushed my feet through the rock.

We began to march, maneuvering ourselves hand over hand across the field of boulders, our progress beyond arduous. Before we had gone too far, we suddenly understood why the Japanese had stacked the corpses here. They were building a road. The piles of corpses filled the gaps between each massive boulder, leveling the path. A wave of nausea and a feeling of absolute terror overcame me. The soles of my feet prickled and I knew only that I wanted to get out of this place as soon as possible.

But you can't always get what you want. There was no easy way across the shoal. We were leaping from boulder to boulder with huge packs, like stuntmen in training. And if we stepped on the gunnysacks? Our entire foot would sink in, catching on the wire and requiring that we be cut free. We gritted our teeth and marched doggedly on, but in nearly three hours we'd gone little more than a kilometer and even the deputy squad leader had reached the limit of exhaustion. Wang Sichuan looked at me, panting for air. "Old Wu, at this rate, we're going to be camping in the mass grave tonight," he said.

He was right. Looking at the darkness up ahead, there was no way to tell how far it went. And hiking for another three hours was not possible. "If we have to, then so be it," I replied. "These are our compatriots. Dead all these years and they still haven't spent one night in peace. Tonight we will watch over them. Now, what's so bad about that?"

Chen Luohu promptly cut in. "I object."

This surprised me. "Well, then what do you propose?" I asked him.

"I think we ought to keep going and rest when we get out of here," he said. "Because…um…because we won't be able to rest well in this kind of place."

I didn't know whether to laugh or cry. "Who wouldn't rest well?" said Wang Sichuan sarcastically. "I'm afraid only you'd have trouble falling asleep. What is it, Luohu, you afraid there's ghosts here?"

Chen Luohu's face immediately flushed a deep red. "Well, I am afraid," he quickly replied. "What's so terrible about that? My mom carried me but six months before giving birth. I've been deficient from the start, a natural coward. Can I be blamed for it? But being a coward never stopped me from serving my country. Whoever wants to laugh at me is laughing at a comrade."

Wang Sichuan and I exchanged a look—there was nothing to be done about this guy. "Spirits are nothing but superstition," I said. "Rock is a form of matter. Corpses are a form of matter. Better just to think of all this as stone. There's nothing to be afraid of. Besides, even if we walked a whole day, we still wouldn't get out of here. We just don't have that kind of strength."

"How do you know?" Chen Luohu replied. "It's pitch-black up ahead. We might walk another fifteen minutes and be out of here."

I thought about it, and he did have a point. If it were possible to sleep somewhere else, I too would rather not have to brace myself for the long night ahead. It was here that Pei Qing spoke: "We need not fight about it. Listen to the noises around us. Up ahead, the water still sounds very calm. The direction and flow of the river are not changing. And even if the edge of the water was just out of earshot, we'd still have another two to three hours to go. Now that we're exhausted, it's going to be impossible to maintain our previous pace or intensity. The road's going to be increasingly difficult for us. To continue would be inefficient—a waste of time and energy." His intonation was neither too fast nor too slow. He was very convincing. "It would be wisest to rest here," he continued. "I'm in support of setting up camp now, but perhaps we shouldn't stay as long as we might normally."

Wang Sichuan didn't care about estimates or anything. He was just pooped. "Three votes to one, majority rules," he joined in.

Pei Qing really does have his own way of doing things, I thought to myself. I wouldn't have expected so much from him. "Little Pei is top of the class," I said. "He looks at problems differently than us dummies. I agree with his analysis."

Wang Sichuan made a few gestures and at once the corpsmen set down all of their gear. Chen Luohu was mad as hell, but there was nothing he could do. His expression was terrible to look at, but we paid him no mind and began searching around for a suitable campsite. Soon enough, we'd located a large rock, dry and flat as a board. After climbing up, the corpsmen began to put our campsite in order while we unloaded our gear. Once we had set down all of our equipment, we felt much more relaxed. Pei Qing and a young corpsman then packed some basic supplies and set off to see just how much farther the rocky shoal went. If it continued for a long way, we'd be forced to leave some of our equipment behind or we'd be stuck here forever and never accomplish our mission. I didn't pay much attention to their departure and merely told them to be careful, but the deputy squad leader acted like he was in a movie. "You take good care of Mr. Pei!" he commanded the young soldier. We decided that if anything went wrong they would warn us by firing gunshots into the air.

We had our own matters. After tidying up the base, we made a fire and began cooking our military rations. Though we all wore waterproof ponchos, we were wet through and through. We stripped off our clothes and let them toast by the fire. My sleeping bag had been provided by the army. It had a big "US" stamp on it, and someone had told me it had been seized during the Korean War. I've never been too obsessed with cleanliness, so as soon as the bag began to heat up, the scent of mildew permeated the air. Wang Sichuan made me put it away.

Chen Luohu continued to sulk and ignore the rest of us, but Wang Sichuan and I talked and laughed between ourselves, and all the corpsmen took a similar attitude. There's a lot of turnover in military units: While it's great if people get along, there's no need to force it. After all, once the mission is over we all return to our respective homes, and who knows when we might meet again.

Our military rations consisted of condensed, dehydrated wheat flour and rice with accompanying packets of sugar and salt.

Unwrapped, it was the size of one's finger, but once cooked it would fill the pot. Wang Sichuan got up to go draw some water, but as soon as he reached the edge of the rock and beheld the field of black bags and twisted wire, he changed his mind. "I think I'll just use the water I carried in," he said. Someone located a kettle and put it to boil. Together we sat and ate our rice-and-flour paste out of a big basin. It was almost inedible and tasted like medicine, but we made do.

As I ate, I began to consider some of the problems we might face. What was I to do once I had drunk all of my water? The more I thought about it, the more vexed I became. At the back of my mind I kept thinking: Should I be on the brink of dying of thirst, would I be able to drink my own urine? Surely that would be no time to be picky.

We'd finished our meal, but Pei Qing and the soldier still hadn't returned. We smoked and waited. The cigarettes I had at the time were an unruly combination of Harbin and Hengda brand tobacco. Either Wang Sichuan's salary or his connections weren't as good as mine, because he smoked Albanian brand cigarettes, which went for eighteen cents a pack. I could see that none of the soldiers were smoking anything good, just generic cigarettes, so I handed over a pack of Hengdas to the deputy squad leader and—no joke—he blushed all over from happiness. Even after smoking for a while, though, we still felt ill at ease. Not a word was spoken. We just gritted our teeth and kept puffing away.

Honestly, I could understand where Chen Luohu was coming from and, in several respects, he was braver than the rest of us. First of all, he had the courage to admit in front of everyone that he was afraid, and even if we weren't as scared as he was, no way were we entirely free of fear. The worst was eating dinner in that place. I could see how each man tried to behave with an air of complete indifference, but I knew how uneasy they really were. The feeling that people were watching us from every direction never slackened. Our shoulders grew tense from fighting the constant urge to turn our heads and look.

Wang Sichuan suggested I tell some jokes to lighten the mood. I'd worked for a long time as part of a prospecting team that included a number of young soldiers. They'd often ask to hear jokes and stories and I'd composed more than a few of them. Wang Sichuan had heard a few while we were living together, so he knew I had a gift for storytelling. Still, being asked out of the blue made me feel a little embarrassed. I usually liked to build up to the story subtly, talking about work, chatting about one thing or another, drawing the listener in, and then bring out the jokes. And of course, I couldn't tell scary stories here. I did have a good bit that I kept in reserve, though. It was about a prospector in Yunnan making a fool of himself with a young woman from an ethnic minority. The routine was truly hilarious, romantic as could be, and with punch line after punch line. I wasn't sure how long it had been since these young soldiers had seen a woman, but hearing this story would absolutely divert their attention.

As I was pondering the best way to begin—*Bang! Bang! Bang!*—three shots suddenly rang out, booming like a series of thunderclaps. We all leaped in surprise. The deputy squad leader clearly knew what he was doing; at once he tossed away his cigarette, hoisted his rifle, and headed off in the direction of the noise, the rest of the soldiers following closely behind. We had none of their superior agility, and I quickly lagged some sixty feet back. Wang Sichuan was too large and too heavy, and before long he had slipped down the side of one of the boulders and caught his foot in a gunnysack. Unable to pull it out, he began to call for my help. I didn't have time to worry about him. I yelled for Chen Luohu— farther back and nearly crawling flat on his stomach across the rocks—to give him a hand. Then I hurried onward.

CHAPTER 10

A Martyr's Death

I ran through total darkness. All I could see were the shaking beams of the soldiers' flashlights up ahead. I had to slow my pace and withdraw my own flashlight to shine the way. I continued on, leaping across the gaps from rock to rock. There was nothing easy about crossing these spaces. A man is not a kangaroo, and as I hurtled on, it seemed that each jump would be my last. Sometimes, if my feet weren't fast enough, I would begin to slide down the side of a boulder. All I could do was try my best to keep up.

They were still firing their weapons in the distance. Soon I could see the course of their bullet tracers as they shot through the dark. I guessed they were still about eighteen hundred feet away. Pei Qing and the soldier hadn't been walking for that long. My strength was gone by the time I'd made it half that far. I came to a stop. I was panting so hard I thought I might vomit, but after resting for a moment, I realized I could wait no longer. All around me was pitch-black, and up ahead the soldiers continued to fly across the boulders, moving farther and farther away. As I looked at the gunnysacks scattered all around me, with the limbs of desiccated corpses emerging at sickening angles, the blood ran cold in my veins. I gritted my teeth and carried on.

By the time I caught up with them, the gunfire had already ceased. I saw that it was Pei Qing who had been doing the shooting. The soldier who'd accompanied him was nowhere to be seen. The deputy squad leader's complexion had turned deathly pale. Along with another soldier he began running back toward camp. "What is it?" I asked, but he ignored my question and ran straight past me into the darkness. I could do nothing but climb over to Pei Qing and ask what was going on. His face was ashen and he made no reply. The soldier at his side began to explain, but he could barely get the words out. He just pointed and stuttered. It took some time before I understood what he was saying. Someone had fallen. The deputy squad leader had rushed back to find a rope.

I could hear the roar of water nearby. Taking a few steps closer, I saw that we had made it to the end. The boulder field had come to a sudden stop. Here the river crossed a fault line and dropped a level straight down, forming a waterfall. It wasn't that high, sixty-some feet at most. As I shined my flashlight along its base, I could see that the bottom was entirely covered in rocks. Then my beam lit upon the soldier. His body was caught between two rocks, his whole face red with wounds and blood. I couldn't tell whether he was alive or dead.

My head began to buzz. All at once the situation had become very serious. I hurriedly asked Pei Qing what had happened. He said that after reaching this spot they had initially planned to go back, but when he saw the waterfall was not that high, and given that they had already come this far—no easy feat, in itself—he decided to climb down and have a look. The young soldier told Pei Qing that he had been ordered by the deputy squad leader to protect him. This was a dangerous situation, the young man had said, so he'd better check it out first. Handing his rifle to Pei Qing, he began to climb down. Before the soldier had even gone two steps, he suddenly slipped and fell to the bottom. Pei Qing had immediately called for help, but after yelling for some time and receiving no response, he began to fire the rifle.

I'd seen this before. Losing one's footing and falling is the most common danger we prospectors faced. I wasted no time in telling the two soldiers waiting next to me to call out the fallen soldier's name. If he was still conscious, we had to keep him from going to sleep. They yelled and yelled—they called him something like "Big Beard"—but the fallen soldier didn't make even the slightest response. My heart sank. The situation looked grim.

Wang Sichuan rushed in, once more exhausted to the point of collapse, but when he heard someone had tumbled over the side, he instantly went to climb down and save him. It took everything the two soldiers and I had to drag him back.

Finally, after twenty anxious minutes, they returned with the rope. The deputy squad leader himself descended, hoisted the young soldier on his back, and we pulled them both up. The deputy squad leader's hands were covered in blood. At first I thought it had to be the fallen soldier's, but then I saw the rips and gashes on his palms. Wire netting had been wound all the way up the falls. It was hidden behind the spray of water. This was why the young soldier had lost his footing. When I went to examine him, his eyes had already closed. He'd died a martyr's death, and before I had even learned his name. Because he'd always worn a helmet, I'd never given this soldier a close look. Seeing him now, I could tell that he was no older than nineteen—still totally naive, recklessly tramping through his youth. He had died rashly, probably without ever having fallen in love, and no one had been there to hear his last words.

The deputy squad leader had served on the battlefield. His only response was to light a cigarette. The rest of the soldiers began to cry, as did Wang Sichuan. He grabbed Pei Qing, saying the boy was still a baby, how could you let him do something that dangerous. Pei Qing said nothing. He didn't resist and his face looked terribly ashamed. I went to console the soldiers, but the deputy squad leader held me back. If they needed to cry for twenty minutes, I should just let them, he said.

The boy's death hit me hard. We've always been conscious of the dangers inherent in prospecting work, and although we may appear relaxed, we're nonetheless highly alert when it comes to these critical points. What a shame, I thought. We'd become so accustomed to taking care of ourselves that we'd forgotten to look out for others. We should have realized that these engineering corpsmen had no experience in geological exploration. Other than their level of physical fitness, they were no different from ordinary people. It was our negligence that killed this young soldier. These were the facts and there was no escaping them. Had it been I who brought the young soldier to this precipice, I wondered, would I have cautioned him before he climbed down? I'm afraid I too would have said nothing. Though all of us are highly skilled at our professions, when it comes to other things we're entirely too lax. Pei Qing alone was not to blame.

That night we carried the soldier's body back to camp and laid him on a sleeping bag. We couldn't bring him deeper into the cave with us. Though we had to give him a proper burial, that would have to wait until we were on our way back to the surface. The deputy squad leader had us tuck in early, but how were we to calm down after something like that? None of us slept a wink.

The next day, not caring whether it was morning or night, we rose from our bags and put all of our belongings in order. After ceremonially paying our respects to the dead, we continued on our way. In 1962, our duty to the country was more important than anything else. Never once did we consider returning to the surface to rest, reorganize, and return again. We thought only of completing the mission. In prospecting jobs nowadays, as soon as something like this occurs, the assignment is over.

We stopped to eat lunch beside the waterfall. Here the body bags had already thinned out. The rocks had become smaller, the distance between them much closer, and our progress was now relatively easy. Wang Sichuan requested to scout ahead and explore the route, but we stopped him—for no other reason than it just didn't feel right. After eating we took a twenty-minute rest. While fishing around in my pocket for a cigarette, I brushed against a crumpled-up piece of paper. That hadn't been in my pocket earlier, I thought. Unrolling it, I discovered it had been torn from a labor-insurance form. There were only four words: "Beware of Pei Qing!"

CHAPTER 11

The Note

I had no idea who had covertly stuffed the note into my pocket. I glanced around at the rest of the group, but no one was paying me any attention. Then I looked over at Pei Qing. He was cleaning the martyred soldier's old rifle. After the soldier died, Pei Qing had begun carrying the gun on his back. Though it had made no difference to me before, I suddenly found something distasteful about the sight.

Things were getting rather frustrating. Back then the country was in a bad way. We'd just suffered three years of natural disasters and were now facing the threat of invasion by the Kuomintang. I assumed the latter was to blame for the strictly enforced confidentiality of our mission. The threats were coming from both sides, however. In those years, "Kuomintang spy" had become a sensitive term on the mainland. Today this must sound like the plot of some second-rate TV drama, but at the time it was no laughing matter. Supposed US-backed spies for Chiang Kai-shek were "found out" within the police force, people's militia, and people's communes. Men and women were being seized at the slightest provocation. Wang Sichuan later put it best: You could look at it two ways, he said. On the positive side, the nation deeply impressed upon the minds of its citizens the importance of national security. Of course, the other way to see it, he continued, was a form of entertainment. In 1962 the country was engaged in class warfare, and as dances and parties disappeared entirely, all that was left to while away one's days was the possibility of catching a few spies.

The sensitivity of the times cut two ways: On the one hand, the activities of these Kuomintang spies had indeed thrown China into turmoil. On the other, they'd also led to a fervor of false accusations and an atmosphere of general mistrust, resulting in a huge number of wrongful arrests and unjustified cases. Some of these stemmed from such insignificant reasons that their absurdity was terrifying. The note writer was probably just swept up in the feverish suspicions of those times. This kind of person was very common back then—the inveterate schemer, overthinking everything. He probably believed that Pei Qing was a spy, that the young soldier had not accidentally fallen to his death, but had been pushed.

But who the hell had written it? The question ate at me. It obviously hadn't been Wang Sichuan, nor could it have been any of the soldiers. That left only Chen Luohu, already withered from fear and having just slunk off to who knows where. He was just the type to have done it. He'd said nothing since the accident, probably because he'd been the one who first suggested we continue on. Since this had most likely influenced Pei Qing's decision to explore the route ahead, and thus had led to the accident, Chen Luohu had to be scared he might somehow be implicated in the soldier's death.

In any case, I didn't take the note seriously. I knew Pei Qing's background. We were alumni of the same department at the Chinese Geological University, though I had been one year above him. At school he'd always been a logical, clear-thinking student. No way would he have ever become an enemy agent. As for Chen Luohu, he already seemed to be a rather useless character, and I had begun to feel a growing dislike for the man. So I threw the note into the fire, pulled out my cigarettes, and began to smoke, unconcerned about anything or anyone else. Before long I had forgotten all about the note. We set off once more, scrambled down the waterfall, and by that evening had traveled nearly another kilometer. Here there were no more body bags and, because we had slept so poorly the night before, we neglected to even eat dinner before heading to bed. It wasn't even five p.m.

I awoke at ten that night. I had slept like a dead man, but once I opened my eyes I could sleep no more. There remained a single soldier keeping watch over camp. He was feeling rather embarrassed about having thoughtlessly fallen asleep while he stood sentry, so I told him I would take his place. He refused to leave his post. I didn't force the issue. I had served in the regular army and understood that mentality. Once again I was starving to death. I found some rations and set them to boil. As the smell of cooking food began to waft through the air, Wang Sichuan and the other two came stumbling over, one after the other. They all crowded around. After having traveled at a fast clip all day and then falling asleep on an empty stomach, everyone was terribly hungry. One pot of food was not enough. I cooked another half pot. Fortunately, our superiors had been generous in estimating how long the exploration would take. Our stock of food would last another week, though none of us believed we'd be down here that long. Although our condensed field rations did contain additional dehydrated vegetable powder, eating too much would undoubtedly be harmful to one's health. As for the few condensed vegetable packs we carried with us, they tasted disgusting.

Our spirits improved with dinner, and after smoking a post-meal cigarette, we felt invincible. Once more we attempted to cajole the soldier on watch into taking a break, but again he refused. Wang Sichuan handed him a few cigarettes, and these at least he accepted. We ached all over. As we relaxed, we alternated between massaging our sore spots and pondering what the next day would bring. Who knew what the rest of our route would be like? If it continued like this the whole way, then we'd better leave our rafts here. Otherwise, if today's progress was any indication, we'd never have enough food or supplies to make it back out.

The way Pei Qing saw it, someone should be sent ahead to investigate the route while the rest of us stayed behind. In six or seven hours, this person would be able to travel a long way. When he returned, we'd have a much clearer idea of what we were facing. This idea didn't sit well with me. After yesterday's events, any proposal that involved splitting the group seemed unsafe. Wang Sichuan, however, agreed with Pei Qing's suggestion. Given how slowly we were progressing, the most pressing issue was the fuel for our lanterns and the batteries for our flashlights. Without those tools, we'd be dead meat in a place as dark as this. Thus, sending someone ahead to explore had an additional benefit: it would allow us to familiarize ourselves with the route and cut down on the use of lights when we continued on as a group. Wang Sichuan said that if I was worried about the danger, we could send half the group on ahead, as opposed to just one or two people. Yesterday's accident had occurred due to recklessness, he said, and added that if he'd been there, he would have warned the soldier to be careful. Pei Qing regarded Wang Sichuan coldly. It was obvious he'd been speaking to Pei Qing. Wang Sichuan was about to say something else, but I stopped him.

Wang Sichuan was a superb fellow in every respect, but he was too righteous for his own good. The accident had already occurred, and now all we could do was accept it. Staring at Pei Qing and blaming him for what had happened was simply a way for Wang Sichuan to escape the reality of the situation. I was convinced that Pei Qing felt awful inside. Moreover, even if he'd managed to stop the young soldier from climbing down and gone himself instead, there was no way to say that a tragedy would have been prevented. Just because Pei Qing was more experienced, it by no means meant that he would have discovered the iron netting before it was too late. In the end, it could very well have been Pei Qing, not the soldier, who lost his footing and fell to his death. But this wasn't something that Wang Sichuan wanted to hear.

Then, as the atmosphere grew tense once more, a metallic clang suddenly rang out. We all jumped. The pealing of metal striking rock was amplified, bouncing off the cave walls, becoming nearly unbearable. Turning, I saw Chen Luohu had dropped the large metal basin he'd been eating from, spraying rice gruel all over the ground. He was looking in our direction, his body trembling all over. Wang Sichuan gave him a look of irritation and asked what the hell was the matter. The sentry turned from behind Chen Luohu and, as he rotated, the look on his face changed. With a *clack* he pulled back the rifle bolt and, his voice quavering, began to yell: "Squad leader! Deputy squad leader!"

We all turned to where Chen Luohu was looking. Cold sweat covered my body. There, standing on the rock opposite, someone had appeared. The stranger stared at us, not moving, not saying a word.

CHAPTER 12

The Stranger

The boulder we were camped on was relatively large, the rocks surrounding it all at least fifteen feet from us. Beneath us we could hear the constant trickle of the river flowing under the rocky shoal. The flickering light of our campfire illuminated the outline of the stranger's body, but the face remained darkened. The members of our group were all accounted for. This person was not one of us. But we were in a section of pitch-black river deep underground, two hundred feet from the nearest point on the surface, the devil only knows how far from the closest village. Who else could possibly be down here?

In an instant, the cold sweat had soaked through my clothes. I hurriedly stepped back. The deputy squad leader and the rest of the soldiers had all been sleeping lightly. As soon as they heard our cry, they rushed from their bags. Seeing our expressions, they turned to where we were facing, gasped in surprise, and loaded their weapons. Quick as could be, five rifles were aimed across the way.

"Who's there?" shouted the deputy squad leader.

The other did not respond, just stood rigidly in place, not moving at all.

We gulped. Wang Sichuan was the bravest among us. "Pei Qing," he called out, "your flashlight—shine it over there."

Pei Qing cautiously raised his flashlight. As the light illuminated the figure, we were all taken aback. Somehow, the uniform matched ours exactly, even down to the Sam Browne belt across the chest. It was the military dress of the PLA, but every inch of clothing was soaked with blood. Though it was hidden beneath a helmet, we could discern a bloody sheen coating the stranger's face as well.

I felt the blood rush from my face. Who could this be? My body had turned ice-cold, as if I had fallen through a hole in a frozen pond.

Wang Sichuan began to curse in Mongolian. Then one of the soldiers cried out, "It's Big Beard! Big Beard's not dead!" Saying this, he made to drop his weapon and climb over to where the stranger stood.

"Stay where you are!" yelled the deputy squad leader, his eyes bloodshot. "Can't you see what he looks like? Look closely now!"

All of us understood what he meant. Had Big Beard truly not died, he would have called over to us as soon as we were in sight. Instead he stood there motionless, stiffly watching us like some reanimated corpse. The soldier lacked the courage to move any closer, and we remained deadlocked. A blue vein bulged across the deputy squad leader's forehead. Clearly, there was no good way to resolve this standoff.

Pei Qing had also hoisted a rifle. Swallowing deeply, he looked straight at me and asked, "What do we do now?"

If you're asking me, I thought, then who am I going to ask? If this person really was the martyred young soldier, then we were all finished. This morning we'd given him his funeral rites, his death already a certainty. Was it possible that the dead could walk? In my mind I rapidly rifled through a number of different solutions, until at last I spied the large metal basin. Picking it up, I handed it to Pei Qing. "Throw this over there and let's see what he does," I said.

Pei Qing replied that his aim was poor. Wang Sichuan should throw instead. As an ethnic Mongolian, Wang Sichuan had been throwing the *bulu*—a lead-tipped throwing stick used for hunting—since he was a kid. While we'd been stationed at the main 723 Project campsite, he'd knocked a wild ring-necked pheasant out of the air. I looked around for Wang Sichuan. He was nowhere to be seen. Looking again, I couldn't believe my eyes: at some point, unbeknownst to the rest of us, he had climbed over to the rock the stranger stood on and was now preparing to pounce. I opened my mouth to try to stop him, but it was already too late. I could only watch as Wang Sichuan bent over, then launched himself forward, grabbing the stranger in a bear hug. A startled cry rang out and several of us gasped. The voice was not Wang Sichuan's—it was a woman's.

Wang Sichuan attempted to force the stranger down, but his opponent was far from a pushover. As their bodies twisted around, the two of them tumbled to the ground and rolled off the side of the rock into the water below. The deputy squad leader dropped his weapon, tore off his clothing, and rushed in to help. The water beneath the boulders was still very deep. If one were to get caught in the crevices under the rocks, there would be no way to come up for air. The rest of us followed after him, first pulling Wang Sichuan from the water, then dragging the stranger out.

The stranger's helmet had fallen off, revealing hair cut in a short bob and a face that had been rinsed clean of some of the blood. Her clothes were soaked through and stuck tightly to her frame, revealing a body of generous curves. We all blushed. Wang Sichuan spit out a mouthful of water, shivered once from the cold, then quickly tore off his clothing and laid it by the fire to dry. He came back and asked if she was dead or not. I moved her hair aside and checked her pulse. Seeing her face up close, I gave a sudden start. I recognized her. Kneeling by my side, Pei Qing saw it too. "My God," he cried out, "is that Yuan Xile?"

CHAPTER 13

Yuan Xile

You, reader, may feel baffled at this point. In fact, that's just how I felt. If this were a novel it might seem absurd. After all, novels are plotted, with a beginning, middle, and end that are supposed to make sense. But my story is simply a record of the facts. I found Yuan Xile down there. That is a fact. I never would have expected to find her in that cave, but that's where she appeared. At first I couldn't believe it, but taking a closer look, I knew it had to be her. My heart raced with the shock of it. How could she be down here?

Yuan Xile was a prospector herself. Although we were more or less the same age, her qualifications were superior to any of ours. She had studied abroad in the Soviet Union and was given preferential treatment when she returned. She had been second-in-command of several of the prospecting teams I'd served on. She was very serious, and people called her the Soviet Witch. Because of my carelessness, I was regularly made to suffer her criticisms, but in private she was a frank and honest woman and we got along rather well. She had led teams all across the country, so Pei Qing's reason for recognizing her was likely similar to my own.

But there hadn't been any women among the twenty-four of us who'd been stationed at 723. And from the wounds that covered her face and body, it was clear that something terrible had occurred. Her body temperature was extremely low. There was no time for us to discuss why or how she got down here. We cast lots and Wang Sichuan was made to remove her clothes. Most of her body was covered in cuts and scrapes, her skin bruised dark blue from internal bleeding. It was a terrifying thing to see. Her hands and knees were a bloody mess. If it weren't for the stones and iron netting that lay all around us, one would certainly have thought that she'd suffered some cruel torture. None of this was fatal, though. The most serious problem was her body temperature. Her clothes had been soaked even before Wang Sichuan knocked her into the water. Her temperature had likely been low for some time. Her lips were already colored deep purple.

Trembling, Wang Sichuan wiped her body dry and wrapped her in a sleeping bag. He heated water for her to drink, then used the fire to help steam her face, continuing to care for her until the small hours of the night. At last, her temperature began to rise, but she remained unconscious and could not be awoken. Still, our voices lost much of their tension. As Pei Qing stood by her side and watched her sleep peacefully, he spoke his thoughts aloud: "How could she have gotten here?"

Once again I thought of what Old Cat had said to me the night before we set out: "Something about this isn't right." More and more, everything seemed like it was going to hell. "We shouldn't keep going," I said.

"What's wrong?" asked Wang Sichuan.

"It's starting to look like we weren't the first ones here," I said. "There's something going on, and that colonel wasn't honest with us."

My mind was in chaos, my specific thoughts and feelings a mystery to me. Still, it was plain what had taken place here. Pei Qing nodded. I could see his brow begin to wrinkle. The same realization must have just occurred to him: Based on Yuan Xile's attire, it was clear she too had been here on a prospecting assignment. She must have belonged to some unknown fifth group. And this fifth team must have entered the cave some time before us. Had they begun after we did, they'd never have been able to overtake us so quickly. Though the specifics were still unclear, we now knew that prospecting activity had taken place here prior to our arrival. Yuan Xile was the ironclad proof. The situation was a mess. All at once, a host of new problems had arisen. For example: If this group had been here before us, why hadn't the colonel let us know? And given that Yuan Xile was a female prospector, there was no way the higher-ups would have let her explore the cave by herself. So where was everyone else?

The deputy squad leader was sitting in silence some distance away from us, surrounded by his soldiers. I went over and asked him how much of this he'd previously been aware of.

"Even less than you," he said, shaking his head. "We entered the cave when you did, but that meeting you held beforehand, we didn't even get that—just orders to accompany you and complete the mission. Nothing more."

Everyone else was silent.

"Why not just ask her when she wakes up," said Wang Sichuan.

I shook my head. Yuan Xile had just been through hell. The scariest thing about it was that she had been without a flashlight. For who knows how long this poor woman had been wandering lost through the caverns in pitch-black darkness. Imagine what she went through: stumbling through the limitless dark of a freezing cave, strange and nameless sounds echoing off the walls. There was no telling what condition she'd be in when she woke up.

"It's useless," Pei Qing added. "Even if she does wake up, she won't tell us very much. Among those of her level, keeping quiet is a point of professional pride. Since she outranks all of us, it would be against protocol for her to say anything."

"So what do we do now?" asked Wang Sichuan. "Goddamn it, what the hell were our superiors thinking? We've never been involved in a mess like this before. The best thing to do would be to just pull out. Is whatever the hell's down here really worth dying for?"

"You should have realized on the long truck ride over that this assignment would be far different from any we'd worked on previously," Pei Qing said, not looking at Wang Sichuan but past him, in the direction we had to travel. I saw a strange sort of anticipation pass through his eyes.

This guy is not normal, I thought. Looking at his face, you'd think what had happened so far made almost no difference to him. I thought once more of the note, but then my mind turned back to our current situation. Indeed, I too was more than a little curious about what was waiting at the end of the river. And why, I wanted to know, was the truth behind our predicament getting harder and harder to grasp the longer we were down here?

"I say you all should just stop discussing it," said Chen Luohu. "If our brothers on the engineering team hear us talking like this, they'll think we're doubting the decisions of our superiors, and that won't be good at all." He had shrunk to one side, but kept speaking in a quiet voice. "We might as well continue on. There's nothing to do but suck it up and keep going."

Wang Sichuan stared at Chen Luohu, but I stopped him before he could say anything. This time Chen Luohu was correct. The engineering corpsmen thought differently than we did. We should take pains to say little in their presence that might make them think we were having second thoughts. "No matter what," I said after thinking about it for a moment, "we can't go anywhere until she wakes up and we ask her what's going on. Even if we only find out a little, that's better than nothing. At the very least, she should be able to give us some sort of explanation."

CHAPTER 14

Madness

A range of thoughts and opinions were swirling about camp that night. None of us had seen a woman in a long time. To have one sleeping in our midst with her underwear toasting by the fire made it tough to fall asleep. I was exhausted, but wild fantasies kept me up. At last, I fell into a deep sleep.

After sleeping for who knows how long, I was nudged awake. I raised my head and looked around, but everything was blackness—the fire had been extinguished. Sitting up, I turned on my flashlight and shined it into the darkness. The sentry must have fallen asleep. I turned my head to see who had shaken me. It was Yuan Xile. She was squatting beside me, completely naked. I felt a jolt of fear. "You're awake?" I asked her.

She made no reply, but moved closer and crawled onto my chest. A strange odor filled my nostrils. I felt dizzy. Yuan Xile was a northeasterner, and like most girls from that region she was voluptuous, her figure incredibly alluring. Though I wanted to push her off, my hands pulled her closer. The soft, smooth feel of her skin beneath my fingers made my hair stand on end, but I dared do nothing more. Unable to go further, unable to go back, I lay paralyzed. Suddenly, she opened her mouth wide. I watched as slowly, very slowly, a long piece of wire emerged from the black recesses of her throat.

I yelled in surprise and sprang off the ground. In a flash everything disappeared. I was still lying in my sleeping bag, the firelight glowing brightly. Chen Luohu, Pei Qing, and two of the soldiers were already awake. Wang Sichuan was nearby, snoring loudly. Yuan Xile had awoken as well and was already sitting by the fire, fully clothed and devouring a plate of food. Her hair was matted and one look at her movements was enough to know that something was wrong.

Laughing to myself, I reached down and felt the crotch of my trousers. Fuck, my old dad was right. The quicker I got married the better. Rubbing my eyes, I rose from bed, washed my face in cold water, and glanced over at Pei Qing. "How is she," I asked him.

Pei Qing shook his head. "Looks like she's had nothing to eat for a very long time."

"Has she said anything?"

He sighed. "You'd better ask her yourself."

Seeing Pei Qing's expression and hearing his tone of voice, I could tell that no pleasant surprises awaited me, but it wasn't until I went over and attempted to talk to her that I discovered how dark the situation actually was. She was curled up into herself and scarcely aware of anything. She seemed absent, her entire being deeply distracted. As soon as I spoke, she turned to stare fixedly at me, but no matter what I asked she never responded. The look in her eyes was somehow dispersed, unable to focus. She'd been wandering in the dark for far too long and was now struggling to adjust her eyes to the light. Still, her face remained delicate and lovely. Just looking at it was enough to make my heart ache. To think what had become of this poor woman.

At last I gave up. Pei Qing brought me some breakfast and sat down. He gave a deep sigh. "It's just too pitiful," he said. Pei

Qing reckoned it had been the lights of our camp that had drawn Yuan Xile to us out of the darkness. He said he'd gone through her clothes and rucksack and all her food was completely gone. Who knew how long she had been wandering through the caverns? Had we arrived just a little later, she would almost certainly have been dead.

I turned to the rest of the group. "We're bound to run into trouble the deeper we get into this cave," I said. "Since at this point we know absolutely nothing about what lies ahead, maybe we should first head back to the surface."

The nature of both the assignment and our team had changed. We now knew the road ahead would be dangerous and that our superiors were hiding something from us. To continue at this point would not be some positive manifestation of stoicism but a foolhardy move, demonstrating a poor understanding of when it's best to adapt to the circumstances.

Pei Qing nodded. "To be honest," he said, "I'm very curious about what happened down here, but I admit that based on the current situation, heading back would be the correct decision. Still, to simply pick up and go back wouldn't be right. If there are others still stranded, we'd just be letting them die. A few of us should advance with a small amount of gear and look around a bit. Maybe we can get some closure on the matter."

He really had a point. My God, this guy was a leader. It made me a little envious. When Wang Sichuan and the rest of them awoke, I told them what we'd discussed. No one had any complaints. In any case, said the deputy squad leader, his orders had been to listen to us.

After everyone finished eating breakfast, we began to discuss how we'd split our ranks. We couldn't bring Yuan Xile. Someone would have to stay behind and look after her. Chen Luohu immediately raised his hand. "I suddenly don't feel so well anymore," he said. "I request to stay behind." No one objected. It was impolite to say it, but he'd been a burden from the start. Worried that Chen Luohu might run into trouble by himself, the deputy squad leader left behind one of his soldiers. Then Wang Sichuan, Pei Qing, the deputy squad leader, two of his soldiers, and I hoisted our lightened packs and set out.

Because we planned to return to the surface after finishing our search, we no longer had any misgivings about wasting our lantern fuel or batteries. We all switched on our flashlights, and at once the cave became bright. The landscape here appeared more or less unchanging, but we didn't have time to take a closer look. With our lightened packs, we were able to practically fly across the rocks. Soon we could no longer see the firelight behind us. The deeper we went into the cave, the bigger it seemed to become. The more we walked, the more we felt strength filling our bodies. It was as if we'd permanently cast off the gloom that weighed us down in the days before, trudging slowly along, burdened by heavy loads. Soon we discovered the crushed stones covering the ground were becoming smaller and smaller, a sign that the shoal was beginning to recede. After walking another two thousand feet or so, we ran into a steep drop-off. The shoal descended for over nine hundred feet. Twenty-foot sheets of iron mesh were stuck patchily across the rock slope. Exercising great caution, we began to pick our way down. Before we reached the bottom, Wang Sichuan suddenly cursed aloud. As expected, the pitch-black river had appeared once more at the foot of the hill, but it was just a short section. As we shined our flashlights along the water, we could see that, some several hundred feet on, it ran into another shoal, this one composed of small, shattered stones.

"What now?" asked Pei Qing. "Do we really have to head back and get the rafts?" Of course, we all knew this was out of the question. The deputy squad leader scanned the water with his flashlight. The bottom was clearly visible. "We can wade across," he said.

He made to leap in, but Wang Sichuan held him back. "Wait a moment!" he said.

He swept the beam of his flashlight back and forth across a secluded corner of the river. There, deposited at the water's deepest point, were a number of iron cages, their interiors hidden in dark shadow.

CHAPTER 15

The Water Dungeon

We had reached a water dungeon. We'd all seen them before in the structures the Japanese built all across Manchuria. The cages were designed so the water would just cover the bars across the top. The prisoner was thus forced to hoist himself up and stick his nose through the gaps if he wanted to stay alive. In the freezing water of the underground river, prisoners would have had to maintain this posture for several days. If they gave up, they drowned.

Iron cages had been sunk all along the length of the river, creating a dense mass beneath the surface, but unless one looked closely, they were undetectable. Bringing the beams of our flashlights together, we could see dim shapes floating within many of the cages. A shiver ran down my spine. Wang Sichuan told us he'd sometimes heard the older generation talk about these things. They said that when the Japanese sealed you inside, there was more than freezing water and exhaustion in store for you. He was sure that leeches and other things also lurked within the river. We couldn't just jump right in.

Hearing this, our hearts dropped. The deputy squad leader protested that it was too cold for leeches, but Wang Sichuan replied

that temperature had nothing to do with it. The Mongolian grasslands were filled with mountain leeches, he said. They would stick
to the underside of fallen leaves and come out as soon as it rained.
We were well aware of the dangers posed by these creatures. They
weren't fatal, but they nonetheless elicited feelings of intense disgust
and their bites could sometimes lead to malarial infections. They
were one of the principal dangers of prospecting. We pulled our
pants and shoelaces tight. Leeches are extremely small before they
fill with blood. Even the tiniest crevice is enough of an opening. We
lined any tears in our pant legs with gauze. Once our preparations
were complete, we inspected each other to make sure we hadn't
missed anything. We then entered the water one by one. Lifting
his belongings overhead, the deputy squad leader led the way. The
rest of us followed behind him, our hands in the air like those of
surrendered soldiers.

The rocks beneath our feet were bumpy and uneven. As we
continued, the frigid water soon rose to the middle of our chests,
soaking through our clothes, stealing our body heat, and causing
our teeth to chatter uncontrollably. Wang Sichuan was freezing at
the back of the line and pressed us to hurry up, but no matter how
much we wanted to quicken our pace, we could go no faster. The
combination of the freezing cold and the deep water greatly hin-
dered our progress. It was all we could do to keep moving forward,
each step requiring an ever-greater effort.

Two of the engineering corpsmen proved more resistant to the
cold. They waded on up ahead, sweeping the beams of their flashlights back and forth across the surface of the water. It wasn't long
before we found ourselves amid the iron cages. They were much
closer here and their details far clearer. As the corpsmen shined
their lights upon the rusted underwater bars, our hearts froze. Hair
hung from them in wispy clumps and the outline of twisted limbs
slowly rocked beneath the surface.

"Terrible," Wang Sichuan said through chattering teeth. "To drown in a place like this…Even in death these men will not find peace."

"Indeed," added Pei Qing, "and how unexpected, to come across a water dungeon this far below the surface. This was one of the tricks the Japanese used to threaten Chinese laborers. The Japanese must have stayed in these caverns for some time. I bet we'll find some long-term fortifications up ahead."

None of us spoke. At last, Wang Sichuan mumbled, "In any case, anything the Japs liked can't be good."

We continued on in silence. All that could be heard was the swishing of water and the men in front and behind gasping for breath. This section of river wasn't long. Soon enough we'd reached the middle. I was already so cold I couldn't feel my feet. My mind swam through a vague tumult of sensations, the swaying flashlight beams appearing like flowers of light blooming in the darkness. I relied purely on reflex to keep going. Whether or not leeches lurked beneath the surface—I had no strength left to care.

Then the sound of swishing water changed. Someone seemed to have stopped. I squinted ahead into the darkness. It was the deputy squad leader. Shining his flashlight at the water just in front of him, he was leaning forward, searching intensely for something. We asked him what was wrong. When he raised his head, we saw his face was pale. "Something down there just grabbed hold of my foot," he said.

"Don't talk nonsense!" cried Wang Sichuan, but I could see the color drain from his face. To say that kind of thing in a place like this was no laughing matter. A moment before we had been merely trudging along, our minds empty from the cold. Now everyone's energy immediately returned.

"I'm not joking," said the deputy squad leader. "There's definitely something in the water." The deputy squad leader was a serious man not given to making friends. No way would he have waited until this moment to finally tell a joke. We all began scanning the water with our flashlights.

"Could it be a cave fish?" asked Pei Qing. "This same water flows all the way from the top of the cave. There would have to be at least some living in a river of this length."

"You find one and I'll believe you," said Wang Sichuan. Then, in the bright spot lit by our flashlight beams, we saw something very long sweep past, moving fast as lightning.

Everyone gasped. Wang Sichuan was the first to react. Panicking, he turned, splashed over to one of the cages, and climbed on top. The rest of us rushed to copy his example. In a chaos of waving arms and sloshing water, we clambered atop the other cages. Only the deputy squad leader thought to hoist his rifle. The *click* of a gun being loaded resounded throughout the cave.

We were all soaked to the bone, cumbersome and clumsy under the weight of our dripping clothes. Pei Qing, the smallest in our group, was unable to steady himself. He slumped down heavily onto the cage, his face even paler than usual, and sat staring numbly at the water. Several people began scanning the river with their flashlights, but nothing could be seen. Small waves and concentric ripples covered its surface, the results of our frantic rush to reach the cages a moment ago. What if the shadowy image had been nothing more than an illusion conjured by our nervous minds? No one was brave enough to jump back in and find out.

For a moment we were unsure how to proceed. Then Wang Sichuan spoke up. "Switch off the goddamn flashlights," he said. "Let's get to the far bank. Then you can look all you want." He stood and began sprinting across the cages toward the shore. We watched him run for a moment. Then some nameless terror overtook us. Unable to think for another second, the rest of us took off after him. The cages were packed tight together, the tops of them relatively flat and only a finger's length away from the water's surface. I had just been wondering how the Japanese had managed to stick their prisoners inside. Now I could see they'd simply walked atop the cage tops. If only we had realized this earlier, I thought, there would have been no need to wade through the water. The old saying was true: only when the situation becomes critical does a solution ever appear.

We ran like the wind, all of us terrified of falling behind. Soon we could see the opposite bank. There were no more cages in the final section of river, and we watched as Wang Sichuan reached the edge of the last one. He leaped like a bear into the water. After struggling to the surface, he took a few short steps and climbed onto the bank. The rest of us followed closely behind. Pei Qing was now in the lead. I was the next man behind him. Then, all of a sudden, he was gone. I gasped and sprinted to the spot where he'd disappeared. The water where he fell began to seethe violently, but I couldn't make out what was going on beneath the surface.

My heart skipped a beat. For a moment I hesitated, then my mind went blank and I leaped into the water. I swam over to where the surface was still churning and dove under. Everything was concealed in a dense swirl of bubbles. Somewhere in front of me, two giant shapes appeared locked in violent struggle. My nerves went haywire. I pulled out my dagger and shined my flashlight into the murk.

It was not at all what I had expected. Once my eyes acclimated to the underwater light, I saw no monster awaiting me. It was Pei Qing. Somehow he'd gotten himself trapped inside one of the iron cages. He was a poor swimmer, incapable of opening his eyes underwater, and though he struggled with all his might to free himself, he was far too agitated. His efforts did no more than vainly stir up the water. After Wang Sichuan ran across the cage's severely rusted top bars, they needed no more than the weight of

Pei Qing to snap in half. He was skinny enough to fall through the gap that had opened, and once underwater, he panicked. Since he was unwilling or unable to open his eyes, all he could do was knock about from one side of the cage to the other.

I had no idea how severe his water phobia was. Some people can drown in public baths. I swam toward the cage, reached my hand between the bars, and tried to calm him down. As I grabbed hold of him, his entire body erupted in a fit of fright. His feet pedaled violently. He smashed them against the sides of the cage. I swam to the surface, climbed atop the broken cage, and reached my hands into the opening to pull him out. At this point, the deputy squad leader and Wang Sichuan both rushed over to help. Wild with fear and adrenaline, we forced apart the bars of the cage and attempted to hoist the half-dead Pei Qing to the surface.

The poor guy was in a terrible way. As soon as we got his head above water he vomited violently, was racked by coughing, and then went completely still, his body soft and limp as clay. Despite all our efforts, we could only get the top half of him above the surface. His legs still dangled in the freezing water below. After attempting to pull him up several more times without success, Wang Sichuan stopped and said that his legs were probably hooked on something below the surface. Someone should go under and investigate. At once everyone turned to me. I alone was entirely soaked from head to toe. There was nothing to say, so I cursed silently and jumped back in.

The water was much clearer now that Pei Qing was no longer tossing about. Treading water, I saw the cages were wound together with coils of iron netting. The Japanese had probably been afraid the strongest prisoners might be able to lift the cage from where it sat and flee while still within its bars. It was this netting that was now hooked around Pei Qing's pant leg. I dove underwater, grabbed his pant leg, and yanked on it with all my might. I was almost out of breath by the time his pants ripped free of the wire. When I released my hand from his leg, Wang Sichuan and the rest were at last able to drag Pei Qing's whole body out of the water. I exhaled deeply, sending forth a river of bubbles. Reaching out of the cage, I was about to kick to the surface, when my flashlight lit upon some shape to the right. There, from out of the darkness, emerged the most hideous face imaginable.

CHAPTER 16

The Water Demon

I've experienced it all in my life, encountered my fair share of seemingly fatal circumstances, and defied death more than once. But, looking back now, I can honestly say there have been only a few instances in which I have felt true fear. This was one of them—though it's likely my terror was due in large part to inexperience. At the time, I had yet to encounter my first real life-or-death situation and therefore didn't know how to react.

Truthfully, I'd only caught a vague glimpse of this face I'd labeled "hideous." I had been shining my flashlight into the pitch-black murk. Turning my head and seeing anything appear like that from out of the darkness—suddenly and very close by—would have been terrifying no matter what it was. I didn't have the chance to look any closer. My natural reflex was to shrink back at once. I gulped a mouthful of cold water. I began to choke and lost my composure. All I could do was flail at the surface. In a moment I was scooped out of the river and back onto the cages.

I had swallowed a lot of water and was coughing so hard I couldn't speak. Nor could I see much of anything, but someone helped me to my feet and pulled me along as we ran across the cages, jumped once more into the water, and then somehow climbed up onto the shore. Only then was I able to regain my bearings.

It was a proper mess. Everyone was soaked to the gills. We quickly found a dry spot and started a fire. Every man removed every article of clothing and placed them by the flames. At last, stark naked, we could do nothing but huddle together for warmth. Wang Sichuan had brought along some *baijiu*, some white lightning. We passed it around and slowly some semblance of normality began to return. It was then that Wang Sichuan asked me what happened down there. Why had I suddenly lost control?

I told him and everyone else what I had seen, but I could tell from their expressions they didn't believe me. Maybe it was one of the sunken corpses, suggested Pei Qing. Perhaps he'd knocked one loose while trapped in the cage, or maybe I was simply mistaken and had imagined the whole thing.

I was unable to respond. I myself had only the briefest impression of that so-called face, and what Pei Qing suggested did seem to make the most sense. Nevertheless, for such a thing to have soundlessly appeared by my side from out of nowhere—there was just something not quite right about it. That moment of extreme fright made a deep impression on me, and whenever I meet up with others from the expedition, we always discuss it. To this day I can still feel some nameless terror building inside me every time I see a channel of pitch-black water. I have the sense that somewhere, hidden under the surface, something awaits.

Of course, that all came later. Even though nobody believed my story at the time, I already felt a sense of dread whenever I looked back upon the still river. And when I realized we would have to cross the pool again on our way out, my blood froze and I forced myself to think about it no more.

We put our clothing back on as soon as it was dry. Feeling its warmth upon my skin, I thought, for the first time since being down here, of the surface and of the sunlight. But then Pei Qing rose to his feet and said that we shouldn't waste any more time. We packed up our things and pressed on once more. At this point, we'd already used a good chunk of the time we'd allotted ourselves. We decided that if we ran into another such pond, we'd be forced to turn back. After we'd walked a short distance farther, the cave suddenly opened up and the river running beneath the rock became noticeably wider. Items left by the Japanese began to appear all around us and in great number. Signs written in peeling Japanese characters lined the walls. Green chests were wedged into many crevices in the rock. They were all ruined, some even smashed to pieces. Inside were piles of black cottonlike material. The deputy squad leader fished several out with his rifle. They were soaked.

The path now became smooth and easy to traverse. We walked on for two hours without encountering anything strange. Then, after passing through a long and narrow enclosure, we climbed atop a terrifically large boulder and shined our lights ahead. Rather than once more illuminating a swatch of total darkness, our flashlight beams instead lit upon the sheer face of a gigantic rock wall.

We stood there gaping for quite some time before we realized what this meant. It was the end of the cave. After we swept our flashlight beams across the wall, it became evident that this was a giant chunk of tectonic limestone. It had been formed hundreds of millions of years ago, when two walls were suddenly forced together by accumulated pressure within the rock strata, creating a single massive rock face. The cave went no deeper. It had naturally sealed itself shut and we had reached the end.

From the pool at the top of the cave we had traveled some four or five kilometers to get here. As far as underground rivers were concerned, this one was rather short. It is much more common to see them stretch for ten to twenty kilometers. Given the amount of water flowing through the cave, we never would have expected it to end so abruptly. All of us prospectors began to talk at once. We felt that for the cave to conclude here was a structural impossibility. Based on the textbook examples as well as on our own experience, this underground river should have extended much farther. The great quantity of water it carried would have to be flushed some-where, most likely into a lake hidden deep beneath the rock. The main thing we kept talking about was how the river had rushed when it reached the stone-filled shoals, how it had been too deep to see the bottom. It's not like the amount of water in the river had been lessening the deeper we got. And once that much water arrived here, it would necessarily keep flowing downward beneath the rock. There had to be a descending channel of water somewhere around here, but from where we stood, the cave really did seem to come to an end. Even after looking for some time, we could find no concealed entrance or tunnel.

We were at a complete loss, so we took a short break to assess our situation. Among us, Pei Qing had the most experience with cave exploration. He had worked in Yunnan, where the landscape is riddled with caves and waterways. Normally, he said, the force of the river would have created a small waterfall here. Over time, the water would then cause the rock around it to collapse, blocking off the rest of the cave. The path ahead still existed, he said. It was just hidden beneath our feet.

Wang Sichuan and I both disagreed. If this were the case, then how had the Japanese been able to proceed deeper into the cave?

"We must have taken the wrong branch in the river," said Wang Sichuan. "One of the other groups is on the right path. But," he continued, "isn't this just what we needed? Now we have every reason to head back the way we came."

I waved off this suggestion. Even if one were to ignore all the signs of long-term Japanese occupation here, the simple presence of the woman having come from this direction was enough to prove that, somewhere around here, there had to be a path that led deeper into the cave.

"Fine," said Wang Sichuan, "let's do it like this: We'll all stop talking, stop making any noise, and just look and listen. If there really is a massive crevice hidden somewhere under the rock, the sound of water rushing through it should be relatively loud."

Having no alternative, we split up and moved around the cave. Lying with our ears to the ground, we held our breath. Little by little, the faint sound of running water became audible. In all honesty, though, if I was able to detect any difference in the sound from one place to another, it seemed random. As I moved about the cave to better gauge the location of the river, the sound itself changed, now becoming louder, now becoming softer. With great care I attempted to track the sound across dozens of feet of cave floor, but without any luck. Sighing to myself, I yelled to everyone that we might as well give it up. One of the soldiers suddenly jumped to his feet and motioned for us to be silent.

Had he found the hidden channel? We tiptoed over, knelt down, and began to listen. We waited a moment, then, rather than the sound of water rushing beneath the rock, we heard something indescribable, almost like the noise of fingernails scratching against stone. We listened in silence for some time, but were unable to discern just what the sound was. We knew only that this noise, like thorns dragging against a chalkboard, was agonizing. It felt like claws being scraped against our hearts, provoking a terrible itch. All we wanted was to scratch it with all our might.

I'm not sure who was first to begin digging, but in a moment we had all joined in and were tearing the stones from the floor of the cave, first big ones, then the small ones. After having lifted several of the rocks, I realized that something was amiss. They were all far too easy to move. Of the shattered stones that lay nearby, some were large and some were small, but they always had much larger stones beneath them. Somehow, though, not a single one of the rocks from this spot was large enough to prevent us from tunneling deeper. What did it mean? In my curiosity I couldn't help but increase my pace. This ferocity infected the rest of the group, and we began to work faster and faster. Then, with an audible *clang*, I knocked against something other than rock.

Everyone paused, stopped what they were doing, and looked over at me. A rust-covered sheet of iron lay beneath the stone I had just pulled from the pit. We stared at it for a moment, our expressions baffled. Then everyone gathered around me, ripping the hole wider. We soon uncovered a massive iron door, fifteen feet long by fifteen feet wide. Mottled green paint peeled from its exterior. The faded outlines of Japanese characters were just barely visible. "Plan 53" was all we could make out. Once the majority of the door had been uncovered, we put our ears to its surface and listened silently. The scratching sound had disappeared and from within the door not a noise could be heard.

CHAPTER 17

The Iron Door

It was a double door made of variously sized sheets of iron welded together. The door was astonishingly thick, with rivets as big as a thumb and overlaid with countless layers of cement and liquid steel. It was set inside a grooved iron frame and was sturdy enough that when we stood atop it, the door neither rocked nor flexed an inch. The two doors would open in unison from the center, where there were three huge torque-operated door handles. They had been welded immobile. Even the tiniest seams between the doors had been welded shut. No matter how hard we pulled, they failed to move at all.

The deputy squad leader gave the soldier at his side a certain inscrutable look, and the latter climbed onto the door and pressed down on it with all his weight. "It's blastproof," he said in a quiet voice. "There's a false layer within the iron sheeting filled with mechanical springs and cotton batting."

"Seems when the Japs left they had already decided not to return," whispered Wang Sichuan. We all nodded.

Having reached this point and unable to go farther, how could we explain the appearance of Yuan Xile? And where were the others who had been with her? Even if they had all died, we should have stumbled across their corpses or, at the very least, some sign of their presence. What if she had entered the cave by herself? No, that could never have happened. Then I had a strange idea. Perhaps I was overthinking, but what if the reason the Japanese sealed the iron door hadn't been to prevent others from getting in, but rather to prevent something inside from getting out?

We'd all seen Japanese bunkers while prospecting in the mountains of Inner Mongolia. We knew that once the Japanese decided to seal off an area, they made absolutely sure it would stay closed forever. Not only would they demolish all tunnels leading to the bunker, they'd also drill into its domed roof and load-bearing walls and set explosives for pinpoint directional blasting. The bunker's entire structure would be thoroughly destroyed. This was the most effective way of ensuring that none of the data or other materials inside might fall into enemy hands and that the ruined bunker would never be usable again. Here the only thing blocking our way was the iron door. This was not at all how the Japanese usually did things.

But there was no use in thinking about it. The simple truth was, we had no chance of getting past the door with the equipment we had. This wasn't a matter of being unprepared; only a massive blowtorch would suffice to open a door like this. Discovering the door had excited us. Surely there was some way of getting it open, we felt. But after kneeling and knocking and feeling about for the better part of an hour, we were utterly flummoxed. We looked at one another in blank dismay.

At last it was Pei Qing who said what we all were thinking: "What do we do now? Are we really going to have to go back like this?"

We all smiled bitterly. At this point, what was there left to do besides head back? It didn't matter how much we wanted to keep going, with the door blocking our path there was no way for us to continue. This prospecting job had reached its end.

Honoring proper work procedure, we gathered hydrological and geological samples, made an approximate description of the iron door, then gathered our things and prepared to head back. The soldiers had grown weary of exploring and were thrilled to be returning to the surface. In addition to what they were already carrying, they hefted some of our belongings as well. After walking only a short distance, though, we noticed that something about the ground had changed. Before any of us could react, the deputy squad leader, marching out in front, realized what was going on. In a low voice, he spoke just two words: "Oh shit!"

We all looked down. At once it became clear: water was bubbling up through cracks in the cave floor, and it was coming out fast. We looked at one another, our faces pale. As prospectors and engineering corpsmen, we understood all too well what was happening. The underground river was rising!

"Run!" someone yelled, and immediately we dropped all of our equipment. We sprinted like mad in the direction we had come. A shiver ran down my spine: the terrain here was far too low!

Prior to beginning river-cave exploration or prospecting work, we were always warned to pay close attention to any rise in the level of groundwater. With torrential rainfall, smaller tributaries branching onto or off of large underground rivers may begin to overflow or flow backward, causing the water level to rise and creating an extremely dangerous situation.

But Inner Mongolia in the 1960s was suffering severe drought. When we entered the cave, the sky had been a clear and boundless blue—no clouds at all. Who would have guessed rain was on the way? And because the course of the river flowed under the rocky shoal, its rise must have been soundless. Suddenly, that sound of fingernails scratching against stone sprang into mind. My God, I thought, there had been nothing strange about that noise at all—we'd read about it in textbooks, just never heard it in real life. It was the sound of water rising up through a dry cave!

We truly were running for our lives. Anyone who lives by the ocean knows how fast the tide can rise, but underground rivers rise even faster. For the first several dozen strides the danger we were fleeing remained in our imaginations, but soon the water had overflowed the cracks and begun to wash across the cave floor.

"To the water dungeon!" yelled Wang Sichuan, running out in front. "The water won't be able to rise that high!"

I knew it was already much too late. The path to the water dungeon was rugged and difficult to navigate. The water would be over our heads before we made it there. By then we wouldn't have strength left to resist the fierce pull of the current. Still, regardless of everything, I sprinted on. Had I taken a moment to stop and consider, I might have realized that gathering together anything that could float and preparing to be overtaken would have been the wisest course of action. At the time, though, only a single word flashed through my mind: *Run!*

We ran as fast as we could. By the time the water reached our knees we still had no idea how much farther we had to go. We could no longer see the rocks that stood in our way. Wang Sichuan was the first to fall. It was not some casual tumble, and when he came up his face was covered in blood, but he didn't stop for a moment. One after another the rest of us went down as well, but we immediately struggled to our feet and kept going. With each fall, getting back up became more exhausting, our hands and knees bleeding and torn. Mindlessly, heedless of everything, we continued on. We were moving so slowly our progress was negligible. The force of the current began to pick up and soon we could barely manage to stand in place. As soon as we relaxed our efforts in the slightest, the river would lift us up and sweep us back the way we'd come. We could go no farther.

It was then that Wang Sichuan, who was still out ahead, finally gave up running and began to scramble toward the side of a gigantic boulder. We knew what he was thinking, and that each of us had no hope of surviving on our own, so we followed his lead. By the time we'd reached it, the water was already lapping at our waists. We toyed with death in every step we took. All we could hear was the thunderous crash of the water all around, the sound amplified by the narrow cavern. The noise was deafening, and we had to shout to be heard. We locked our palms together, Wang Sichuan stepped on them, and we hoisted him atop the tall rock. Then he leaned over its face, reached down, and pulled us up one by one.

After climbing to the highest point of the rock, we huddled together and looked down. Any hint of the dry land we had crossed only a short time before was now thoroughly hidden beneath the waves.

CHAPTER 18

Rising Water

The boulder was fifteen feet tall. The water would be that high in ten minutes, though I doubted our nerves could stand to wait that long. Sitting there, watching the water move closer and closer, feeling our hearts thumping fast enough to burst in our chests, having not the slightest idea of what to do next—it was a hellish kind of torture.

Among us, the deputy squad leader remained the most calm. He seemed to have already made his peace with the world. He moved to the side of the rock, sat down, and pulled out his cigarettes. They were soaked to ruin. He tried to light one several times, but finally threw them into the rising water. Wang Sichuan had the greatest resolve. As he shined his flashlight across the cave wall, he yelled for me to come and look for evidence of a waterline. We might determine approximately how high the water would rise, then make whatever preparations remained to us. I hurriedly searched and at last I found it—far, far above our heads.

One of the young soldiers began to cry. They were simply too young, and though we tried to console them, it made no difference. As for me, I felt only restlessness awaiting my death. I didn't have long to wait. Soon the water was above our feet, and with it a feeling of terror spread through us. Everyone held their breath. With faces pale as ghosts, we waited for that final moment when the water would wash over us and all would be gone.

It was then that Wang Sichuan, who had never given up for an instant, suddenly roared and pointed at a section of the cave wall. There jutted the rocky spine of a waterfall. "If we swim over there," he said, "we can climb up as the water rises. At least we'll be able to survive a little while longer."

He had us shine the way with our flashlights, and without another word, he leaped into the swift current. He was swept along, now sinking, now submerging, before he righted himself, got his bearings, and began swimming hard for the waterfall. It wasn't far. With the speed of the current pushing him along, he was soon able to grab hold of the rocks and climb up. He switched on his flashlight and signaled to us that he was all right, that we'd better get over there fast. The deputy squad leader jumped in with his young soldiers. In a moment, they too had made their way over to the waterfall, almost as if there was nothing hard about it. I was ready to go. I slapped Pei Qing on the shoulder, said to him, "Let's go for it," and prepared to jump.

He grabbed me back from the edge, his face deathly pale. "Stay out of the water!" he said.

I was astounded. "What's wrong?"

He pointed at the white water swirling just beyond the rock. "Look!" he said. "There's something in there!"

I switched on my flashlight and shined it on the water beside the rock. There, out of nowhere, was a long black shadow, silently riding the current, its body absolutely still.

Words cannot describe the urgency and disorder of that moment. The white-capped rapids were already above my ankles, Wang Sichuan was bellowing our names from his perch atop the waterfall, Pei Qing was gripping my arm as if he would rather die than release it, and there, in the water just beyond the rock, some dark apparition seemed to be waiting for us. I didn't know what to do even before the thing appeared. I had no energy left now to consider an additional factor. "You see ghosts and spirits everywhere," I shouted at Pei Qing. "Even if there were sharks in the water, we'd still have to go for it!"

Pei Qing refused to listen. With a death grip on my arm, he rolled up his pant leg and yelled, "Take a look at this!"

I lowered my head and looked. A dark black mark had appeared on his calf, like a bruise where something had grabbed hold of him. "I didn't fall into that cage back in the water dungeon," he continued, "something pulled me down. I'm telling you, there's something wrong with the water here."

Nonsense, I thought, but I remembered what I'd seen in the water and my words caught in my throat. Wang Sichuan continued to yell for us. He couldn't understand what the hell was taking us so long. After hesitating only a second longer, I realized it didn't matter whether we jumped in or waited. The water was already at our knees. Regardless of what kind of thing had grabbed Pei Qing, regardless of whether he was willing or not, I gripped his arm and leaped desperately into the river.

The current picked us up in a flash. We were flipped over and around in the waves before I found some measure of stability. All I could see of Wang Sichuan was the beam of his flashlight shining over the water, but that was enough. I took a deep breath and, with all the strength in my body, swam in his direction. I swam wildly, absent of any technique. My eyes saw only the beam hovering in the darkness while my arms worked as hard as they could to get me there. I knew neither how long I swam nor how much farther I had to go. My mind was a blank and I heard only silence. At last, I felt something grab hold of my arm. Wang Sichuan and the others pulled me ashore. Gradually I regained my senses. I could hear once more the thunderous roar of the water crashing all around us.

I wiped the water from my eyes and looked around. The rock waterfall was not much higher than the cliff we'd just left. As I looked back, I saw Pei Qing slowly making his way over to us, pulling himself hand over hand along the wall. He was slow as an old man, but didn't appear to be in any trouble. Once more the strange black shape flashed through my mind. It was nowhere to be seen. Could I have been mistaken again? I wondered. Was it perhaps some trick of light and shadow? Enough, I thought. I calmed myself down and watched as Pei Qing arrived safe and sound. He was pulled up onto the bank and, gasping for breath, immediately lay down against the rock, his face in his hands.

I berated myself for being so gullible, though it was pretty funny that I'd believed Pei Qing's excuses. Now that we'd all made it, Wang Sichuan asked me what the hell had taken us so long. Still panting, I told him to ask me later. I didn't have the strength to get into it yet. He clapped us on the back and said we'd better keep climbing, all the way to the waterline if possible. The water continued to rise with menacing speed. Soon this platform would be submerged as well.

We all nodded. With a burst of energy, the deputy squad leader rose to his feet and began to climb. One by one the rest of us followed. I was still exhausted and waited until almost everyone else was on the wall before beginning. Pei Qing was in even worse shape, so I clapped him on the back and attempted to rouse him. If he were the last to go and somehow fell, there'd be no one left to help him back up. He sat looking at the water, as if some fear still lingered in his heart. Then he stood up, slapped me on the back, and, grinning at me, began to laugh. He turned to the wall and started to climb. Something was wrong. Pei Qing never laughed. What was there to laugh about, and why so strangely? Could he be embarrassed about what had happened? Then Wang Sichuan swore loudly at us from above, complaining that we were always the last ones, so I hurriedly began my climb.

Most underground waterfalls are created by large cracks that open within the rock strata above a cave. Once enough water has poured through these cracks, the calcium carbonate that lines the rock walls is worn away, leaving curtains and flowers of curling stone. These formations were our hand- and footholds as we ascended the falls. Many of them were soft and brittle, splitting beneath our feet, any remaining sense of security fleeing as they crumbled. We continued this slow and nerve-racking ascent until we reached the highest point of the falls. It seemed barely an improvement over the precipice we'd just left. Still, the feeling of imminent doom began to ease slightly. After each of us had found a stable spot to stand on, we began to scan the opposite wall with our flashlights, searching for an escape from the rising water. Our luck appeared to have run out. The wall was almost entirely bare. There was a single outcropping that looked as if it might support our weight, but it was some distance upriver. Given the ferocity of the current, it was clear we'd never make it. The hope we'd felt climbing the falls only amplified our current despair. Any chance of survival had been utterly dashed. Even Wang Sichuan gave up trying. All of us just sat there in silence, glumly watching the water continue its relentless approach.

Then, just as the water had risen to our heels, Wang Sichuan began to sing:

> *The valley wind swelled our red flag.*
> *The raging storm washed our tents.*
> *With blazing passion, we conquered weariness and cold.*
> *Our gear on our backs, we roamed the rolling hills.*
> *Filled with boundless hope,*
> *We sought riches for our motherland.*

The heavenly star lit our way.
The forest bird woke us at sunrise.
With blazing passion, we conquered weariness and cold.
Our gear on our backs, we roamed the rolling hills.
Filled with boundless hope,
We sought riches for our motherland.

As the winding river joins the billowing sea,
So we give our wisdom to the people.
With blazing passion, we conquered weariness and cold.
Our gear on our backs, we roamed the rolling hills.
Filled with boundless hope,
We sought riches for our motherland.

This was "The Prospector's Song." It was the romanticism of this song that made me first decide to become a prospector. Now, these long, dull years of work had all but worn away that youthful passion. I would never have expected Wang Sichuan to sing it now. Though we were facing death, I hadn't felt much of anything, but listening to Wang Sichuan sing with his harsh, gonglike voice, I felt once more traces of the romanticism I had sought as a youth. The rest of us joined in, almost involuntarily, and as we sang that familiar song, our fear began to slip away.

Our situation didn't change, however. No matter how beautifully we sang—nor how awfully Wang Sichuan did—the water continued to rise. In a moment it was above our ankles. Closing our eyes, we sang with all our might. When Buddhists or Christians face death, they can use texts given to them by God to pray their fear be lessened. For us atheists, all that remained was to hope the remembered passion of our younger selves might somehow banish death. Huddled tightly against the rock, we waited for the end to come. The water rose above our knees, our waists, our stomachs.

When it reached our chests, the pressure was too great and we could sing no longer.

Suddenly I heard Wang Sichuan yell out, his voice hoarse from singing. I couldn't hear what he said, but I noticed something strange on the water. From somewhere in the distant dark there appeared a blinding light. A moment later, four oxskin rafts floated into view. At first I was sure it had to be an illusion, but as the boats drew closer I could see that none other than Old Cat was squatting at the head of the first raft. A cigarette dangled loosely from his mouth. As he beheld our looks of utter terror and despair, I could see him smirk.

CHAPTER 19

Rescued

One by one we were lifted onto the raft. Wang Sichuan knelt down and kissed its old, worn exterior—just as his ancestors had once knelt and kissed the vast grasslands. I, on the other hand, lay stock-still, my head resting on the side of the raft, darkness slowly filling my vision. All that had just happened: that strange and gravelly sound, the rushing water, the bitter cold, the terror, and our final song—everything, everything!—swirled together as a kind of vortex or whirlpool. I watched as it slowly spun farther and farther away from me. Death had been so close at hand. Now it seemed like only a dream.

Just as I was about to faint, someone propped me up and helped remove my clothes. Only then did the cold I had endured for so long begin to hurt. After taking off our clothes, we wrapped ourselves in blankets and slowly regained some of our spirit. Shivering, I looked around at the men who had rescued me. Two of them were fellow military prospectors, though I barely knew them. The rest were engineering corpsmen I had never met before. The only familiar face was Old Cat, still crouched at the head of the boat.

After drying himself off, Wang Sichuan asked what was going on—how had they managed to arrive just in time? According to one of the engineering corpsmen, the main campsite had sent out a cable this morning saying there had been torrential rain at the upper reaches of the Kachar River, some twenty kilometers away. The cable cautioned that a spring tide—during which the river would rise to its highest level—was likely. Old Cat was at camp when he heard this news. He went at once to find the colonel and tell him it was probable that the underground river would rise. At first the colonel didn't believe him, but Old Cat persisted, and so a rescue team was organized. And just in time too, said the corpsman. If they'd arrived only a little later, this wouldn't have been a rescue mission. They'd just be dredging up bodies.

"Thank goodness," said Wang Sichuan, "and may Tengri protect us. Old Cat, you're like a father to me. Come here and let me give you a kiss."

Old Cat just laughed and said nothing. He continued to look at us, first Pei Qing and then me, his face deep and inscrutable.

Suddenly I realized we had not turned back toward the surface, but instead were continuing deeper into the cave. "Old Cat," I asked, lips trembling, "where are we going? This cave runs into a dead end."

As soon as they heard my question, the rest of our group chimed in. "He's right!" they called out, their faces pale. "The cave dead-ends up ahead."

"The terrain here is too low," said Wang Sichuan. "We'd better head for the top of the cave. If the water rises too high, this place will become an underground water cavity. The path back will be entirely submerged and we'll be stuck here."

The corpsmen manning the rafts all looked at Old Cat. Not paying us the slightest bit of attention, he took a puff on his cigarette and said, "Keep going."

Like assault boats, the four oxskin rafts charged forward. We all raised ourselves up to see where we were going. Wang Sichuan's face shook with worry. We had just barely escaped with our lives and had no desire to risk them once more. The rafts sped over the waves. Soon we reached the end of the cave. Old Cat gestured for us to be quiet and pointed at a spot on the cave wall. Floating atop the rising water, we were now at least ninety feet above where we'd discovered the iron door. From the start we'd paid little attention to the uppermost reaches of the cave, for the darkness there was at its most impenetrable. Here the roof of the cave was dim but visible. It formed an acute angle with the cave walls. Countless rows of shadowy stalactites hung down like the pearly teeth of some wild beast. There, at the top of the rock wall we'd taken for the end of the cave, gaped a thirty-foot hole in the rock. Water rushed in with the force of a galloping horse, obscuring the opening behind a sheet of white spray.

We understood: The tectonic activity that had occurred here had not completely sealed off the cave, just blocked off the bottom. The cavern with the iron door was a water cavity. Though too small be called an underground lake, it served the same purpose: helping to regulate overflow from the underground river. Because of successive years of drought, the river was already at its lowest point when we arrived. It was only natural that we had been unable to locate the path onward—we had been searching for it on the lake bottom. Who would have thought that the path onward had actually been on the cavern's roof?

I wanted to ask Old Cat how he'd known where to go, but there was no time. We were rushed forward by the speed of the current, and as we charged toward the opening, our raft began to spin. One of the corpsmen yelled for us to get down and hold tight. Hardly had his voice faded when we burst through the opening and smashed into a wall along the narrow channel within. One of the corpsmen was knocked halfway out of the raft. Luckily Pei Qing's reflexes were lightning fast. In an instant he'd grabbed the soldier and dragged him back into the boat. Then, spinning along in total darkness, we continued down the channel.

By the end I couldn't tell if the raft was vertical or horizontal. After experiencing the extremes of exhaustion and terror and then having to contend with the speed and violence of the rapids, I had nothing left. Gritting my teeth, I attempted to rouse myself, but darkness filled my vision once more and I gave in.

CHAPTER 20

R&R

By the time I awoke, the roar of water was gone and all around me was quiet. Wrapped in blankets, I felt warmth like I hadn't in days. Wang Sichuan and the rest had fallen fast asleep. They were pressed close together and looked much more comfortable than they had ever been sleeping alone. I carefully sat up and looked around. Through the hazy lamplight, I discovered I was sitting on a pebbly shoal. Blankets had been laid to suck up the groundwater. Nearby a very small fire flickered in the dark. Several indistinct shapes sat beside it, evidently the sentries on watch. As soon as one of the figures saw I was awake, he came running over. It was one of the engineering corpsmen Old Cat had brought along. "How are you feeling?" he asked.

Stretching out my limbs, I noticed my hands and feet felt unusually stiff. Reaching down, I discovered they'd been tightly bandaged. Except for this I felt all right. I'm fine, I told him.

The corpsman helped me to my feet and I walked with him over to the campfire. "Where is this place?" I asked.

He told me we were still beside the river, on a piece of jutting rock. We had floated for four hours after I fainted. He wasn't sure where exactly we were either. Saying this, he handed me a plate of food. I looked around the cave as I ate. The ground was terraced like rice paddies, like steps climbing out of the river till they met the steep walls. Originally, the rock would have been smooth and sloped at a gradual angle, but over the last ten thousand years it had eroded into these angled formations. We were camped in the middle of one of the terraces. The upper levels were driest, so that's where our belongings were stacked. Though the terraces were not wide, they ran for a very long way. The rafts had been run aground off to the side. I discovered that the bumps beneath my feet were not pebbles, but rather tumorlike protrusions in the rock that jutted sharply upward. It was lucky we'd been able to fall asleep at all. I shined my flashlight across the water, but it failed to illuminate the cave wall opposite. The river had widened significantly. Those still awake staggered about in a daze, while snores from the sleepers rose and fell. Except for the sound of our voices, everything here was quiet. Even the burble of the river had been silenced. It was rare to come upon such a tranquil place. It would be a waste to not rest up here. Gradually, I felt myself relax. After eating my fill, I took a piss and curled up beside Wang Sichuan. After a moment I was in dreamland once more.

This time when I awoke everyone was already up. Water for tea and food was being boiled on three vigorously burning bonfires. Several of our group sat around the flames tending their wounds. Our clothes had also been toasted more or less dry. Old Cat was over by the fire, sitting across from Pei Qing. Wang Sichuan was there too. Rubbing my eyes, I walked over and joined them.

Wang Sichuan clapped me on the back. "Goddamn if you don't enjoy a life of ease and comfort!" he said. "You passed out at just the right time, giving me, your close comrade in arms, a chance to render great and meritorious service! Do you know who hauled your ass all the way up here yesterday? It was me. So remember to tell the higher-ups I deserve a third-class merit when we get back!"

I nodded my head in embarrassment. It's not like I wanted to faint, I thought to myself. I was born this way. To be honest, my body was never suited for this line of work. When it came time to enlist, I forced myself to drink three big bottles of water and just barely managed to make weight. The recruitment officer thought I had contracted some stomach-swelling illness. Normally I was so thin my ribs stuck out like piano keys. But whenever I was ordered to go all out, whatever I lacked in physical power I made up for in spirit. This is where my strength has always lain. Fortunately my body has also become much hardier.

Fainting from exhaustion was very shameful. I tried to change the subject and asked what they'd been talking about. Pei Qing said Old Cat had drawn a contoured map of the cave. Now they were figuring out what the rest of the river might look like and how best to proceed. Hearing this, I was perplexed. "Why are we continuing?" I asked. "Aren't you all the rescue team?"

They were silent. Old Cat continued to smoke his cigarette, the ember glowing brightly in the dark. Then he sighed. I asked again. At last, Wang Sichuan responded. His voice was dry and constricted. "Old Cat said we're not the ones they're here to rescue."

CHAPTER 21

The Real Rescuees

The bonfire flickered before me, crackling as a light breeze fanned the flames. The firelight distorted the faces of those sitting around it, Old Cat's most of all. I could make out no more than a dim outline of his features, their expression a mystery to me. We weren't the ones they were here to rescue?

At first I didn't quite understand, but when I thought of Yuan Xile, a slow realization crept over me. Still, I had to be sure. "Then who are you here to rescue?" I asked, looking over at Old Cat, hoping he would give a clearer explanation.

The two new prospectors had been chatting a short ways away. As soon as they heard my question they stopped talking and turned toward us. Wang Sichuan and Pei Qing stared into the flames, not making a sound. Evidently, this question had already been asked.

Old Cat regarded me from across the fire. Tossing his cigarette butt on the ground, he said in a low voice, "It's not up to me to say. You'll know when we find them."

Silence descended once more. No one spoke. At last, Wang Sichuan whispered, "This time, I don't agree with the military."

Old Cat responded brusquely. "It's a soldier's duty to obey orders. If you have a problem, take it up with Rong Aiguo after we're out of here."

We all sighed. It wasn't that Old Cat didn't want to tell us. He just couldn't reveal such confidential information in front of so many people. That kind of slip could lead to a court-martial. In any case, we were all military men. Though we might serve in a relatively unusual capacity, we had to obey orders. Every aspect of the military relies on this basic tenet, and we knew that when we enlisted.

So Wang Sichuan cursed once and said no more. The two prospecting specialists who had been looking over at us went back to their conversation. To lighten the mood, I spoke up again. "Well, never mind all that. So what have you figured out so far? I'd like to hear it."

Pei Qing also wanted to ease the tension. He handed me the map Old Cat had drawn. "We just showed him where the iron door was located," he said. "We were discussing what might be hidden beneath the door."

I thought once more of that strange door. By now, it must be deep underwater. Old Cat's map was a long, hastily sketched passageway. It was easy enough for me to identify the places we'd been. Old Cat had drawn a big question mark where the iron door was. Pei Qing said they'd asked the engineering corpsmen about it. The engineering corpsmen had replied that there were two possibilities. The first was that it wasn't a door at all, but rather the cement base of some temporary crane. Should it be necessary to lift some relatively large airplane component—an engine, for example—a heavy-duty crane would probably be required. The iron door might very well be a remnant of the crane's concrete-and-steel base.

I paused for a moment to recall the place. Bullshit, I thought. It was definitely some kind of door.

"What about the second possibility?" I asked.

"Now this one is interesting," said Pei Qing. "The corpsmen said that if it's not a concrete base, then it's definitely a precision-blasting site, meaning it's filled with explosives. They're certain that in the space behind the door deep holes were drilled into the load-bearing layer of cave rock, then filled at key points with an extremely large quantity of water and shock-proof explosives. That way, if the situation ever became critical, the Japanese could seal the cave off at a moment's notice, buying themselves some time. Only a select few higher-ups would know the detonation codes required to carry out this 'sacred' task. For some reason, however, the Japanese sealed the iron door shut when they left. Clearly they hadn't wanted to block the cave off entirely. Or maybe the only people who knew the detonation code had already died."

"You're saying that we were standing on a heap of dynamite?" I asked.

"No," interrupted one of the corpsmen behind us, "a *huge* heap of dynamite."

The engineering corpsman who spoke up was relatively old, perhaps even older than the deputy squad leader. He pushed his way in between us. Old Cat introduced him as Tang Zeding, company commander of the engineering corps and a veteran just returned from the Chinese-Indian border. Obviously the two of them knew each other. Old Tang had a completely different personality from the deputy squad leader, and perhaps due to his higher rank, he never hesitated to engage with us. After sitting down, he began to speak: "They say that back then, the Japanese generally used Type 97 explosives, a synthesis of TNT and some shit I can't remember—benzene or something. They're hugely powerful in water." He added that we shouldn't worry. The Japanese had plenty of experience rigging explosives. They weren't going to go off by accident. He also believed that the location of the explosives showed that the

Japanese considered the cavern a key strategic point. The explosives were a fail-safe in case the Japanese lost control of the cavern. If this assessment was true, then the rest of the underground river should be comparatively safe to travel.

"I'm glad you think so," Wang Sichuan said sarcastically, patting Old Tang on the back.

"So that's what we've been discussing," said Pei Qing, "but there's something else we need to address. I'm talking about the issue of Yuan Xile and Chen Luohu."

What is he talking about? I thought to myself.

"What issue?" I asked. "Aren't they still waiting for us upriver?"

Pei Qing shook his head. "Old Cat said that when his group arrived, they found our equipment and the corpse of the martyred soldier, but Yuan Xile, Chen Luohu, and the engineering corpsman were nowhere to be seen."

How could that be possible? Pei Qing said they had two hypotheses: either Old Cat somehow missed Yuan Xile and the other two, or the three of them realized the water was rising, came to rescue us, and ran into some sort of trouble. "In any case," he said, "we can't go back and look for them now. All we can do is pray they're all right."

My heart was overcome with worry. Chen Luohu and Yuan Xile were both unable to care for themselves. Would that young soldier really be able to look after them?

The discussion moved on to the course of the river. Some suggested we use *mise-á-la-masse* (a contour map created by measuring how electrical current passes through minerals) to map the area around us, but this data was only approximate and we needed detail. Then a noise suddenly echoed across the cave. We turned our heads. Two of the engineering corpsmen had walked a great distance away from the camp along one of the terraces. All we could see were the beams of their flashlights bobbing in the dark.

The deputy squad leader yelled for them to return, but they waved for us to come over, pointing with their flashlights at the roof of the cave.

Wang Sichuan's eyes lit up and we jumped to our feet. Everybody ran over to see what it was. There, on the ceiling, amid a profusion of stalactites, was the U-shaped form of a power cable. It was thick as a man's arm, extending down the cave in one direction and to the foot of the cave wall and into the water in the other. As I stood beside the cable, I began to hear the sound of fingernails scratching on stone, just as we'd heard through the rocks atop the iron door. This time, however, the noise was the static produced by electricity coursing through the cable. The corpsmen became very excited. The existence of this cable meant there was some kind of electrical equipment nearby. Whatever generator the Japanese had used, it wouldn't have produced enough power to go very far. A power cable thus meant we weren't far from our goal. But how could an electrical cable here still have power? Could the generator still be running? Old Tang had several of the corpsmen form a human ladder to raise him up. The cable was decayed from decades of water erosion, and calcium carbonate had formed thickly around it, pinning it to the stalactites. It could not be pulled free. Old Tang ordered the deputy squad leader into the water to see what the cable connected to.

The deputy squad leader removed his clothes and followed the layers of rock terrace to the river's edge. With one hand tracking the course of the cable, he dove under. We watched as he swam out, submerging one moment, coming up for air the next. Soon enough his flashlight beam was swallowed up by the dark of the cave. We hurriedly launched one of the rafts and paddled out after him. In a moment we'd rowed to the middle of the river. We could see the deputy squad leader's flashlight shining from beneath the water. We watched as the beam moved back and forth, then stopped and began to float toward the surface. Seconds later there was a splash of water and the deputy squad leader emerged, gasping for breath. In one fell swoop he hauled himself into the boat.

We anxiously helped him sit down and gave him a towel to dry his face. Unable to bear the suspense, Wang Sichuan asked what was down there. It took the deputy squad leader a minute to regain his breath. Then he stammered out, "A plane! The wreckage of a plane is lying on the river bottom!"

CHAPTER 22

The Night Fighter

A plane? Could we have reached the end of the cave, thirty-six hundred feet underground? Impossible! According to the barometer, we weren't even halfway there. And if the mysterious bomber really was lying on the river bottom, at least some of it would break the surface. Our flashlights would definitely have been able to illuminate the cross of its shadowy hulk, but here the river was a sheet of darkness. We could make out nothing.

"Is it the bomber?" asked Wang Sichuan.

The deputy squad leader shook his head. "It's a little puddle jumper," he said. The plane, he said, was sturdily chained to an iron track running along the river bottom and seemed to have been completely destroyed.

Being freshly injured, I had to stay out of the water. Although I was burning with excitement, I could only watch as those around me jumped into the river one after another, each vying to be the first to the bottom. They had been inspecting the wreck for about an hour when Old Tang called us back to shore. Once on dry land, the swimmers breathlessly described the underwater scene while they dried themselves off. We made a sketch according to their description of the plane. It wasn't until much later that we learned this was a very rare model indeed. An aerodynamics engineer at the Air Force Academy recognized it as a smaller version of the Ki-102 series. If we'd really discovered one down there, the professor said, it would demonstrate how seriously the Japanese regarded this place. Back then the Ki-102 was still a relatively new model of night fighter.

At the time, though, we'd seen only a small number of planes, and our understanding of them was limited. All we knew for sure was that the power cable led to the wreckage of a small plane lying atop an iron railway at the bottom of the river. There was also some strange piece of machinery wedged into a crevice in the rock. Presumably it was the control for the mining track. The wings of the plane had been snapped completely off and the nose was smashed beyond recognition. Perhaps it was the victim of some crash landing. The real question was, however, what was it doing here? To keep finding things where they shouldn't be is the definition of strange. "Strange." That still seems the right way to think about the whole situation.

Wang Sichuan went so far as to ask whether the Japanese might have constructed an underground arsenal here, storing the planes that they didn't have time to transport. Should they ever have to repel an assault on their position, they would be ready.

I couldn't see the point of spending so much effort storing a bunch of planes in a cave. The Japs might do things a little strangely, I said, but they weren't fools. We shouldn't turn them into stereotypically idiotic movie villains who could do nothing more than run around cursing "*bakayaro*" all the time.

Those who'd stayed behind wanted to take a look for themselves, but Old Tang didn't want to take any further risks and sternly denied them. They had no choice but to crowd around Wang Sichuan and implore him to keep talking about what he'd seen. He was only too happy to oblige, continuing to brag and boast about the experience.

Old Tang and Old Cat were also excitedly discussing what had just happened. Now that we'd located a power cable, they guessed the path ahead would be much smoother. The existence of the iron track also suggested that the terrain should begin to even out. Rather than waste any more time here, they decided to continue on immediately. As soon as the order was given, we quickly organized our belongings, dressed, and set out once more.

We followed the cable along the cave wall, advancing slowly, and before long came upon an emergency light. This part of the cave had once been highly developed. It would be a smooth road ahead. Now Old Cat felt there was no need for delay. We floated for two or three kilometers without break, finally coming across a giant tangle of power cables converged on the roof of the cave. Old Tang inspected it for a moment and said there was definitely a generator somewhere nearby. Turning the next corner, we saw a large two-story concrete scaffold erected on the side of the cave wall. Just a little farther down from this scaffolding, level with the river, gaped the black maw of a sinkhole, fenced on all sides by iron railings. A chaos of power cables emerged from within. Old Tang said this was a power distribution center and that the generator was located somewhere inside. He was positive one of the power cables snaking their way out of the sinkhole would lead to the end of the cave. I noticed a guard post perched atop the scaffold. It had a searchlight and was covered in iron netting. Then someone cried out and we all snapped to the direction he was looking. On the lower level of the scaffold were two army tents, along with packs and sleeping bags of the kind we were used to. With one glance we knew this gear didn't belong to the Japanese. It had been set up only recently.

Old Cat immediately stood up. "Get closer," he said to Old Tang.

Even though it was built by the Japanese, I nonetheless felt a sense of comfort climbing onto the concrete base. After all, we'd been traveling through barren and inhospitable terrain for some time now. Painted on the scaffold were partially rubbed-off characters that read: "____saki Heavy Industries____Joint Unit 076." The first floor of the scaffold was dry, and we discovered that, sure enough, these were PLA tents. This was someone's temporary campsite. As suspected, another prospecting team had entered the cave before us. Even though I had long been sure that this was the case, to have the proof right in front of me set my mind much more at ease. None of our groups had brought tents. That this team had kept theirs suggested there were women among their number, and most likely more than one. Yuan Xile and the rest of her unit must have made it all the way here.

Old Cat ordered a search of the area. After climbing the ladder to the scaffold's second floor, we found a bunker concealed behind a pile of sandbags. The small lounge inside stank of mildew and mold but was otherwise in fairly good order. Crisscrossing electrical wires ran throughout the room. There was a bed, an army-green writing desk, a military-use candlestick telephone, and even a gun rack with a single rifle, so rusted it resembled an iron club. Had there been spiders here, this room would have long since become a snarl of webs. A pity there were none. The place felt almost too immaculate—no dust or dirt, just a collection of mildewed furniture. The whole scene gave me a terribly creepy feeling, as if the Japanese had only just left.

On the writing desk was a mess tin and canteen identical to our own. Evidently the people Old Cat was looking for had held a meeting in here. Nothing else grabbed our attention. After thinking it over, we decided the engineering corpsmen should station themselves here and continue to search the area. A number of daily necessities had been left at the camp, so we figured whoever was staying here wouldn't have gone far. Then, just as we were about to leave the bunker, a shrill ring reverberated from behind me. The noise was clear and sharp, as abrupt as a clap of thunder sounding within the bunker. The hair on the back of my neck stood up. We all turned around. There, on the wall at the back of the room, the ancient telephone was ringing.

CHAPTER 23

The Unknown Team

Wang Sichuan and I stared at one another. I looked over at Pei Qing. He and Old Tang were doing the same thing. I had deeply hoped that at least one of us would not be wearing a look of inexpressible terror, but even the eternally unflappable Old Cat had turned deathly pale.

The phone continued to ring, though the sound soon changed to a low rattle, almost like a belch. The decrepit bell clapper must have split off. There was a young soldier standing beside the telephone. He had no idea what to do. As he looked over at us, his hand began to tremble—his conditioned reflex to grab the phone from the receiver. It continued to ring for a long time. None of us did anything, just stood there stock-still, deadlocked. We remained frozen until the phone stopped ringing. Though even then we didn't know whether the call had finally stopped or if the phone had simply broken. Still, once that strange, rattling noise was gone, we immediately relaxed.

Again we looked back and forth from one man to another. We couldn't pretend this had never happened, but what was there to do now? We prepared to leave. A few soldiers walked over to the phone. Old Tang turned back and called to one of them, "Little

Zhao, weren't you a communications soldier? Well, go on then. Take a look at the phone."

The young soldier nodded, but as he was about to pick it up— *brring!*—the phone suddenly began to ring again. We jumped in fright. Old Tang whipped around, instantly set his feet in horse stance, and fluidly pulled his gun. Many soldiers who'd studied martial arts were like this. I'd seen monk soldiers—able fighters and rather skilled with a gun—but as soon they were frightened, they reflexively shifted into a martial-arts pose. Their feet hit the ground and they'd be in horse stance, but with their gun raised out. It never failed to amuse me.

No one was about to laugh now. We were frozen once more, staring stiffly at the telephone. Then Wang Sichuan yelled, "Who are you scared of?" strode over, and grabbed the phone from the receiver. "Hello!" In the black depths of that crack in the earth, within the ruins of a secret installation abandoned by the Japanese, hearing an ancient telephone suddenly ring—and then Wang Sichuan marches over and takes the call? Our hearts were going to beat out of our chests.

Wang Sichuan went silent. The sound that came in response was utterly inhuman. We all heard it: a series of quick bursts of static electricity and a host of indescribable noises, as if someone were coughing very, very rapidly. One after another we each picked up the phone and listened. We had no idea what it might be, but we knew it had to mean something. There was a definite pattern amid the noise.

Now, reader, I know what you're thinking: Morse code. We all jump to this conclusion because all those foreign adventure movies and novels overstate the frequency with which that simple telegraphic code is used. To be sure, explorers from other countries have and still do employ Morse code as a way to increase their chance of survival, but for us that was an impossibility. Morse code uses the Roman alphabet, and in the China of that era, Russian was the language to learn, from the first day of school all the way through graduation. It wasn't until the late 1950s that Chinese-Soviet relations soured and English became the required foreign language. We only began to learn some elementary English in the reeducation classes we took at the workers' university once the Cultural Revolution was over. So even if it had been Morse code, none of us would have been able to understand it—we didn't even know the ABCs.

The noise continued for another forty-five seconds before disappearing again. Wang Sichuan then hung up the phone, though the rest of us remained circled around it, waiting for it to ring again. For the next two hours, it made not a sound.

Old Tang ordered all corpsmen in the vicinity to check the phone line. He then asked Little Zhao, the former communications soldier, just what the hell was going on. Little Zhao explained that hand-crank telephones are in fact a sort of generator and can receive (and send) two kinds of calls: from another telephone or from a routing room. Just crank the lever and the other end of the line will start to ring. Because this phone had just done so, there could only be one explanation: the telephone wire still had power. The indistinct sound we heard was most likely the result of a disjunction between a dry cell that was out of power and a telephone wire that wasn't. These wires can last for a very long time, but the dry cell was certainly already ruined. And since this sort of telephone can communicate across a relatively large distance, it would be very difficult to estimate where the call was coming from.

The group of soldiers Old Tang had sent to follow the telephone line tracked it for about one hundred feet, only to find that after joining up with the giant power cable, it too extended deep into the sinkhole. This gave Old Tang the basis for a materialistic explanation. The power cable and the telephone wire, he said, had undoubtedly begun to affect one another. When we got here, he'd sent a couple guys to check on the generator. While fiddling with it, they must have somehow enlarged the electrical current, which then penetrated the insulation of the telephone wire and caused the phone to ring. As for the patterned regularity of the noise, it was probably just the sound of static electricity running through the circuit. This felt like a sensible explanation. Wiping the sweat from our faces, we were so relieved we nearly congratulated one another.

Only Pei Qing refused to accept it. Continuing to stare at the phone, he shook his head at Old Tang, his face unfathomable. Old Tang asked Pei Qing what was the matter. Pei Qing looked at us for a moment, then, taking the phone in hand, he began to cautiously rotate the crank, gradually gaining confidence and quickening his pace. Somehow, the call went through! Placing the phone against his ear, he looked at us, brought a finger to his lips, and motioned for silence.

Describing the event later, we would all say this call had been placed straight to hell. The call continued soundlessly for around ten seconds, and I thanked God for not giving us any further scares. Then, once more, the phone released that indescribable noise.

Pei Qing listened for a moment, then brought the phone up so we could hear: that continuous high-frequency cough, no different than before. "Have you ever seen *The Eternal Wave*?"[1] he asked.

---

[1]Released in 1958, *The Eternal Wave* is a classic Chinese movie about Communist revolutionaries secretly operating an anti-Kuomintang broadcasting station—sending messages in Chinese telegraphic code—in 1939 Shanghai. It should be noted that Chinese telegraphic code, while sounding similar to Morse code, uses an entirely different system for encoding messages.

CHAPTER 24

The Eternal Wave

It wasn't that we were stupid, we just didn't know what Pei Qing meant. At the time, nobody knew anything about telegraphs except for that *di-di-di* sound they made in the movies. And you young folks born after the seventies, even if you'd watched a bunch of old movies, would you therefore know, upon hearing a rhythmic series of knocks, that it was some kind of meaningful signal? I doubt it. Thus it was truly incredible to us that Pei Qing could make some kind of connection. Finally, it was Little Zhao who said something. "Engineer Pei, do you mean that the sound we're hearing is a telegram?"

"Listen," said Pei Qing. "Do you hear that—*pa-pa-pa-pa, pa*. It starts over every thirty-four seconds." He raised his arm and glanced at his watch. "Each time the duration is exactly the same." He looked over at us. "It's not a person on the other end of the line. It's an automatic transmitter on a loop."

"Are you sure?" asked Old Cat, narrowing his eyes at Pei Qing.

Pei Qing nodded several times, then turned to Little Zhao. "During basic training, did you communication soldiers memorize telegraphic code?"

Little Zhao nodded, chagrined. "But I've pretty much forgotten it all."

"Will it come back to you if you listen to the code?" asked Pei Qing. He gave the phone to Little Zhao and asked us for a piece of paper. I had no idea what was going on, but I took a workbook from my pocket and handed it over. Little Zhao's brows wrinkled as if he were being forced to do something against his will. With a great show of effort he put his ear to the phone and listened for the code.

To this day I still have that notebook. Here is what he wrote down:

28171653060471452397275720530226025529720522232

After he finished, we stared uncomprehendingly at the string of numbers he'd written. Looking over the numbers once more, Little Zhao stated confidently that it was a message in standard Chinese telegraphic code. Chinese telegraphic code has codes for about seven thousand different characters. Even a professional telegraph operator often needs a codebook to interpret lesser-used characters. What hope was there for Little Zhao, who'd been trained in no more than the fundamentals? Still, he split the numbers into groups of eight, giving him six phrases, though among these he could understand only the most commonly used codes.

Extreme28171653
—06047145
—23972757
Us20530226
Stop02552972
—05222232

Based on these few characters, all we could determine was that the person or people who'd set the automatic telegraph weren't Japanese. We passed the text around so everyone could take a look, but it was only for show. We merely took it up, moved our eyeballs symbolically, and passed it on, like the text of a long presentation being passed around some basic-level meeting. Only two people—I remember this very clearly—examined the text in great detail. One was Old Cat; the other was Pei Qing. Old Cat scanned it once, his brow wrinkling immediately. Pei Qing, on the other hand, stared at it, biting his lower lip all the while. Then, suddenly, he spoke up: "I think I understand it."

We all turned to him at once. "My father was our town's telegraph operator," said Pei Qing. "When I was little, I would translate messages for him. I've probably seen codes for more than a thousand different characters. Now, when I send telegrams, I write the code directly. I don't need a postal worker to translate it for me."

We looked at him as if he were some kind of supernatural being. Old Cat's face had turned pale. "What does it say?" he asked.

Pei Qing leaned over the desk, snatched my notebook from me, and began to scrawl. We crowded around, several of us fishing out cigarettes. As he worked, we smoked and observed his progress. He had memorized the translation for the code and was writing the correlated word next to each group of eight numbers. At last, he handed us the notebook to see what he had written:

Extreme28171653
Danger06047145
Save23972757
Us20530226
Stop02552972
Prospecting05222232

"The telegram is a cry for help!" several of us gasped.

Everything then happened extremely fast. As Old Cat looked at the translated text, faint beads of sweat appeared on his forehead. He told Old Tang to gather everyone together. We had to set off at once. They were in danger, he said, and we couldn't delay for an instant.

In reality, we were all aware that this ghostly transmission had been sent some time ago. The sender had probably already suffered some untimely fate. Still, it was our duty as the rescue team to assume the best. We had to believe the people we were tasked with rescuing were still alive. While we were readying our equipment, Old Cat stopped a few of us and said we had to stay here. Something bad had surely happened up ahead, he said. We were completely in the dark about the danger awaiting us. If we all entered together and whatever happened to the other team befell us as well, our entire group would be annihilated. A few of us needed to stay behind and form the second echelon. Once the first unit made it safely, they would send someone back to notify us.

We objected. How could they expect us to go along with this? "Why don't you guys be the second echelon?" said Wang Sichuan. "I'd never do anything so cowardly."

Old Cat just shook his head. "Right now this is a military operation," he said, "and Old Tang has the most weight around here. This is what he wants. Obey orders! In any case, all of you are injured. Staying behind is in your best interest."

Saying this, he walked off. Wang Sichuan bristled, but after Old Cat mentioned the word *orders*, he could no longer protest. Everyone knew that Old Tang was a softie. These orders must have come from Old Cat himself.

He hadn't gone more than a few steps when he suddenly turned back. "You can understand telegraphic code," he said to Pei Qing.

"That'll probably come in handy. They'll stay here, but you come along."

Pei Qing seemed to have been expecting this. Smirking, he turned to us. "Take good care of the place!" he said, his voice sickening. Wang Sichuan was so angry he was almost spitting blood.

We watched them board the three boats and quickly push off from the bank. The person at the head of each shined his flashlight along the cave walls, searching for the power cables. Twenty minutes later, all three had disappeared into the dark of the cave, their noises moving farther and farther away. I was not accustomed to the sudden quiet that descended upon us. Looking around, we discovered that, in addition to Wang Sichuan and I, the deputy squad leader and three engineering corpsmen had also been left behind. All at once I felt a kind of sadness.

What should we do now? Wang Sichuan asked me. All I could say was that Old Cat had a point. We were injured. There was no denying it. In a way he had been doing us a favor. All five of us squatted down. Even the deputy squad leader looked crestfallen. A soldier doesn't fear death, only that he might be unable to join the battle. There was nothing to do but look for a few cigarettes to console them with. As I reached into my pocket, I was given a start. I withdrew my hand. There was another note.

CHAPTER 25

The Second Note

The note was superficially identical to the one I had been given on the rocky shoal, both torn from our worker's insurance documents. Paper back then was thick, yellowed, and rough, not at all like today's high-quality stock. Opening it, I saw, once again, only a few small characters: "Enter the sinkhole."

The three characters were written in an exceedingly sloppy manner, so sloppily that it took me a while to figure out what they said. They'd been jotted down in a terrific rush. I could feel my heart thump heavily in my chest. Enter the sinkhole? I turned and looked to where it yawned amid the circle of iron railings. It wasn't far away. All of the power cables hung from its mouth like the tentacles of an octopus, winding together in thick bundles. Between these river water ran down into its black depths. Enter this sinkhole? I was confused and reached inside my pocket once more, but besides my cigarettes, I found nothing else. Who could have slipped it in there? When I discovered the first note, warning me to "Beware of Pei Qing," I had disregarded it, assuming it was some trick played by Chen Luohu. Now, having received a second one, I was forced to take it seriously.

Wang Sichuan and the rest were all squatting nearby. They saw the mix of emotions that played across my face. They all crowded around to take a look. Knowing I wouldn't be able to resolve the matter myself, I handed it over. Maybe one of them could figure out just what the hell was going on.

Wang Sichuan gulped and said it had to be a clue, but damned if he knew who it was from or why they'd given it to us like this. Could our team be harboring an enemy spy? We all agreed that was a possibility. Otherwise there would be no need to convey information so surreptitiously. Wang Sichuan then jumped to his feet, saying, "Comrades, the chance to win honor has arrived! It looks as if there's something fishy going on in that sinkhole and the enemy spy cannot be allowed to find out about it. Thus it was we who were covertly appointed to investigate. This shows the confidence our comrades have in us. Come on then, there's no time to waste—let's begin at once!"

I stopped him. "Something's not right. We need to make some kind of plan first. We don't even know who placed the note in my pocket. Let's first go down to the mouth of the sinkhole and take a look. Even if we really are going to explore it, we still shouldn't make that decision hastily." Wang Sichuan nodded, adding that, in fact, this was just what he had intended all along. So we turned on our flashlights and made our way over to the sinkhole.

The engineering corpsmen who'd just surveyed this area had left their anchors and locks. With these we made our way smoothly down the wall to where the sinkhole opened. To be honest, I hadn't looked at the sinkhole too closely until now. When we first arrived, I'd noticed straightaway how slippery the rock was around the entrance and so hadn't dared get any closer. The mouth was big enough to drive a jeep through, though the tangle of electrical wires took up almost half the space. The remaining gap was pitch-black, and out of it blew an intermittent cold wind.

Thanks to the soundness of my exam-based education, I could already tell what it would be like inside just by looking at it. Indeed, *sinkhole* was a rather apt description of the thing. Despite being located deep underground, it was fundamentally identical to sink-holes on the surface, having been formed by erosion as water flowed down a vertical crack in the rock. I didn't know how deep it went, but once the surface water had penetrated to a certain depth, the sinkhole would either begin to slope down along the rock strata— descending gradually into the earth like a set of stairs—or form a tilted joint, becoming winding and complex. This sinkhole was a kind of cave within a cave. The water most likely exited through some hair-thin crack at the end to become groundwater, but it was also possible that beneath our feet there was another cave system or that somewhere down below was an even deeper tributary of the underground river.

Seeing the sinkhole up close, we hesitated. Geological prospec-tors always retain some thought of safety, and we knew that this type of cave would be dangerous to explore. The water level was also high, and the spray it kicked up as it rushed into the hole greatly reduced our field of vision.

What now? I asked Wang Sichuan. The situation inside the hole was anyone's guess from out here, he said. He would descend first and check it out. The deputy squad leader immediately inter-jected that he should go instead, but Wang Sichuan stopped him. "That son of a bitch Pei Qing and I are different," he said. "I'm a geological prospector, and climbing into caves is my specialty. It's up to me to explore it first. Don't argue about this."

At this my temper flared. "Don't pull this hero shit now," I said to Wang Sichuan. "That note was stuffed into my pocket. It's up to me to handle it."

I've always found these kinds of arguments infuriating, but this was how everyone acted in all of the revolutionary movies, and that's where we learned how to behave. What could you do? In the end, it was decided that I would be the first to descend. Wang

Sichuan was too big. Even with three corpsmen holding the rope, we were afraid they still wouldn't be able to pull him up.

We had originally been carrying equipment for this sort of thing, but we'd dropped it while fleeing the rising water. Luckily the people who'd been here before us left their belongings behind. We put all the gear in order, and I strapped on a headlamp. This was my least favorite piece of equipment. Wearing it makes one's forehead burning hot, and this affects my thinking. Looking into the deep cave, I felt a twinge of regret. Being the trailblazer has never been my forte. But there was nothing to do now except grit my teeth and take the plunge.

I hooked myself in and climbed over the iron railing. Stepping onto the tangle of power cables, I slid into the cave. With the torrent of water splashing all around me, I could see nothing but the thick black cables. The cave wall behind them was completely obscured. The uppermost portion of the sinkhole was narrow and cramped with power cables. After descending a short distance, I began to hear a creaking sound. Scanning below with my headlamp, I could just make out a dark form somewhere far below my feet. It appeared to be a platform with some kind of machine. The men up above continued to lower me down. I turned my head to escape the water's spray, but I was soon drenched and freezing. After another twenty or so feet, my headlamp illuminated an iron sign, rusted to ruin, hung amid the power cables: *Station-0384-Line 8*. More Japanese was written on the back, but I couldn't understand what it said. The sound of rushing water filled my ears. I finally descended deep enough to get a clear look at the machine. You could see the traces of where the engineering corpsmen had peeled the calcium carbonate from its exterior. The generator had been erected on a platform of iron bars laid across the hole like a protective filter. Looking through the gaps I could see the utter blackness below. Another iron sign had been placed on the platform: "No Entry."

Little by little I continued to descend, until at last I dropped onto the platform. It immediately let out a fearful groan and began to buckle. I stepped onto the "No Entry" sign. The sign was so rusted, it split apart and tumbled through the cracks. The nerves on my back tingled. I took another step. Again the platform groaned, but this time the sound clearly suggested it would hold, so I dropped my whole weight onto it.

The generator was water powered and hidden beneath a layer of calcium carbonate. Even the propeller blades were covered in the stuff, but they still managed to slowly turn as water rushed past them. Knowing little about such things, I decided not to investigate it any further. Instead I took a quick, exploratory lap around the platform. Behind the machine, I found a space on the floor where one of the iron bars had split off, leaving a gap big enough for a person to descend through. I squatted down and shined my flashlight into the breach. Sure enough, thirty feet down the cave was no longer vertical. Here it sloped into a kind of staircase that ran deep into the earth. Perfect, I thought. From here on the way will be easier. Even if I fall, I probably won't get seriously injured. So I pulled on the rope—telling them to let more of it out—squatted next to the opening, and took a careful look down. Kneeling this close to the platform, I began to detect a thick, foul chemical odor. Covering my nose, I leaned in close and looked down. A layer of iron netting had been wound underneath the platform and a hole torn through it. Something had clearly passed through here, but this "something" was a good bit smaller than Wang Sichuan.

I yelled up to the top several times, asking them to toss me down some pliers. A moment later a pair slid down the rope. Grabbing them, I extended my arm into the opening, felt around a bit, and began cutting through the netting. At this angle the work was strenuous. After a few minutes, my back started to cramp. I continued to cut, tearing off pieces of the netting as I worked. At last the job seemed more or less complete, so I bent over and wriggled my upper half through the gap, scanning about with my headlamp to see what was waiting for me underneath. The iron mesh beneath the platform was very dense, like close vegetation. I turned my head to illuminate the darkness. Then I saw it. There, tangled deep in the wiring, was a thick clump of hair.

CHAPTER 26

The Clump of Hair

J ust beneath the hair, I saw a dark, curled-up shadow, but it was sunk too deep in the mesh for me to make it out. As I brought my head closer to the object, the stink grew even stronger. In my heart I already knew what it was. I brought the pliers through the gap and, gripping the clump of hair, gently pulled it away, revealing a sickeningly pale face, swollen with water. Just as I'd thought. Even though I knew what I was going to find the moment I saw the hair, it was still a shock when my suspicions were confirmed. At once I pulled my head out and began to yell toward the surface. At last, someone else rappelled down—one of the corpsmen. He descended until he was hanging just above the platform. "What is it?" he asked. I gestured for him to quiet down. Having someone else down here filled me with newfound courage. Covering my nose to block the awful smell, I leaned back in for another look.

The corpse was entirely wound in the iron netting, his uniform identical to our own. He must have belonged to the same unit as Yuan Xile. The corpsmen had just searched this goddamn area, yet none of them had discovered the dead body. Did this mean that rather than continuing deeper into the cave, Yuan Xile and her team had stopped here and descended into the sinkhole, just as we were doing?

I felt a chill in the air and drew back out of the gap. After telling the young soldier that there was a dead body beneath the platform, I yanked on the rope, signaling to the others to lift us up. Back on top everyone was stunned. This is a clue as well, said Wang Sichuan. He asked me if I'd recognized who it was. I shook my head, but seeing as he'd died here, the sinkhole probably didn't lead anywhere good. We'd better lift the corpse out and take a look first, I said. Then we could figure out our next move.

We spent the next three hours taking turns cutting away the iron mesh that bound the body. By the time we'd raised it up, all of us stunk of death from head to toe. The man's hair was very long and covered his face. The face, although slightly swollen with water, remained well defined. He had very dark skin and looked to be about forty—he was probably the team elder. Wang Sichuan had been looking closely at the corpse. Once we washed its face clean, his expression abruptly changed.

"My God," he stammered, "I know this guy. How did he end up here?" When he said the name, our faces all turned white. We stared at the corpse, none of us daring to believe it was true.

Forgive me for not revealing his name here. Within the world of geological prospecting, he was a famous expert, really more of a geologist than a prospector. In the history books, it states that he defected to the Soviet Union, but in reality he died a martyr's death, here in the depths of the cave. Given the man's identity, it became apparent that the quality of the first team was superior to anything we'd imagined. Had their standards been any higher, the only people left to include would have been legends and icons like Li Siguang and Huang Jiqing. We were stunned. If these were the people Old Cat was rescuing, it was a grand mission indeed.

Wang Sichuan searched the corpse's pockets, but they were all empty. Next we inspected the body, hoping to learn how he'd died. He appeared to lack any external injuries, but his extremities—especially the fingers and toes—had taken on a greenish hue. Stranger than that, the gums in his wide-open mouth had all turned black and his entire body twitched. He was in a severe state of rigor mortis.

"Seems like he was poisoned," I said, basing my judgment on folk knowledge.

Several people nodded their heads. What about poison gas, said Wang Sichuan. He suggested the Japanese had hoarded chemical weapons down below and they had begun to leak. It was hard to deny this possibility. In fact, after considering it a moment, the correctness of it struck me like a revelation. Yes, I thought, that's exactly what happened. What if this cave was actually one of the sites where the Japanese stored their chemical weapons? To hide the fact they'd used them during the war, they'd buried those it was too late to destroy down this sinkhole. As for the plane, maybe it had only been transported here by chance. At the time of the Japanese surrender, war criminals were said to have revealed that nearly 2 million chemical warheads were secretly hidden around China. To this day the Japanese have divulged neither the locations of these bombs nor their total amount. It's rumored the majority are scattered across what was once Manchuria.

After Japanese prospectors discovered and reported the underground river, their superiors must have realized that, although they'd located no mineral resources, this spot was suitable for storing chemical weapons. They then constructed a weapons storehouse within the cave. As this area was within the defensive zone maintained by the Japanese military against the Soviet Union, there were clearly strategic reasons for storing chemical weapons here as well. On the face of it, this explanation seemed entirely rational.

Then, as quickly as the thought occurred to me, I realized how unlikely it was. Why would the Japanese have bothered to haul their weapons so deep into the forest? Concealing them like this didn't seem worth the effort. How much time would it take to transport chemical weapons to such a remote place? Moreover, using an underground river as a storehouse was patently unsafe. No matter what, a dry cave would have been found for such an operation. The deputy squad leader agreed this probably wasn't the case. According to him, the netting beneath the platform was a measure to prevent workers from escaping. He pointed out that the "No Entry" sign suggested that an as yet unexplored area lay below. If it were gas bombs down there, the sign would have said something different.

Everyone let fly with a hundred different opinions at once. There was another problem as well, Wang Sichuan pointed out. How had this person managed to die on the underside of the platform? He couldn't have been swept down there by the water. He would have landed atop the iron platform, not under it. There was only one possibility: In his final moments, he'd attempted to head back the way he'd come, but the strength of the poison had blurred his senses. He'd tangled himself up past any point of extrication, and there, at last, he died.

It now seemed as if not only had the earlier team descended into the sinkhole, but something terrible had happened to them down there. Had the person who slipped me the note already known about this?

After we'd covered the corpse with a sleeping bag, Wang Sichuan said we had no choice but to go down there and investigate. We were on to something, he said. And if these were the people that Old Cat was here to rescue, then he had already gone the wrong way. Having been given a clue, we couldn't just ignore it. We placed country above all else in those years, and, given that people's lives were at stake, none of us felt the slightest hesitation about completing the job in Old Cat's stead.

"There's probably poison gas down there," said Wang Sichuan. "We have to be extremely careful. Since we don't have any gas or protective masks, we'd better prepare some wet towels."

In the end, we all tore off pieces of cloth to use as masks. Thinking back on it now, it sounds so naive, believing that these would actually protect us, but back then, that's what they'd taught us in Attack Preparation class: hide under your desks if there's nuclear war, and a wet towel is a replacement for gas masks. Anyway, we geological prospectors weren't used to using gas masks. Any caverns that produce poison gas are also generally combustible. What use would a mask be? You'd be blown to smithereens long before the gas had time to get to you.

We passed one by one through the breach in the iron platform. The deputy squad leader led the way down to the staircase-shaped slope that lay below. We continued down for a very long way. The sides of the cave had been washed so slick that the moment you stopped paying attention you'd fall. Making our way with great care, we soon arrived at a narrow tunnel with eroded limestone walls. Running water covered the floor. Although this tributary was still expanding, it was still too small to be called anything but a subterranean brook. The water rose no higher than our ankles, and the space was so narrow we had to stoop to proceed.

As expected, there were few signs of Japanese presence down here. After we'd been walking for some ten minutes, covering our noses with cloth all the while, one of the young soldiers suddenly paused and said something was wrong. We all stopped and looked at him. What is it? we asked. He didn't respond, but used his flashlight to illuminate his boots. Then, somewhat anxiously, he rolled up the bottom of his pants. His legs were covered in a black, uneven mass of soft, writhing flesh. We looked closer: leeches, and already filled to bursting with his blood.

CHAPTER 27

Leeches

My mind buzzed as I shined my flashlight around the water. At first I could see nothing, but when I squatted closer, my hair stood on end. The water was all leeches, their color similar to the cave bottom. They crowded around our feet. Inch by inch, they crawled over to us, hoping to burrow into the cracks in our boots. Goose bumps rose all over my body. Without second thought we began frantically pulling them off of us, Wang Sichuan using so much force that he flung one directly onto my neck. I cursed violently and told him to get it off me. The deputy squad leader then raised his pant legs. We gasped. Black leeches bulging with blood covered every inch of his legs. We checked our own. They were no different. "How the hell are there so many of them here?" asked Wang Sichuan.

"It's the water temperature," said one of the young soldiers. "It's much warmer than the main river."

Leeches may be disgusting, but they're not fatal. Still, watching them squirm all around us made me deeply uncomfortable, for after latching on to you, they become very difficult to remove. While in the South, I once heard that leeches will sometimes burrow into a man's reproductive organ without him feeling it. This scared the hell out of me. I immediately began to brush off the area around my groin. Wang Sichuan asked me what I was doing. When I told him the story, his face turned pale with fear. "Should I not just take it out and wipe it off?" he asked.

"Try to be a little more civilized," I said, but then the deputy squad leader announced that we had to keep going. There were too many leeches for us to wait here any longer.

We ran like the wind, none of us paying any attention to what was beneath the water. Then, after sprinting about a hundred feet—*whoosh*—the deputy squad leader suddenly disappeared from out in front. Neither Wang Sichuan nor I had time to react, and in a moment there was nothing but air beneath our feet as well. I cried out, but it was too late. The cave had suddenly sloped downward, right out from under our feet.

Everything went dark. We tumbled together down the slope, somersaulting over and over each other until we were wrapped together. Within seconds my knees, head, butt, and every other body part had been smashed so many times I wanted to vomit. My flashlight was knocked loose. With his great strength, Wang Sichuan tried desperately to grab hold of something to stop our descent, but the drop was far too sheer. A chaos of light pulsed before my eyes. For an instant my body ceased its tumbling, but I had no time to realize the change before air was once more beneath me. The rock was gone, and I was in free fall.

It's over, I thought to myself. Am I really about to die? Is there some jagged cliff below me? Before I could finish imagining this miserable plight, there was a loud boom and my body went cold—the shock went through me as soon as my butt hit the surface, then all at once I felt the force of it—I had plunged deep into a pool of water. The current picked me up in a flash and washed me onward. Wang Sichuan was still holding me in a firm bear hug and wouldn't let go. I gathered my strength and kicked him off, then swam for the surface. With effort, I finally made it to the top. It was pitch-black, and the water seemed to be continuously spinning me around. From the speed I was moving and the sounds that filled my ears, I could tell I'd fallen into the raging rapids of some second underground river. Judging by the roar of the water and the speed of the river—each of them far in excess of the channel we had initially traveled down—this seemed to be the true underground river!

I struggled against the waves and cried out, but my voice was lost amid the crash of the water. Caught up in the current, I was rolled end over end and rushed who knows how far to some dark and distant corner of the cave. There was nothing fun at all about this experience. To be honest, I don't have any direct memory of what occurred, for I could see nothing and heard only the roar around me. Whatever image I have of the place originates almost entirely from my imagination. I remember only utter panic at the thought of being sucked deep underwater. I was washed along in total darkness, knowing neither when nor where my life would finally come to an end.

Then, from somewhere off to the side, the deputy squad leader turned on his flashlight. The sight of it shook me from my stupor. In the extreme blackness of the cave, the beam's radiance was like a beacon of hope. I mustered all the strength I had left and swam hard in its direction. Upon reaching him, I saw his face was covered in blood, though he didn't seem much affected by it. Fighting through the waves, the two of us began to search for the rest of our team. Wang Sichuan was nowhere to be found, and we didn't know whether the three soldiers had fallen in or not. As the deputy squad leader shined about with his flashlight, I saw it was just as I had imagined: the river was extraordinarily wide. I couldn't even make out its sides, only a vast expanse of billowing water.

"What is this place?" shouted the deputy squad leader, his voice hoarse and quavering.

But I had no idea and could only hold tightly to him. With a great deal of effort, we managed to right ourselves and began to float atop the water, though just barely. The speed of the current was astonishing. Great torrents of water rushed us toward the lower reaches of the river. Soon enough I realized I could struggle no longer. The freezing waves had sapped all of my energy. Fortunately, the deputy squad leader did not lack for strength. It was he alone who continued to fight through the water, towing me along beside him. I tried to tell him to forget about me, but I lacked even the energy to utter those few words. Who knew how long the current drove us on? At last we were both completely spent, like dry lamps with no oil to spare, when something suddenly struck my back. As the rapids flowed on around us, we were brought to an abrupt halt.

I was already numb from the cold, so although the collision was severe, I gasped for only a moment and felt not the slightest bit of pain. We felt around. Our way, we discovered, was blocked by an iron lattice sunk beneath the rapids—a screen to keep out any stray objects floating down the river. I could feel a number of branches and twigs and other pieces of debris. Thank heaven, I thought. With tears rolling down my face, I pulled myself up the latticework and clambered desperately atop it. The deputy squad leader did the same, then pulled out his flashlight and illuminated the water around us. The lattice dam was fragmented and washed away in spots. That we'd run into it at all was truly a stroke of luck. We looked at one another, our expressions indescribable—neither joyful nor sad. How strange, I thought, that a dam had been laid here. Had the Japanese been through here as well?

Just as I was thinking this, the deputy squad leader and I both noticed that something in the area beyond the dam seemed to be reflecting the beam of his flashlight. Angling it up, he directed it farther on. Our mouths dropped open. It was a gigantic bomber, the Japanese Shinzan, submerged in the river past the lattice dam.

More than half the fuselage was underwater, leaving a great black shadow, while the nose and one of the wings stuck out above the surface. Most astounding, the plane had obviously been ruined in some terrible crash. All that remained before us was the wreckage.

CHAPTER 28

The Distant Mountain in the Water

My breath caught in my throat as I stared at the huge black cross the Shinzan's wingspan formed underwater. As the flashlight beam illuminated the rust spots covering its body, it resembled some legendary animal of tremendous size, raising its head above water to breathe. It was the most magnificent thing I had ever seen. For anyone other than members of the mysterious "Plan 53" unit, coming across a plane this colossal in mainland China would have been impossible in those days. Back then, when a plane flew across the sky, children would all crane their necks to catch sight of it. Now, even if a fleet of fighter jets streaks overhead in formation, no one pays them any attention.

Stacked all around the bomber were the same corpse-filled gunnysacks we'd seen earlier, but here their numbers were even more astonishing. They formed a dense mass underwater and extended in every direction farther than the eye could see. They were piled one atop the other, some remaining in neat condition, others already caved in from decay, their appearance similar to the large seaside rocks that buffer the ocean waves. It was between these bags that the plane was wedged. We gingerly tiptoed onto the gunnysacks.

Though they would sink down when trod upon, there was always some spot that would support our weight. Holding each other up, we began to make our way across. "What the hell were the Japanese doing here?" said the deputy squad leader.

I could say nothing in reply. Neither side of the river was visible. The flashlight illuminated only a black expanse. Soon I began to question whether this wasn't in fact the middle of some giant subterranean lake. We made our way across the piles of unevenly stacked corpse bags. At last we reached the twisted length of one of the wings, rising above the surface. It was severely corroded, and rusty water covered our hands as we scaled its side. Thank goodness the top was dry. As we stepped upon it, the wing sank slightly under our weight. If Wang Sichuan were here, he probably would have snapped it in half, I thought to myself. I couldn't help but take a look around, searching for him. There was no sign of the big guy, only whitecap rapids. I didn't even know if he was alive or dead.

We were exhausted, truly on the point of collapse, my only comparable experience being the seven-day deathwatch I kept after my father passed. After reaching the top of the wing, darkness descended upon me, and I nearly crumpled to the ground. But resting was something we absolutely could not do. To rest was to die. We removed our clothing, both of us turning away at the sight of the leeches. Our blood visibly pulsed inside them, some so filled they had turned amber. In a moment I began to vomit.

For leeches a cigarette is best, but all that remained of mine was a thick paste in my pocket. I'd have to scald them off with my lighter. At the time, most people had only matches, but when used in the field it was too easy for them to become damp or start a forest fire. Those of us who could, made sure to buy a lighter. Old-fashioned lighters burned kerosene and were unusable while the wicks were damp. We had to let them dry for a long time before they would finally light. Then, one by one, we roasted the leeches off of us. Once they began to burn, we flicked them back into the water, blood spilling from our open cuts. With great difficulty we disposed of them all, bloodying ourselves in the process until we were truly frightening to look at. Only when we'd thoroughly checked each other, and made sure they were truly gone, did we finally relax. After wringing my clothes dry, I picked up the deputy squad leader's flashlight and went to inspect the sunken bomber.

The flashlight had already dimmed considerably, but even still, from atop the wing I had a much clearer view of the plane's lower half. The Shinzan must have hit the water unevenly, tail end first. The nose still rose above the surface. The tail was some distance off, too far away for me to see clearly. I stood atop the broken wing between its two giant engines. I could make out the twisted shapes of the three-bladed propellers below, sunk halfway into the river and already too rusted to spin. The front of the plane was divided into upper and lower sections. The bottom section, just above the nose, was the machine-gun cabin. Its glass-and-steel exterior was smashed to pieces, leaving only the frame, half of which was underwater. Above this was the cockpit, its windows at least partially intact. A rotating gun turret sat atop the plane in the middle of its body, seemingly undamaged. The parts of the plane that had sunk underwater were already so rusted none of their original green coating could be seen. Holes had opened in the walls of the engine room. It had been sitting here for more than twenty years, getting water-washed the whole time. Above the surface it still looked all right. I could see a vague "07" written along the nose in huge characters, though the rest of the marks were unclear. I had seen this plane on a filmstrip just three days ago, the image smaller than a fingernail. Standing upon it now, deep beneath the earth, I couldn't believe it. There really was a giant plane! That's what I said to myself at the time. My God, I thought, there really is a bomber down here!

But we were told it had been disassembled before being moved into the cave. Why did it appear to have crashed down right here? Had the Japanese tried to fly it over the underground river and failed in the attempt? I craned my neck and shined my flashlight upward, trying to see how high the cave went. The beam failed to illuminate the ceiling, but it was obvious there wasn't nearly enough room for a plane to take off. Why on earth would the Japanese have wanted to fly a plane down here?

CHAPTER 29

Exploring the Shinzan

My perspective of the plane was limited from my perch atop the wing. Moreover, the flashlight was gradually dimming and would soon go out. I had no choice but to stop and figure out my next move. By now I had regained my strength, or should I say that in my curiosity I forgot the terror and exhaustion I had just felt? I also knew that we'd be done for without a light down here. I proposed to the deputy squad leader that we climb into the plane and take a look around. Perhaps there'd be something inside we could use to light our way. At the very least we needed to see if it would provide us with some shelter from the wind. To remain bare to the waist out on the wing was a terrible idea. The deputy squad leader had used up far more of his strength than I. He was out of his mind with exhaustion, as if comatose. I asked him what was the matter, but he just nodded and said nothing. I had no choice but to knead his body to warm him up. Only after his skin had reddened was I comfortable letting him stay behind. Then I headed for the cabin.

The section between the wing and the nose had sunk into the river, forcing me to wade across. I cautiously stepped from one gunnysack to the next. Once more I caught sight of that massive "07," as well as the smaller characters written underneath, but they were much too vague and I had no time to closely examine them. After wading all the way to the machine gunner's cabin, I wriggled in through a gap in the twisted steel.

The cabin interior was pitch-black, but it felt different from the darkness outside, not as hopeless. In here at least there were objects for my flashlight to illuminate. I could feel the distorted steel plates of the cabin walkway through my shoes. The first thing I saw was the ruined remains of a machine gunner's chair, its leather cover already unrecognizable, leaving only a rusted iron form. All around me the inner walls of the plane were riven with cracks and hung with snaking electrical wires, the majority of which had already bonded together into a dark and indistinct mass. In front of the seat was the half-destroyed remnant of some kind of stand—probably a mount for the machine gun, but now all that was left was the frame. Standing on the machine gunner's seat, I looked back down through the plane. The passenger and cargo compartments were too flooded for me to proceed, but the iron ladder to the pilothouse overhead was somehow still intact. Taking great care, I began to climb.

The tail end of the plane had received the brunt of the impact. The pilothouse was therefore relatively undamaged. After climbing in, I first came upon the copilot's seat. A layer of rust and shattered glass had fused together across the floor. I shined my flashlight around the cockpit. Leaning over the top of the captain's seat was a leather aviation helmet of the Japanese air force.

It was the pilot's shriveled corpse, as I had expected. As the body rotted it had melded with the seat behind it and now they were stuck together, a single form. Its mouth was especially distended, gaping wide open. This corpse was indeed Japanese, and from many years past. I shined my flashlight slowly along its length, inspecting it in detail. I gasped. Looking around the pilothouse, I could tell there hadn't been a fire, but the corpse had somehow turned bluish black and was covered all over in deep hollows. At first glance, it resembled nothing so much as a honeycomb. Initially I assumed the hollows were caused by machine gun fire, but after taking a closer look, I realized I was wrong. These things weren't "hollows" at all. They were holes opened by the contracting flesh as the body rotted away. This corpse had decomposed very unevenly—some parts of its body had rotted very severely, while others seemed almost untouched.

I grabbed a sheet of iron from beside me and used it to cover the body. Then I returned to the wing, hoisted the deputy squad leader, and carried him back to the pilothouse. Once there, I gathered together everything I could find that seemed as if it might burn—the corpse's leather helmet and shoes, things like that—and set them alight. Luckiest of all, amid the wreckage of the cabin I found a hydraulic pressure tube. The oil inside had completely dried, leaving only a layer of black mudlike substance. After I scraped it out and burned it together with the tube itself, the temperature in the pilothouse became quite satisfactory. The flame was small, but for us it was some kind of salvation. Our cuts stopped bleeding, our clothes began to dry, and the two of us gradually warmed up.

I still hadn't decided what our next move should be. Given the situation we were in now, nothing we did would really be of much use. All we could do was wait to be rescued, but who knew whether that was even a possibility. After a while we could find nothing else to keep the fire going. Fortunately our clothing had dried by then. After picking out the leeches that were still inside and throwing them into the coals, we got dressed, crowded around the fire, and lay down. Despite the strangeness of our surroundings and the hundreds of things that might have kept me awake, though my mind was filled with question after question, I fell asleep immediately.

When I opened my eyes again, I saw only darkness. I had no idea how long I'd slept. The fire was out. I'd been warm the whole time I'd slept, but as soon as I opened my eyes I knew something was wrong. Why had I awoken so abruptly and what was this pain in my ears? From outside the wrecked plane came a series of incredibly loud, droning, *weng-weng-weng* wails. What kind of noise is that? I wondered. After listening for a moment, I realized—it was a siren! What was a siren doing here? I felt the blood drain from my face. What the hell was going on? Could the power have been restored? During our Attack Preparation classes we'd become all too familiar with this sound. Wasting no time, I climbed through a hole in the pilothouse and on top of the plane.

Darkness was all around me. Resounding over the river from some dark and distant part of the cave came the wail of the siren, like the voice of some evil spirit. The air had begun to vibrate, as if with a kind of extreme restlessness. I had no idea what was about to happen. The deputy squad leader had been startled awake as well. He climbed up and asked me what was going on. I listened to the sound of the alarm. The noise, I suddenly realized, was speeding up, becoming more and more urgent. All at once an extreme foreboding burst forth in my mind.

CHAPTER 30

The Siren

The siren resounded through the vast cave, the noise continuing to intensify, but we could see nothing within that darkness. A great unease filled us, the kind that makes one want to flee at once, but there was nowhere to run. All we could do was stand anxiously atop the plane and await the arrival of whatever danger the siren was warning us about.

After sounding for roughly five minutes, the alarm abruptly went silent. Before we could react, there was a tremendous roar, as if some piece of machinery had been twisted apart. From the darkness downriver, the sound of water became audible once more. I looked uneasily in the direction of the machine sound, knowing neither what it was nor where it had occurred. The wreckage of the plane underfoot began to tremble slightly. I looked down. The force of the current had picked up and the water level had unexpectedly fallen. A dam! It suddenly became clear to me. The siren and crash were a dam's sluice gates opening. Had the Japanese actually dammed the underground river? At first, this was hard to believe, but if a bomber could "crash" deep beneath the earth, then to build a dam down here seemed comparatively reasonable. The deputy squad leader and I looked at one another, then back down at the river. We were both at a loss.

The water level fell rapidly. After half an hour it was already below the gunnysacks. Together with the rest of the fuselage, countless corpse bags were now revealed. It was a terrifying thing to see. In the darkness it was easy to feel that the water level hadn't dropped, but rather the corpses had floated to the surface. They extended in an unbroken expanse across the cave. Looking at them, I felt my breath catch in my throat.

A previously submerged road of planks and wire mesh appeared amid the gunnysacks. It was still underwater, but the water was no more than thigh high. We didn't know whether the decrease in water level was manually operated or some automatic mechanism, but we saw an opportunity to escape. We climbed down from the plane at once and clambered along the gunnysacks until we reached the plank road. Although seriously decayed, it was nonetheless able to hold our weight. Quickening our pace, we hurried onward.

The water level had soon dropped beneath the plank road, and we no longer needed to wade along. Once we'd run for about three hundred feet, the roar of the water became much louder. We could feel the dam nearby. We couldn't see the plane anymore, though. A pair of giant iron rails then appeared along the river bottom, more than ten times as wide as ordinary train tracks. As I looked at them and at where the plane had been, I could tell they'd been the latter's transport. Huge electrical transformers, the kind used in large-scale hydraulic power generation, appeared on either side of the tracks. Some of them seemed to be in operation, the crash of their components blending with the sound of the rapids. They were indistinguishable if one failed to listen closely. There was also a crane, a searchlight, and a collapsed sentry tower. As the water level swiftly diminished, all sorts of heavily corroded structures were revealed. Never would I have expected so much hidden beneath the waves. Why had all of it been built in the middle of the river? Then, up ahead, we finally caught sight of the dam.

In fact, calling it a dam would be somewhat misleading. Only one long section of concrete with rubble remained, towering overhead and laced with cracks. Still, on an underground river it would be impossible to build too tall of a structure, and this "dam" had probably been developed for only temporary use. At the foot of the dam we saw a massive iron loudspeaker, though who knew if this had actually produced the siren? At the end of the plank road was a rickety-looking iron ladder that led to the top of the dam.

I craned my neck and looked. At the most, it was only one hundred feet tall, but seeing the still-damp waterline along the dam, I felt a lingering sense of fear. The deputy squad leader motioned to me to ask whether we should climb up. I was anxious to see what lay beyond, so I nodded. The two of us began to climb, one in front, one behind, cautiously making our way up the dam. Fortunately, the ladder proved quite sturdy, but as soon as we reached the top a violent wind began to blow, nearly knocking me off the dam. I quickly squatted down to keep my balance. I'd already heard the roar of a waterfall as we scaled the ladder. Up here the noise reached its peak, but there was more than just a waterfall. After finding my footing, I saw that after the dam stretched a deep abyss. It was into this that the underground river ceaselessly surged and fell. Incredibly, there was no sound of the falls striking bottom. I had no way of knowing how deep the abyss really went. More than that, the opening of the abyss—a vast and empty expanse—yawned as wide as it was deep. There was nothing for my flashlight to illuminate here, just some kind of giant subterranean void.

An oppressive sense of emptiness came over me, something that hadn't occurred while on the river. Then as a cold, powerful wind came sweeping out of the darkness, we had to move away from the edge. "Why does it seem like there's nothing out there?" the deputy squad leader asked me. "It's like outer space. What is this place?"

I searched the geological lexicon, but my brain could find no term suitable. I could think of only one way in which a place like this could have been created: after the limestone cave system had reached its final stage, an enormous portion of it had collapsed, forming this cavity. It was a marvelous geological spectacle. That I should actually see such a rare phenomenon in my lifetime made me feel, quite abruptly, as if I were about to cry. I continued to stare at it in astonishment when a loud boom suddenly rang out and several beams of light appeared from the side of the dam facing into the abyss. In a moment, all but two were extinguished. They then began to pivot side by side, seemingly from a fixed point, the beams sweeping through the darkness. A searchlight had been switched on. Someone was inside the dam!

The deputy squad leader immediately became alert. "Could there still be Japanese soldiers here?" he asked in a low voice.

Impossible, I thought to myself. "No," I said, beginning to smile. "It's probably Wang Sichuan!" I wanted to yell aloud to let him know we were here.

Before I could utter a sound, dread enveloped me. My body went stiff. As I watched the searchlights probe that endless dark, I was unable to move a single step. I've always felt there are marked differences between the sensations of fright and dread. Fright originates from sudden occurrences. Though whatever causes the fright might not, in and of itself, be scary at all, it manages to become so by either suddenly appearing or disappearing. Dread is different. Dread results only after reflection and requires some time to ferment in the mind. For example, this dread I felt watching that unending dark, it manifested only after I'd begun to imagine what might be out there. In itself there was nothing scary about the dark.

If you asked me what I saw down in that abyss, I could say only dread. For in fact, I saw nothing at all.

How vast was the abyss? I had believed it would be comparable to something I'd seen or heard about, but as I watched the searchlights shine across it, I realized the word *vast* was entirely inadequate to describe its size. Military searchlight beams generally reach forty-five hundred to six thousand feet, meaning they can illuminate objects from over a kilometer away. This searchlight illuminated nothing, extending out into the abyss until at last the far end of it was swallowed up by the darkness. It was as if the beam had been aimed into the night sky. A moment later I understood. My jaw dropped open. The deputy squad leader saw my shocked expression. After hearing my explanation, his eyes went wide. Cold sweat trickled down my back. At once I understood why the devils had endured such hardships to transport a bomber down into this cave. They'd planned to fly it into the abyss.

CHAPTER 31

The Abyss

The whole thing was beyond strange—not just the scene that lay before me, but also what the devils had done. It was all so creepy. It gave me a profound understanding of the deeply irregular way the Japanese behaved. I'm afraid that only a people as paranoid as them could have carried out such an affair. A gigantic Shinzan bomber took off from an underground river thirty-six hundred feet underground, flew into a black abyss, and then disappeared. Over the many years that have passed since then, this image has stayed with me, like a nightmare that never goes away. I'm unable to shake it from my mind.

I imagined the Japanese prospectors reaching this point. Certainly there were no natural wonders like this on an island nation like Japan. How must they have felt? Probably just as I did now. As they looked out at that boundless darkness, were they seized by an intense desire to explore it, to see what was hidden within?

I continued to watch the point where the searchlight vanished. For a long time I was spellbound. At last a cold wind broke me from my trance, and I began to shake all over. I pulled myself together at once, muttering that this was no time to get excited.

Romanticizing requires an environment both safe and secure. This place was neither.

The searchlight beam began to move again. It has to be Wang Sichuan, I thought to myself. Helping each other along, the deputy squad leader and I made our way toward the light. In a place like this, finding another person was no small thing. We wanted to meet up with him as soon as possible and come up with a way out of here. Our assignment was finished. Although I feared the military would attempt to replicate whatever the Japanese had done, right now it had nothing to do with us.

The searchlight was surely located within the facility's machine room, a place filled with the valves and mechanisms used to regulate the water level. We just didn't know where the entrance was. The deputy squad leader yelled out, "Engineer Wang," several times, but he knew his voice would never reach. As soon as the words left his mouth, they were swept up by the wind and carried away. Once we were right above the searchlight, we could see the beam was shooting from somewhere within the body of the dam, but there seemed no way in from up here. There was only a vertical iron ladder, like the one we'd just climbed, leaning against the outside of the dam, but it was honestly too terrifying. As brave as Wang Sichuan was, even he wouldn't have dared to descend from here into the black abyss. After walking a while more, we came upon a ruined part of the dam. A large section had caved in. Within the breach was a set of emergency stairs. Making our way down, we came upon an iron door on the side of the dam. We went inside.

The room was pitch-black, but given how dark it was outside, this was nothing I wasn't used to. Sure enough, it soon became clear that the dam really had been designed for only short-term use. The concrete walls were covered with spreading cracks and exposed steel bars. The machine room might have been better termed a "machine facility." It was divided into a number of stories. The concrete floor was pockmarked with holes, looking similar to those in the half-torn-down buildings you see today. There were a number of wooden boxes near the entrance, covered by a dry oilcloth. Dust filled the air as we pulled it off. Through the holes in the floor we could make out a faint light, many stories down. It had to be the tail end of the searchlight. The primary machine room was probably at the very bottom. I could feel some vague sense of the gigantic apparatus down there. The wind had died down, but from outside the sound of water was still frighteningly loud. We called for quite some time, but there was no response. He couldn't hear us and we couldn't find a way down.

"What now?" I asked the deputy squad leader.

Each of the dam's floors was much taller than average building stories. Jumping was out of the question. The deputy squad leader dropped a piece of concrete through a hole in the floor, but we could neither see where it landed nor hear the sound it made. There was still no response from below.

"It seems we can't get down from here," he said. "We'll have to find another way."

I cursed to myself and shined the flashlight around the room. The light was almost out. This flashlight's lifespan was already way above average. It should have gone out much earlier, back when we were first exploring the sinkhole. There was no point placing any outsize hopes on it working much longer. I turned to the deputy squad leader. "First we have to find a new light source," I said. "Otherwise, when our flashlight goes out, we'll be stuck."

We looked around. There were more than a few things we could burn, and who knew what was inside those wooden boxes stacked in the corner? The deputy squad leader forced one open. Inside were mostly power cables and welding rods, as well as a bag of already-hardened cement. These had probably been used to maintain the dam. Cement mortar has to be reapplied to the base and body of a dam every year, otherwise it will gradually push outward, becoming incredibly dangerous.

After we'd taken four or five boxes apart in quick succession, the most useful things we found were a steel helmet and a cotton overcoat. The coat was exceedingly damp, almost as if I'd found it in a coffin dug up from the ground. The helmet, however, was still in fairly good shape and blocked some of the wind. We also discovered a box of water canteens. Having long since lost my own, I took one of these as well. At the time this little plundering spree didn't feel particularly notable, but in hindsight I get nervous just thinking about it. The canteen was key. It's the reason I'm here reminiscing and not still in that dam beneath the earth, slowly rotting away.

The room itself was not large. After making a lap, we'd turned over just about everything in it. We could barely breathe from the dust and decay. We broke off several wooden sticks and wrapped them in oilcloth in preparation for when our flashlight went completely dead. As we were getting ready, there came a sudden droning wail from outside. The instant I heard it, I knew it was the siren. As we were so much closer this time, the noise was deafening. I'd already mentally prepared myself for this. Were the sluice gates closing? I wondered. What was going on? Could there be some automatic maintenance system installed in the dam? Luckily, we didn't have to worry about the water rising while we remained stuck on the wing of the wrecked bomber.

Hoping to see what was happening with the river, we walked back outside. Suddenly, the deputy squad leader's brow wrinkled. "Engineer Wu," he said to me, "listen closely. This siren is different from the one we just heard." I listened, but could detect nothing new about it. "The sound is much longer," he said. "Now it can reach much farther away. This one sounds like the early-warning siren for an air raid."

An air raid? There are air raids here too?

CHAPTER 32

Air Raid

I believed what the deputy squad leader said. After all, this was something the army drilled nearly every day. As I spent most of my time in the field, I knew little about air-raid sirens. Although there had been mandatory evacuation drills—once or twice a year—back when I was in school, we all knew it was just practice. We followed the teacher and it was a fun diversion. No one was paying attention to the frequency of the siren.

There was not going to be an air raid here. That was beyond doubt. I was much more inclined to believe the alarm had some other function—warning, for example, that prisoners had escaped. The deputy squad leader told me that the early-warning air-raid siren would ring for thirty-six seconds, then stop for twenty-four seconds. It was an advanced alert for when an air raid was still only a possibility. As the planes approached, the siren would speed up, ringing for six seconds, stopping for six seconds.

Hearing the alarm from within the machine facility was enough to make us tremble. We climbed back on top of the dam. Walking into the wind, we made our way back to the point above the searchlight beam. It had changed direction and was now strafing the gigantic open space overhead. In theory, the roof of the abyss could not possibly be more than thirty-six hundred feet up. Indeed, the faint bulge of cliff rock could be seen at the uppermost end of the searchlight, but the area of illumination was too small and I was unable to make out their actual shapes.

There was no sign of any air raid—as if the frantic siren was all a joke. And though the searchlight swept back and forth above the void, there was nothing to see but rocks. After a while, its operator seemed to realize he was wasting his time. We watched as the beam again went level, then tilted down and began to illuminate the lower reaches of the abyss. We couldn't even hear the falling water hit bottom. How could this searchlight possibly illuminate anything that far down? I wondered. But when I crawled to the side of the dam and looked over, though the far end of the searchlight was rather dim, it was nonetheless able to illuminate the very bottom. The abyss was not that deep at all. Then I took a closer look: it was not the bottom being illuminated, but rather a huge sheet of mist that was floating slowly upward. It was as if the beam was shining upon a cluster of clouds in the sky. Although it might sweep back and forth, it could not penetrate their outer layer—like when we were young and we believed a lid must have been placed over the world. The mist was far from still. You could tell, albeit only vaguely, that it was slowly, almost rhythmically roiling and floating ever higher. This strange sight, matched with the immense and extraordinary background, only increased our agitation. Just what exactly was producing this mist? And what sort of geological formation was underneath?

I'm ashamed to admit it, but despite hearing the chaotically ringing siren and watching what was happening, I somehow didn't connect the two. I just continued to stare, my mind filled with excitement and wonder. Little by little the mist rose ever nearer, the searchlight beam becoming shorter and shorter, until the early-warning alarm suddenly stopped and abruptly changed to a much more urgent air-raid siren. Startled, I finally realized what was going on—the alarm was warning us about the mist! And it was now only six hundred feet below the dam. I remembered the corpse with the blackened gums in the sinkhole. My toes curled in fear. I could have slapped myself. How had I not realized this earlier? The mist carried some deadly poison!

We had to get out of there at once. I grabbed the deputy squad leader, wanting to flee back the way we had come—at least to the wrecked plane, but the farther from here the better. He was even thicker than I—he didn't realize at all the danger the mist posed—but when I explained it, his face turned white with fear. Still, he wouldn't leave. He grabbed hold of me. "Not yet!" he said. "Wang Sichuan is still down there. We'd just be letting him die. We have to go save him. Otherwise we'd never be able to live with ourselves later."

I felt both ashamed and worried, but it was too late to search for a way down. I looked again. I still couldn't see any sign the searchlight operator knew what was going on. The searchlight continued to focus on the mist below, swaying ever so slightly. What was he looking for? Then we both saw it—the iron ladder leading down into the abyss. It was only a few feet from us. We looked at one another. The deputy squad leader stretched his foot down onto the first rung. "Get out of here!" he said. "I'll go inform—" Before he could finish, the rung broke beneath him. His feet pedaled air, he dropped downward, and then he was falling.

CHAPTER 33

The Iron Chamber

There was something supremely valiant about the way the deputy squad leader spoke that final sentence, like some hero in one of those old War of Liberation movies. Unfortunately, I was roused too late. All at once he dropped away. A split second later, I instinctively shot my arm out to grab him, but his fall had been too sudden. He dropped directly onto the nearly vertical wall of the dam and slid downward. I froze, terrified, then, in a flash, I lost my balance and very nearly tumbled down beside him. Fortunately, the dam was sloped, if only just barely. After hitting the wall, he slid no more than eight or nine feet before he managed to grab on to a section of the iron ladder's concrete base. This alone stopped him from immediately falling to his death, but his momentum was too great. He was barely able to grip the concrete, and his hands began to slip.

I yelled to him not to panic, I was coming to get him. I got down on my stomach and leaned over the side, but my arms weren't long enough to cover even half the distance. I leaned out farther, until half my body was over the edge, then farther still, but even when I was about to slide down, there still remained a huge gap between us. The deputy squad leader was a soldier, his strength and reflexes far superior to those of the average man. Seeing me stretch out my hand, he kicked off the wall with his feet, using this split second of momentum to leap upward, just high enough to grab hold of my hand. I took a deep breath and tried as hard as I could to pull him up, but I had misjudged both my strength and my position. I was extended too far over the side. His weight yanked me free from my perch and together we began to slide over the edge. Panicking, I swung my free arm desperately, but the way I was stretched out, even if I'd managed to grab something, I would never have been able to hold on to it. My surprise lasted for only a moment, then the deputy squad leader pulled me down. In that instant I saw his eyes register some complex emotion, but my mind was completely blank. Everything had happened much too fast.

My chin immediately scraped against the rough concrete. I somersaulted and began rolling downward. My head knocked against the iron ladder, sending a terrible burst of pain through me. I reached out to grab it, but it was already too late. Down we tumbled, covering forty or fifty feet in the blink of an eye, all the way to the source of the searchlight. In a flash I saw a square window open on the side of the dam, a beam of white light shooting out of it. I couldn't open my eyes in the glare, and then I'd already rolled past.

God protect me, it was then that I felt a sudden jolt. My shoulder tightened and somehow I stopped falling. I shook my head and looked up. A vertical line of steel bars, their sharp ends pointing out, jutted from the wall of the dam. They were set into the concrete two palm-lengths apart from each other, probably installed while the dam was being built to give workers something to hold on to. The end of each had been curved into a hook. The strap of the canteen I'd so recently plundered had looped around one of these steel hooks and had actually managed to hold me up.

The deputy squad leader was nowhere to be seen. The flashlight and torches we'd prepared were all lost. Darkness surrounded me.

If the searchlight had not been so close by, I really would have been finished. I composed myself and pulled myself up the canteen strap. The hooked steel bars were very strong, but so narrow they supported only my toes. Trembling, I climbed from one to the next until I'd reached the bay window where the searchlight shined. As I grabbed on to it, I found that all my strength had left me. I could exert myself no further. This was a very familiar feeling. I'd probably broken a bone. Just as I began to give up, a hand suddenly extended from within the window, grabbed hold of me, and pulled me inside.

I slumped to the ground, barely able to keep my head up. I saw only a faint figure behind the beam of the searchlight, but from that glance alone I could tell this person was very small and thin. Definitely not Wang Sichuan. At first I believed my eyes had to be mistaken—I was sure Wang Sichuan had been controlling the light. The shadowy figure then moved out of the darkness behind the tail of the searchlight and walked over. He was wearing an old-fashioned gas mask. After looking me over he helped me up. Who was this person? Some Japanese man who'd been left behind? My next thought was to hide somehow. He called out to me, his voice made incomprehensible by the gas mask. Though he made several attempts at communication, I could only shake my head. At last he removed the mask. My mouth dropped open. It was the young soldier we'd left behind to look after Chen Luohu and Yuan Xile.

After getting over the shock, I felt a surge of happiness. I tried to give him a hug, but my arm lacked even the tiniest bit of strength. Instead I asked him what had happened to the other two. He ignored my question, and with an agitated expression said only: "Come with me right now!" He put the mask back on and supported me as we moved toward the back of the room. I told him the deputy squad leader was probably still out there, that I didn't know whether he'd fallen all the way or was still hanging somewhere.

The soldier nodded and told me that he'd go look in a moment. We continued on. The space here was illuminated by a dark-red emergency light. This was likely the dam's machine level. The floor was made of iron grates and concrete. Through the grates I could see the river and a gigantic piece of old-fashioned machinery. It looked like a huge iron spindle cast in concrete. Rusted iron pipes and power cables wrapped around it, crisscrossing as they extended upward. At the end of the room was an iron wall with a circular iron door built into it. The door was airtight, triple-proofed, and rusted the color of a fried-dough twist. The private turned the spinner handle in the middle of the door, the assistance mechanism kicked in, and the door swung open. He helped me inside.

We entered a ready room. Japanese-style hazmat suits hung on the walls. When the door closed, the air in the room was automatically changed. The soldier ran ahead to the end of the room, where there waited an identical triple-proofed door. He opened it in the same manner as before. Inside was a sealed chamber smelling of rust. Everything was made of iron. There was an ironwork chair and writing desk with a mess of papers stacked atop it. Maps were hung all around, and a Japanese slogan was draped across one of the walls. Small cup-shaped emergency lights lit the room. The young soldier told me to wait here, that he would return in a moment. Yuan Xile was shrunk into a corner of the room, her body curled into a ball. Chen Luohu sat on the iron chair. When he saw me, he nervously stood up. His eyes were all bloodshot, his mouth opening and closing, not knowing what to say.

I too was at a loss for words. Never would I have expected to find them here. We'd split up less than a day ago, but already it was as if a lifetime had passed. Far too much had happened. I asked Chen Luohu how they'd gotten here. He said that when the river started to rise, they'd blown up the oxskin raft and set out. With the river at a high point, a number of new branches had opened up. The water was too fast and they'd been swept down one of the branches. In the end, they found themselves here. Then Chen Luohu's responses stopped making sense. He seemed to have reached his mental breaking point. Not that it was his fault. If I hadn't already been scared into a kind of numbness when the water rose, who knows how I would have reacted when I saw the Shinzan?

We were silent for a moment. "What about everyone else?" he asked me. "Have the higher-ups sent in a team to rescue us?"

I didn't know how to explain what I had experienced and could give him only a rough idea of what had happened. Hearing that Old Cat had come, his expression changed and all at once he relaxed. Then it occurred to me: If this place was our assignment's intended destination, then where had that strange telegram led the others to?

As I was about to say this, the triple-proofed door opened again. In rushed the young soldier, the deputy squad leader slumped across his back. Covering his nose and panting heavily, he yelled to us, "Close the door now!" Before I could react, Chen Luohu had already jumped to his feet and swung it shut. Together we spun the handle dozens of times without stopping. At last we heard it click. Only then did we drop our hands and relax. Through the glass aperture atop the door I looked into the airlock. The door at the far end was wide open and gray mist floated slowly in, filling the room.

CHAPTER 34

Trapped

I t's hard to describe the mist, and since then I've never seen anything like it. What I remember most was how gray it was. It appeared extremely heavy, yet nevertheless it managed to float. The mist continued to pour through the outer door. It moved at an even speed, its pace calm and unhurried. Because of the light I could make it out only dimly. I then turned to help the soldier lay the deputy squad leader down. When I looked back, the ready room was already pitch-black. Mist had covered all the lights.

The door was sealed tight. The mist could sprawl no farther. The quality of this decades-old triple-proofed installation was better than I could have imagined. Still, I didn't dare stand too close to the door. The feeling that the mist might seep in through some crack never left me. I bit my lip and thought, if I was still outside right now, would I look like that corpse in the sinkhole?

Chen Luohu called for me to help. We lifted the deputy squad leader onto the writing desk. His face was covered in blood. The young soldier was panting and frantically checking him for wounds. I asked him where he'd found the deputy squad leader. He said that only a very short distance down the wall was a water chute, above which there was a concrete buffer strip to prevent people from falling. The deputy squad leader hadn't been as lucky as I. He'd tumbled all the way down and smacked into the buffer strip. That area was reachable from this level of the generator facility, and the young soldier had immediately rushed down. The mist was almost at their feet. The deputy squad leader had lost consciousness, but kept a death grip on his flashlight. As soon as the soldier saw how close the mist was, he picked him up and ran like mad back the way he'd come. The mist nearly overtook him, leaving him no time to shut the outer door.

We all had experience giving emergency medical treatment. This kind of thing happened often in the field, and injuries from falls were particularly common. By now my hand was killing me and I could barely lift it, but I ignored the pain and helped undo the deputy squad leader's clothing. He had a heartbeat and was still breathing, but out cold. His whole body had gone soft, and there was a huge gash on his head. It's hard to tell how serious head wounds are. I've seen people fall from tall trees, hit their heads and bloody their faces, then wrap the wound and climb back up the next day. I've seen others fall dead after getting knocked on the head by a fist-sized rock while picking pecans. Miraculously, the deputy squad leader had otherwise suffered no major external injuries.

The young soldier's face crumpled. Seeing the deputy squad leader like this, he began to sob. I told him not to worry and patted him on the back, although the pain in my hand was agonizing. Rolling up my sleeve, I could tell for certain that it was either not a break or only a minor one. My wrist was heavily swollen and hurt like hell. I'd probably sprained it, but there's no good way to treat a sprained wrist. I just had to endure it.

We stopped his bleeding and let the deputy squad leader rest. I asked the young soldier how, after reaching this place, he'd found the triple-proofed chamber. With a blank look, he said it wasn't he who'd found it. Yuan Xile had led them here. The current had swept their raft all the way down to this dam. They'd found a place to dock, and as soon as they climbed out, Yuan Xile took off running like a madwoman. The soldier and Chen Luohu ran as hard as they could after her, but she didn't stop until she'd reached this chamber, where she immediately curled up in the corner and hadn't moved since.

I was dumbstruck. The average person has learned to navigate buildings based on the layouts of those they're most often in. These habits are useless when it comes to structures designed to serve some specific and unfamiliar function. It is for this reason that, when coming across ruined buildings while prospecting, we sometimes decide not to explore too deeply. Within a chemical plant, for example, you might start running somewhere, but not get a hundred steps before hitting a wall. Places you assumed to be walkways turn out totally different. Hydroelectric plants are especially unusual. The structural design of such facilities takes into account only the pressure they must bear and the machinery they will contain. That Yuan Xile could enter a place this complex and sprint all the way here without stopping could only mean one thing: she'd already spent a lot of time here. Remorse skewered me. She'd gone through so much to return to where she'd met up with us, and then what did we do? Goddamn it! We led her right back here. Had she not already lost her mind, I suspect she would have tried to strangle us.

The private told me the mist had already come up once. That time it had also been preceded by a discharge of floodwater, but the mist hadn't risen nearly so high. Yuan Xile had practically gone mad when she heard the siren go off and went immediately to shut the door. As an engineering corpsman, the soldier knew quite a bit about poisonous gas and the measures taken against it. He'd quickly realized that the mist was toxic.

There had to be some kind of induction machine here to regulate the water level, he said. Once the river reached a certain height, the dam would automatically open the sluice gates. Either this facility had been in continuous operation for the past twenty-some years, or it had recently been switched back on. When the discharged water crashed into the depths of the abyss, it disturbed the mist, allowing it to ride the crosswind up to the dam. (Later, after making it back out, we would agree that this was the only possible explanation.) As to what the mist was composed of, he had no idea.

I asked his name. Ma Zaihai, he said. He was a soldier from Yueqing, in Wenzhou, a three-year veteran of the engineering corps who'd never once taken a leave. "Then how are you still a private?" I asked. He said his family's class wasn't good. Every time a squad leader mentioned him for promotion, his file was ignored. His squad leaders had changed four times, yet he remained a private. The deputy squad leader was just like him, he said. He too had a bad family background, but having fought against India, he'd been risen one rank. The two of them had stayed within the squad this whole time while each of their leaders was promoted. If I felt bad for him, he said, I should help him out and talk to our superiors. No matter what, he was determined to become at least a deputy squad leader.

I laughed hollowly and made no response. Given the situation we're in now, I thought, let's think about making it out alive first—not that I'd be able to help him, anyway.

The mist persisted. Outside the airtight door, it was pitch-black, and after two hours there were still no signs of it beginning to disperse. From our hiding place in the iron chamber, we could only observe the situation through the small window in the door. We couldn't see anything clearly. Fortunately, the sealed chamber was relatively quiet. We could hear the roar of the current, but the most distinct sounds were our own breathing and the groans as pressure bore down on the dam's concrete structure.

None of us knew when the mist would retreat. At first we talked among ourselves, but then we quieted down and took to resting within the chamber. After lying comatose for an hour and a half, the deputy squad leader finally came to. He was groggy and listless but nonetheless awake, and there seemed to be nothing seriously wrong. Ma Zaihai was so happy he cried again, and I too felt a sense of relief.

Later, I began to worry we'd exhaust the room's oxygen supply, but I discovered an old-fashioned ventilation system installed behind the baseboard. While visiting a captured Japanese submarine on display at a naval base in 1984, I would run into a similar system and realize this chamber's ventilation system had probably been based on submarine models. This chamber seemed designed to withstand the mist. But I had no one to discuss these observations with. I could only silently ponder the events taking place.

Given Yuan Xile's familiarity with the area, her prospecting team must have stayed within the dam for some time. Though I didn't know what exactly had happened to them, it was clear that whatever they encountered, we were soon to face as well. Yuan Xile had lost her mind and a man had been poisoned to death. Whatever had happened here, it was nothing good. But where was everyone else? Was Yuan Xile's extreme terror because the mist had already killed the rest of her team? And, again, what had the Japanese been up to? There was no thread to follow. My mind flashed to an image of the gigantic Shinzan bomber, then to the abyss and the mist rising out of it like some evil ghost. Thinking about this gave me a splitting headache. These were our only clues, but I couldn't make heads or tails of them.

I considered the situation for nearly three hours. The mist still hadn't dispersed. The pain in my hand was indescribable. I thought again of Wang Sichuan, of whether he was alive or dead, and I wondered where Old Cat and the rest were now. And how were we supposed to get back? Our problems were endless. In this anxious state, I fell into a muddled sleep. I didn't know it at the time, but this was the last bit of rest I would get for a long while. It was only after the bad dreams that filled this short sleep that the real nightmare would begin.

When I awoke, I tried once more to talk to Yuan Xile, but again got nowhere. The poor woman seemed to have reached the very limit of fear. Even the slightest sound would set her off. She'd immediately curl up tighter whenever I tried to speak to her, her eyes involuntarily avoiding mine. Instead I began discussing with the deputy squad leader and the rest how we'd get out of here and what route we should use. The one thing worth celebrating was that Ma Zaihai said their raft should still be where he left it. If the current wasn't too strong, we could paddle it back upstream. We didn't know whether we should travel back up the main underground river or try to locate the sinkhole where we'd fallen in. The wisest route would be the one Yuan Xile had taken, but which was that? Had she still been in her right mind, she might have led us some of the way.

"If only we had some kind of blueprint or map," said the deputy squad leader. "There's definitely one around here. If we can find it, we'll know how the Japanese planned this place out and will be able to find the shortest, safest way back. Many of the facilities here are already ruined," he said. "It wouldn't be smart to just heedlessly rush back." I nodded. These engineering corpsmen can glean a lot just looking at a blueprint, though I suspected that all such materials were destroyed when the Japanese left.

As we discussed the matter back and forth, my mind gradually emerged from its stupor. I began to relax. We were heading back. We knew what awaited us at our destination, and, moreover, we had choices. No matter what, it's always good to be given a choice. That little aphorism was something I thought up later.

None of us, however, had realized the most essential problem: It wasn't our journey back. It was right before our eyes. Ten hours later, after settling upon an approximate plan and counting how much food and fuel we had left, we once more looked through the small aperture in the door. Outside was still pitch-black. Suddenly we realized the true crux of the matter. How long would the mist remain out there? A day or a whole month? Nobody else had considered this problem until I brought it up. They all assumed that soon enough it would begin to dissipate. Even after I raised the issue, there was a slight nervousness, but everyone remained hopeful. Ma Zaihai said that while the mist had not risen all the way up last time, it had retreated quickly. He was sure it would be gone within a few hours. And if not, the crosswind would have thinned it out considerably. I took it for granted that he was right. In this sort of situation, it is always better to find a reason to feel relieved than to look for gratification in having suspected the worst. Still, the force of the river smashing against the bottom of an unfathomably deep abyss had caused this demonic mist to rise, and even now the water continued to fall. So long as the sluice gates remained open, the mist would continue to roll upward. How could it do anything else?

We passed the next five or six hours in a state of silent unease. The mist continued to fill the air outside our chamber and showed not the slightest sign of having begun to disperse. The indistinct panic we'd felt earlier gradually intensified. We had no choice but to admit that the mist would not be disappearing anytime soon. Once more we discussed our options. The plans we'd made and the rousing rhetoric we'd spouted ten hours before now seemed no more than a joke. The atmosphere had become rather awkward.

The deputy squad leader and Ma Zaihai asked whether we shouldn't just be patient. Wouldn't overthinking just further confuse the situation? I told them that we had to face reality. So long as the floodgates stayed open, the mist would only get thicker and thicker—no way would it dissipate. "That being the case," I said, "there are a few steps we'll have to take: First, we'll need to distribute the water and grain rations. We need to do our best to survive as long as we can and hope that we'll be able to wait until the mist dissipates. Second, we have to actively think of a way out of here. The first measure is particularly important," I said. "Even though the mist might be gone in an hour, we need to prepare as if we won't be out of here for a month."

Ma Zaihai looked embarrassed. "Actually, we've got plenty of rations," he said. They had abandoned the majority of the equipment in their hurry to come rescue us but had kept the food, bringing along several bundles of hardtack and condensed vegetables. But he and Chen Luohu only had two canteens between them, one of which wasn't even full. My heart fell as I heard this. At once my throat felt parched. Our pant legs were already dry, otherwise we could have wrung the water out of them. I remembered how, shortly after entering the cave, I'd wondered what I would do should we run out of water and whether, if need be, I could drink my own urine. I cursed my naïveté. Now I would be put to the test. My mind turned at a dizzying speed, but it was no use and I soon despaired.

I had had only a few similar experiences being trapped, the most dangerous being one time in eastern Sichuan in 1959. I'd only recently begun working as a prospector. On a cave-prospecting job organized by the local geological bureau, we were trapped inside an air cavity by rising water for three days and two nights. Luckily, the water finally receded. There were ten or twenty of us at the time, and our food and water rations were abundant. What we had lacked most was experience, and soon the tears began to flow. Really, though, it wasn't so bad. Now we were full of experience, but had almost no water. Compared to this, being stuck for a few days and going on a bit of a crying jag was hardly a big deal.

"Waiting in here until the mist retreats will require a huge amount of luck," said Ma Zaihai, "but if one of us can get out, he might find something useful. What if we find an old-fashioned water or steam pipe, for example, and there's still water inside? Shouldn't we give it a try?"

Where are we going to find something like that, I thought to myself, only to see him squat down and point to the air vent running along the baseboard. "This vent is connected to the filtration system," he said. "The technology was used by the Germans during World War II and later studied by the Soviet Union. Today, the majority of our underground fortifications use an improved version of this system. There's probably a water pipe somewhere inside." Hearing this, I seemed to catch sight of survival, but the vent was just wide enough for a person's head. How was anyone supposed to wriggle his way in?

Ma Zaihai said he had a small frame, so it shouldn't pose too great a problem. He lay facedown, removed the anti-mouse grate, and began to squirm into the vent opening. I too dropped down, but with one glance I knew he'd never make it. He was a man, after all, and a small soldier is still not that small. After performing a number of odd and amusing movements, Ma Zaihai could still do no more than stick his head in sideways, while the rest of his body remained outside. At last he wrenched his neck and gave up. As for the rest of us, Chen Luohu had a large head, I've got wide shoulders, and the deputy squad leader already had a head injury. Yuan Xile was hardly worth mentioning. This idea was a dead end.

Disheartened, I slumped to the floor. No one spoke. Chen Luohu madly hugged his water canteen to his chest, seemingly afraid we'd snatch it from him. I was not in the mood to deal with him. My mind had gone blank. Then there was a sudden bang.

As if only to further compound the hopelessness of our situation, the chamber's emergency light abruptly went out. A scorched odor wafted through the air. The decayed electrical wires must have finally shorted.

CHAPTER 35

Vanished

The sudden darkness caught us all unawares. In the blink of an eye we could see nothing. Chen Luohu was so shocked he fell over. The rest of us were left stupefied for a moment. I heard Ma Zaihai curse *"gousheng"* from within the darkness. Whatever this meant, it wasn't polite. The deputy squad leader sighed. I could hear him laugh bitterly to himself. I felt a sudden annoyance. We'd already been at an impasse. Was it necessary that we be more thoroughly screwed? At least it fit our profession to die in the dark.

After about five minutes, I heard what sounded like small broken objects being fumbled about. Not long after, a flashlight beam shot across the room. The sudden brightness left us unable to open our eyes. Ma Zaihai had flipped it on. He brought the iron chair underneath the emergency light and stood on it, examining the lighting case. I knew this sort of emergency light—and especially one so rarely used—wouldn't ordinarily break. Even after being left alone for dozens of years, its simple design meant it should still be good as new. Breaking open the power storage box underneath the light, Ma Zaihai discovered there'd been a short in the old electrical line.

We had none of the tools or parts required for its repair. Using his bare hands, Ma Zaihai fiddled about with it, burning himself as a result. He swore again from the pain and was berated by the deputy squad leader. Neither recklessness nor cursing is encouraged in soldiers. Ma Zaihai was very submissive toward the deputy squad leader and apologized for his mistake at once.

We were all greatly disheartened and felt at a loss. Being knocked down over and over like this wears on a person's willpower. Our sole source of consolation was that, now that the chamber was dark, we could see a very faint ray of light shooting into the room through the aperture in the door. Before it had barely been visible, but now it was quite conspicuous. The light in the ready room was still on.

The deputy squad leader had Ma Zaihai turn off his flashlight to preserve the batteries. It was already low on power, the beam very dim. Ma Zaihai waved it gloomily about, lit at last upon that old-fashioned emergency light, then turned it off. Watching the light sweep around the room, I had the sudden feeling that something strange was afoot. I seemed to have caught sight of something, as if the room had somehow changed now that the light was off. Though I couldn't be sure what it was, a cold sweat broke out across my entire body, as if by reflex.

What was it? I wondered. I yelled for Ma Zaihai to turn his flashlight back on and shine it around the room. Ma Zaihai jumped in surprise, then immediately switched on the flashlight and scanned the chamber. This time all of us could see the problem. The deputy squad leader began to cough violently. A backpack was all that remained in the corner where Yuan Xile had been. She was nowhere to be seen.

Without wasting a second we jumped up and circled the room, shining about with the flashlight. We checked the corners, under the desk, even the ceiling, but Yuan Xile had disappeared! How much time had passed since the light went out? I counted it out on my fingers and was sure it hadn't been more than ten minutes. In that dark time, we'd sunk into such a state of gloom and depression that no one had paid any attention to the sound of Yuan Xile's movements. Logically, however, I knew that no matter what she did, there was no way she could have left this sealed-up chamber.

At first we couldn't believe it. Ma Zaihai's light was already dim. We were sure we must have simply missed her. Chen Luohu took out his flashlight and we searched the room for nearly twenty minutes. The chamber was not large. After I'd scanned it once and then again, my whole body was soon soaked in a cold sweat. "She's really gone," groaned Chen Luohu.

I had a sudden splitting headache—none of this made any sense. What the Japanese had done down here was already abnormal to the extreme, and now someone had inexplicably vanished from within a darkened room? It was more than I could take. I put my head in my hands and shrank against the wall. Was I having another nightmare? I suddenly wondered. Even this question felt beyond me.

The deputy squad leader was deathly pale. Each of us turned from one man to the next, our expressions dumbfounded. Ma Zaihai and the deputy squad leader both squatted down and looked back into the air vent. I felt as if I were losing my mind. There was absolutely no way a person could wriggle into a space that small. It was truly preposterous. But the iron chamber was far from large, and besides the main door, there was no other way out. We'd just watched Ma Zaihai attempt to squeeze inside before the light went out. Our eyes were all drawn to this spot. I thought of Yuan Xile's build. People back then were generally quite slight, especially young women, though I didn't know exactly what kind of physique she had. Still, no way was she petite enough to fit into a space like this.

Ma Zaihai was first to lie flat in front of the opening. He switched on his flashlight. Sweat ran down his face. We watched in silence, our attention concentrated on the beam of light. Rather than fading, the sudden terror we felt had only increased. My heartbeat was like thunder. I'd felt like this only once before: the first time I stole an egg from the production brigade. Still, we never would have expected that the moment Ma Zaihai shined his light down the shaft, he would suddenly scream out in fear.

It was a terrifying sound. Ma Zaihai jumped up as if he'd been given an electric shock, his face ashen. He stumbled and fell back down. Despite being scared half to death, I quickly scooped up his flashlight and crouched down to take a look. My mind was buzzing. Goose bumps ran from the top of my head down to my heels. My whole body was so cold it was like I'd fallen into a giant icehouse. While the emergency light was on, we'd been unable to see anything past the mouth of the air vent. Now the beam shot into the air vent, illuminating its deepest recesses. Then it appeared. It was a face, crushed and terribly deformed—whether it belonged to a person or to some "thing," whether it was that of Yuan Xile, I couldn't tell, but in my heart I found it impossible to believe that whatever was stuffed back there could really be human.

CHAPTER 36

The Air Shaft

The three of us gulped. It took me a long time before I was brave enough to take another look. I don't know whether it was from the buildup of psychological pressure or if the face really was that terrifying, but as I examined it in detail my fear somehow became even more intense. I felt as if I were suffocating.

It had a nose like an eagle's beak and an abnormally tall forehead. Had it been squashed into this form or did it normally appear this strange? If it was a person, he had to be dead, his brain matter crushed into tiny pieces. There was not the slightest trace of Yuan Xile in this demonic face. That was good at least. A long time passed as we looked at one another in blank dismay. No one knew what to say.

Ma Zaihai was first to react. He stood up, went over to his backpack, and pulled out a rope with a three-pronged pig-iron hook at the end. Then he made to dismantle the long iron desk. He wanted to use one of the desk legs as a handle for the hook. Unfortunately, the desk was too solid. It was welded to the floor. Though we tried for a long time to move it, the thing never even flexed. We rummaged about for a while, until at last the deputy squad leader found a length of iron wire—thick as a thumb—welded to the wall. We tore it down and wrapped it around the base of the grapnel. Then we all squatted down, curious to see what was really back there.

It was a chaotic scene. The deputy squad leader was still injured, so it was I who took the flashlight and illuminated the vent, while Ma Zaihai reached in with the hook. In fact, Ma Zaihai was far from willing, but he had to obey orders. His lips trembled as he lay prone. We told him to be careful, but what use was that? All three of us lay down in front of the opening and watched as bit by bit the hook moved farther in.

The whole thing took less than half a minute, but I felt as if I'd been staring for a whole day. At last, when the hook was about to bump into the strange face, my eyes were already sore. By then we were ready for anything—the thing suddenly moving or dodging quickly backward—but the hook knocked into it and the face didn't move in the slightest. No matter how we prodded it, the thing made no reaction. "It seems all flopped over," said Ma Zaihai. "The feel of it is wrong." He finally caught the grapnel around the thing's neck. The point dug in, giving him a tight hold around the head. There was almost no resistance as it came sliding toward us. My heartbeat abruptly quickened its pace. All of us stood up at the same time, each preparing to jump backward at a moment's notice. No one wanted to react too late.

The pale white head was first to emerge. Next came the body. I saw things like feet and hands and in that moment my mind went numb. How incredibly strange, I thought. Its whole body has gone soft, like some enormous mollusk. My heart gave a leap. Then I realized what it was.

This was no monster. It was a strange rubber suit. It was time-worn and probably left by the Japanese. The twisted face was no more than a squished gas mask attached to the top of the suit. The mask was really more of a helmet. It had a very high forehead and an odd-looking design. The clothing and mask were one piece. It was a model I'd never seen before and presumably protected against much more than just poison gas. Ma Zaihai poked at it with the iron hook. There appeared to be nothing inside. Seeing this, he relaxed and made to swear once more, but he seemed to remember what the deputy squad leader had said and his jaw snapped shut. The deputy squad leader's countenance remained imposing. Ma Zaihai wanted to take a closer look, but the deputy squad leader grabbed him. "Leave it alone for a moment," he said.

But nothing happened, so we crowded back around it and the mood eased up. Spreading it open with the hook, Ma Zaihai poked and shined his flashlight over the thing. I remembered the time a gold-striped snake had gotten into my clothing. My mother had whacked at the clothes until the snake slithered back out. There was nothing like that, nothing hidden or the least bit amiss, about this suit.

At last Ma Zaihai turned the suit over. The spot where the rubber body connected to the helmet was already torn, most likely the autograph of Ma Zaihai's hook. The area around the suit's chest was also rotted. It had probably been sticking to the bottom of the shaft and ripped open when we yanked it. Inside was absolutely empty. Everyone relaxed. False alarm. Ma Zaihai knelt down and began ripping off sections of the suit. He tore it to shreds. There truly was nothing inside.

"Strange," said the deputy squad leader, "who would have stuffed this thing back there, and toward what purpose?" As he said this, Ma Zaihai squatted back down and shined his flashlight into the air shaft.

CHAPTER 37

Another One Gone

I squatted down beside him. A faint breeze was blowing out of the air shaft as we shined our flashlights inside. It was utter blackness. Who knew where it led? A strange odor floated up from somewhere far down the shaft. I still remember that scent. It was much lighter than what I'd smelled in the sinkhole, but I could tell it was the same odor. Although I had no idea what it came from, that odor appearing at this moment made me feel uneasy. Had someone used the suit to seal up the opening? Was there a leak in the ventilation system? This blockage had been merely a temporary measure, but now that we'd removed it, would the poison outside begin to leak slowly into the room? As I thought about this I began to feel a little unwell. Ma Zaihai and I piled up a stack of odds and ends and, in a symbolic gesture, used them to block up the air shaft. At least this way we felt somewhat more secure. We sat down, all of us severely dispirited. Such a succession of frights was far too wearing.

In a soft voice, Ma Zaihai asked, "If she didn't leave through here, then how exactly did Engineer Yuan get out?"

Looking at the opening, I shook my head. We'd been deceiving ourselves. Even if Yuan Xile had managed to crawl inside, she was too big to have advanced any farther. So where had she gone? After all, this was a sealed room. Besides the vent, none of the other openings were big enough for even a cockroach to crawl through. As I thought about this, I involuntarily raised my flashlight and shined it once more around the chamber. The chaos of our search had thrown the entire room into a terrific mess. The extent of our alarm could be seen from the complete disorder, but there was still no Yuan Xile. The four of us were all that were left.

As this thought of "the four of us" occurred to me, I felt a sudden mental jolt. Something had changed. This sensation felt very familiar, as if I'd just experienced it. Again I shined my flashlight around the room. For a long time I was puzzled. Then, all of a sudden, I realized what it was: in addition to us three, the fourth person was Chen Luohu. I assumed he'd been curled up in a corner this whole time. As I swept my flashlight across the chamber, I realized that—for who knows how long—I hadn't seen him at all. I stood up. Once more I shined the flashlight around the room. Chen Luohu had vanished as well!

Then I really began to fall apart. My blood pulsed in my veins and I could no longer support my own weight. I was rocked by a burst of dizziness and felt as if my brain was swelling in my skull. I was tottering, hanging on by only a thread. I wanted to slump directly to the floor. Luckily, Ma Zaihai helped steady me. "What is it?" he and the deputy squad leader both asked. Stammering, I managed to get it out. I watched as the color drained from their faces. In an instant Ma Zaihai was sweeping his flashlight around the room and calling out, "Engineer Chen!"

The way our excitation continued to increase made us seem like mere pieces on a chessboard, being manipulated by some unseen, diabolical hand, led little by little toward the point of collapse. Every move was perfect. In the flickering flashlight beam, all of us quickly sank into a state of hysteria. I have already forgotten what we felt in those moments, though dread was certain. Thinking back on it now, however, given that we'd encountered something that went beyond any rational explanation, what was there for us to dread? Was I scared of disappearing myself, or scared of being abandoned here?

We pounded our fists against the walls of the iron chamber and yelled at the top of our lungs. Then we lay down and examined the floorboards. The already messy room became even more chaotic, but all our efforts were futile, and the sturdy, utterly flawless walls only increased our panic. We did this again and again until we were completely exhausted. The deputy squad leader was the first to stop, then the two of us gradually calmed down. Ma Zaihai grabbed at his short hair and sat dejectedly in the chair. I rested my head against the wall, brought it back, then smashed it savagely back down.

Any sense of order had now been lost. Could there really be ghosts in here? No one spoke. We could hear one another breathing heavily. And the atmosphere, well, our minds had all gone blank, so there was no atmosphere to speak of. Time passed little by little. Perhaps it was two hours, perhaps four. No one spoke a word. Now that the agitation had passed, exhaustion surged over us like an ocean tide. There came a long period of semiconsciousness, but I was far from asleep. In all my life I'd never felt weariness like this. As a geological prospector, there'd been numerous times I did not sleep for days, but I was always able to regulate my level of exhaustion. We were all born not long after the beginning of the War of Resistance. Even in childhood, we had to labor under conditions so arduous they would be difficult to imagine. Physical tiredness meant little to us, but this sort of total psychic fatigue was something else entirely.

Slowly, though, my mind did become more placid. I don't know precisely how long it all lasted. I'd imagine that what brought me back was the chill that ran through my body once the cold sweat had dried. Or it could have been the hunger. I took a deep breath, turned off my flashlight, and looked around for a place to sit. How long since I'd last eaten, I wondered, and how long had I already been inside this chamber? Here there was neither night nor day. Everything had been thrown into disorder. In those days, watches were considered home appliances. Given that even the supply of lighters was restricted, you can imagine how much harder it was to acquire a watch. As my senses returned, I began to think deeply, almost as if forced. The details of the entire circumstance were released into my mind with no way for me to stop their advance. I later told Old Cat that it was only at this point that I really began to consider what was going on. You could say that the way I thought about things somehow opened up. I've always felt that the moderate professional success I've achieved since then was catalyzed by this very experience. Though it might seem incomprehensible to many, there were a lot of people like me in those days—simple and naive, our problem-solving methods unfailingly direct. This was probably because our news and information was severely limited. You can ask your parents to relate how simplistic the plots of our movies and model-theater performances were—persons good and bad could be clearly distinguished based solely on what they looked like. Back then we almost never considered issues of too great complexity. It was this immaturity on our parts, this belief that things should be simple, that allowed the Ten-Year Calamity (the Cultural Revolution) to be so destructive.

At first, my mind was filled entirely with scenes of Yuan Xile and Chen Luohu's disappearance, all occurring beneath the swaying beam of a flashlight, until I felt dizzy. Then my mind began to move. Just how had it all happened? There had to be something unusual about this chamber that we were unaware of. In a deep recess thirty-six hundred feet underground, within a strange airtight chamber built into a ruined installation abandoned by the Japanese decades before—in a situation in which it was absolutely impossible to disappear—two very alive people were suddenly nowhere to be seen. Assuming they really were gone, then at some point during the several minutes when our attention slackened and we weren't watching them, something must have occurred. But what?

I tried as hard as I could to recall anything that had felt even the slightest bit amiss. When Yuan Xile disappeared, it had been amid total darkness. All of our attention had been focused on finding a flashlight. We'd ignored any sounds that might have been occurring around us. Yuan Xile could have used that moment to do anything she wanted. When Chen Luohu disappeared, the room had been only half dark, but all of our attention had been focused on the opening to the air shaft. We were completely blind to anything happening behind us. Both times somebody disappeared, all our attention had been concentrated on a single spot. I sighed and a preposterous thought appeared in my mind. Was it possible that in here, as soon as you stopped thinking about someone, they would vanish?

This was truly absurd, but as soon as the thought occurred to me, my whole body suddenly went cold and I realized: I wasn't paying attention to Ma Zaihai and the deputy squad leader! With a start I came back to reality, hurriedly twisting my head around, looking for the two of them. Darkness surrounded me. At some point, their flashlight beams had been extinguished, but I hadn't noticed. A wave of panic rushed over me. I groaned involuntarily. I sank into a state of extreme, irrational fear. I was so scared that my entire body curled in on itself. I was unable to force a single breath into or out of my chest. I made myself scream out, though the barest sounds were all I could manage. There was no response. I truly was the only person left in that pitch-black room. I felt another splitting headache, as if my skull were bursting open. The brief calm I'd experienced disappeared at once. I cried out as loud as I could and switched my flashlight back on.

For the briefest moment, I genuinely believed that I was looking at an utterly empty room. I alone had been abandoned within these hellish ruins, trapped inside a secret pitch-black chamber, poisonous mist just beyond the door, and everyone who was with me had vanished like ghosts. A more awful plight could not be conceived. Had it truly been as bad as all that, I'm afraid I would have promptly gone mad. The difference between novels and so-called reality is that, while novels often go to extremes, in reality people are rarely forced into such desperate straits. As soon as I switched on my flashlight, I saw Ma Zaihai standing before me, having seemingly appeared out of thin air. His face was white as a dead man's and he seemed to be groping around the wall for something. I yelled in fright as soon as I saw him. He immediately shrank back several feet. The beam of a second flashlight shot across the room and swept toward me. It was the deputy squad leader, standing in another corner of the iron chamber and watching us with a perplexed look on his face.

Though I relaxed a little, I was still furious. "What the hell were you doing?" I asked them. "Why did you turn off your flashlights and not say a word?"

Ma Zaihai had gone totally stiff. I had scared him half to death and he was speechless. The deputy squad leader stepped in and explained. He'd realized that when the other two disappeared, the iron chamber had been almost totally dark. He wondered if there wasn't some sort of mechanism that turned on when all the lights were off. So he'd asked the two of us to turn off our flashlights and see what we could find. I'd turned mine off just as he'd said this, so he'd assumed I'd heard.

Seeing that the two of them were still here, I began to calm down. "I thought you two had disappeared as well," I told them.

The way their eyes widened said they'd had the same worries. Being regular soldiers, though, they were different from me. They had just taken their feelings, placed them in the back of their minds, and ignored them.

"Did you find anything?" I asked them. Ma Zaihai shook his head.

In this we were deceiving ourselves once more. If we were unable to find anything in the light, then how could anything be found in total darkness? But for a man like the deputy squad leader to have thought of this was still rather impressive. The educational level of engineering corpsmen was far from high. At most they would have received a bit of training in their specialty, and that was it. It's like they used to say about the three treasures of the heroic railway corps: a spade, a pickax, and a worn-out quilted jacket. That's how the special-engineering divisions were back then.

We gathered together and sat down. Each of our faces wore the same serious expression. "Let's not panic," I told them. "From now on, we three will stick close together, so if someone else disappears the rest of us will be sure to know what's going on!" They both nodded. It was gratifying to see our morale rise. The situation hadn't changed a bit—my stomach rumbled its intense hunger, and the problems we faced remained legion—but seeing the two soldiers before me I felt secure.

According to materialistic thought, all these strange things we encountered had to have rational explanations, no matter how far-fetched these rationalizations might be. Admittedly, we did often discover that these seemingly forced interpretations were in fact correct, but right now I feared materialistic explanation would simply no longer suffice. I began wondering what would happen if Yuan Xile and Chen Luohu never reappeared. Assuming we made it out of here alive, how would we explain that? The two of them had vanished like ghosts, and where were they now? Had they disappeared completely, or ended up in some other place?

I raised my head and looked around. Not once had I considered the purpose of the iron chamber itself. Based on how it was furnished, it seemed to be either an alternate command center or some kind of safe room, a temporary refuge when the poison mist rose up from the abyss, but was this really the case? It was unimaginably fantastic what the devils had built here. At the end of an enormous natural grotto, we'd found a massive dam and warplane, their presence basically inexplicable. So, given that the Japanese intent was still unfathomable, was it possible this iron chamber was part of some overarching plan?

I stood up and looked at the four walls around me. Suddenly a question appeared in my mind: What was behind them? Concrete? Or something I couldn't even guess? I ran my fingers along the iron. It was bumpy and rough, as if corroded by some strong acid. Traces of white paint remained, none larger than a fingernail. The wall was ice-cold. As soon as I placed my palm to it, all the heat was sucked from my body. No, I suddenly realized, this was much too cold! The temperature was like that of the underground river, so cold as to be unendurable.

I stuck my ear to the wall. The deputy squad leader and Ma Zaihai stared. "What is it?" Ma Zaihai asked.

I raised my hand to tell him to not make any noise. I had already heard something. At first I couldn't identify it, then a moment later it dawned on me. It was the sound of water, but not the roar of the river crashing against rock. This was a noise I was familiar with. I come from a family of fishermen. It was the dreary swooshing of the underwater current rubbing against the sides of a boat. In my astonishment I listened again, and indeed I was not mistaken, but I knew it was impossible. The iron chamber was above the generator room. I distinctly remembered the water level was many floors beneath our feet. Even if the sluice gates had closed while we were in here, the underground river would never have risen this high. I related my discovery to Ma Zaihai and the deputy squad leader. They were both perplexed, but when they pressed their ears to the wall, they could hear it as well. Smiling bitterly, Ma Zaihai asked, "So what does this mean? Are we underwater now?"

I grabbed the grapnel and struck it forcefully against the iron wall. There was a bang. Sparks flew off the wall. The sound was low and deep, totally unlike the cry emitted by hollow metal. We truly were surrounded by water. I was stunned. Then I realized that beyond this chamber, beyond the water, there was sure to be another gigantic iron wall. The iron chamber was independent from the rest of the dam and wrapped in a huge iron chute. I slapped myself. How had I not thought of this earlier? What part of a dam's interior installation would require a thing like this? It was all too simple. As far as I knew, there was only one device that would necessitate just such an iron shell!

CHAPTER 38

The Caisson

On several of the large-scale dams the Japanese built in the thirties and forties—for example the one in Fengman on the Songhua River—the electrical generating units were located roughly thirty feet underwater. During construction, these dams required a special kind of freight elevator—called a "caisson"—to take workers and machinery underwater for installation and generator maintenance. These caissons were generally steel-bar-reinforced iron boxes in vertical cement chutes. Although usually dismantled once testing on the dam had been completed, they sometimes continued to serve as the only way to reach the dam's lower levels during periods of maintenance and repair. To my knowledge, the only kind of rooms you ever find completely encased in iron are these freight elevators—these caissons. I looked around the room. Was this iron chamber just such a device?

If so, then that triple-proofed iron door was really the entrance to an elevator. My mind seemed to abruptly open up and a number of things occurred to me all at once. The creaking sound I'd heard within the chamber—the one I'd thought was pressure bearing down on the dam—had it been the chamber rubbing against the iron elevator tracks? Could it be that after we stepped into the room, the caisson had actually begun to move? As I listened again to the sound of water outside the chamber, I wondered: In the time it took us to enter the room, could someone have started the thing up? Was it possible that, unknowingly, we'd already descended beneath the water to the dam's lowest level?

This guess seemed absurd once I thought it all the way through. If it really did happen, how had we completely failed to notice? But as I thought back on what had just taken place, I couldn't reject the idea. For if it really were as I surmised, then there was now a highly rational explanation for the disappearances of Yuan Xile and Chen Luohu. I focused my attention on a single portion of the iron chamber. Oddly, not once during my recent panic had I taken any note of this area. Why had I never thought of this place when, in actuality, it was the most likely place someone could disappear to? Far, far more likely than the lunchbox-sized ventilation tunnel. I'm referring to the airtight door, of course.

I walked up to it and looked through the small aperture. I could see a faint bit of light, though this light appeared not to be coming in from outside, but rather the reflection of our flashlight beams on the glass. The scene appeared no different than when we had first entered. As I looked at the door, I became lost in thought. This idea was very simple—that people might leave a room through its door. We'd neglected to think of it because we'd believed that outside the door was toxic mist. We believed that if Yuan Xile and Chen Luohu had exited through this door, not only would they have died, but the mist would have invaded the room. We reasoned that since none of us had died, the door must have remained shut, but if the iron chamber had already dropped to the lower levels of the dam, then there was no poisonous gas outside. Therefore, once the emergency light went out, Yuan Xile would have been able to slip through the darkness, open the door, and step through. The same went for Chen Luohu. The problem was whether a certain prerequisite to my whole line of reasoning had been fulfilled: Was there really no poison gas outside the door?

I told the deputy squad leader and Ma Zaihai my idea. Ma Zaihai shook his head at once. Impossible, he said. If a thing as large as the iron chamber really did descend, the people within it would have to notice. And how had Yuan Xile managed to find the door with such precision in the dark? And what about the sound of the door opening—why hadn't we heard it? The deputy squad leader was silent, his head down, but based on his expression it was evident he agreed with Ma Zaihai.

He had a point. How had Yuan Xile known so clearly where the door was located? And how had she managed to avoid the chaos of everyone's arms and legs within the darkness, passing right beside us without making a sound? She wasn't a cat. I sat perplexed, staring at the layout of the iron chamber. There, in the center of the room, was the long iron table. It was covered in the papers we'd thrown about as well as fragments of something unidentifiable. The table stretched a long way, from the corner Yuan Xile had curled up in to right in front of the door. None of us had gone so far as to climb on top of the table during the earlier chaos. As long as Yuan Xile had crawled along the table, she would have been able to make it to the airtight door with great speed and ease. And when Chen Luohu vanished, all of our attention had been focused on the ventilation shaft.

Ma Zaihai went over to look at the table. It was a wreck. Of course, no trace of such an exit could be seen. In other words, there was nothing whatsoever to support my idea.

The three of us stared blankly. I had become rather uncertain how to proceed. My hypothesis did nothing to mitigate the anxiety we all felt. Rather, it added a number of new reasons for agitation. We began to waver and our distress became like a web we had woven around ourselves, the circumstances behind the black iron door like some constant nightmare, ceaselessly pressing down on us. If it really was as I said and no toxic gas remained, then we should open the door without hesitation and figure out where exactly Yuan Xile and Chen Luohu had run off to. But if I was wrong, then opening the door would be suicide. We passed this time in spiritual torment. The development that made us feel most helpless was that there were no developments at all. In the chamber, time passed bit by bit, our hunger growing increasingly intense. Having no other choice, we were eventually forced to make one of the corners a makeshift bathroom. It soon stunk to high heaven. It felt as if time had stopped moving, every minute seeming to last for an eternity. No one brought up what we were supposed to do next. We were all watching the door, each of us knowing that, once it was opened, all our questions would immediately be answered.

As a matter of fact, we were caught in a kind of battle between materialism and superstition, as if the purpose of all this was to see which side we would choose. Could we rationally go through the possible choices, or, overwhelmed by fear, would we resort to belief in ghosts and the supernatural? As a devout Communist Party member and officer in the PLA, the choice should have been obvious for me. In reality, though, I was just as afraid as any ordinary person would have been. All manner of complex emotions swirled within me.

From a certain perspective, given that three of us were men—especially men born into destitute peasant-class families—to stay in a sealed room stinking of piss and shit for a couple of hours, with hungry stomachs to boot, wasn't actually that terrible. If our plight had had a definite endpoint—one day, for example, or one week—it absolutely would have been bearable, especially if it were an integral part of some official assignment. Compared to getting dragged off to India to go war, this was considerably more leisurely.

What was unbearable was that our predicament had no defined limit. So long as no one opened that door, this would all continue until we died. As I thought about it, the pores all across my body seemed to burst open.

At first we talked it over, then we became fidgety, felt a burst of calm, then another rush of agitation. Ma Zaihai and I took turns looking out through the aperture, feeling around the iron walls, and doing a great deal of things that were utterly pointless. The deputy squad leader continued to sit in the same place, his eyes closed, pondering who knows what. We waited for approximately seven hours, suffocating under our agitation and the choice we faced. At last it was the deputy squad leader who suddenly stood up, walked over to the airtight door, and grabbed hold of the wheel lock. Slowly, he began to turn it.

I remember the deputy squad leader's expression with total clarity. I wish I could describe it as filled with that calm, composed, and fearless sort of revolutionary spirit, but in reality, he was no different from us—his mind was barely able to bear what he was doing. It's just that those who've served on the battlefield become accustomed to life and death hanging in the balance. It becomes easier for such people to take the pivotal step. Only after he'd rotated the wheel halfway did we really understand that he meant to open the door. It was then that I did something pretty worthless: I actually made to rush over, grab hold of him, and prevent him from going any further, but before I moved, the deputy squad leader stopped on his own. His expression was very calm as he turned and waved over at us, saying we'd better get against the interior wall. If something was wrong, he could still quickly shut the door and we would be saved. Ma Zaihai insisted they open it together, but the deputy squad leader refused. That's the difference between those who've served on the battlefield and those who haven't, he said. Those who've served would never just give away their lives for nothing. They know as long as they remain alive they might still be of some use to their country. Ma Zaihai didn't listen, so I grabbed him tightly and dragged him back. The deputy squad leader became annoyed and yelled at us to shut up. Only then did Ma Zaihai calm down.

He and I retreated to the back wall, our eyes on the deputy squad leader. We watched him take a deep breath and then, with almost no hesitation, spin the wheel one full turn. From within the door came a faint *creak* and a sort of sucking noise as the air lock broke. It quietly opened a crack. I hadn't fully readied myself. I began to shake all over. The three of us went stock-still. Time seemed to stop and my mind went blank.

Nothing happened. Everything was just as it had been before. I held my breath for a long time before discovering that, in fact, we were OK. I was right after all. I relaxed and, from his place in the doorway, the deputy squad leader let out a deep breath. Ma Zaihai did, too. I was about to say thank goodness, when the deputy squad leader's entire body suddenly slackened and he crumpled softly to the floor, his hand pulling the door halfway open. I watched as, in an instant, a roiling cloud of mist poured through the doorway and into the iron chamber.

This is it, I thought to myself. In a moment, the dense, heavy mist had filled the room, rising and spreading as if it were some enormous soft-bodied organism taking over the iron chamber. My nerves were stretched to their limit, a single thought playing in my head: Fucked. The wall at my back was ice-cold. I could retreat no farther.

Perhaps, if given a bit more time, I would have felt both furious and regretful. Because of my baseless inferences, my comrades in arms and I were going to die. Those minutes of remorse would have been far worse than any pain that dying could bring. I probably would have slapped myself viciously and torn off my own scalp.

There was no such time. Within ten seconds of my having realized that, in fact, things were no longer looking so bright, the surging mist had already closed in on me. Ma Zaihai rushed into the dense mist to help the deputy squad leader, but I knew it was futile. As the mist blew in against my face, I instinctively held my breath and turned my head away, wanting to stay alive if for only a second longer. What was the use? I smelled some ice-cold scent and the mist wrapped itself around me.

CHAPTER 39

The Mist

I closed my eyes. I was surely about to fall down, froth at the mouth, and die. Looking back on it, how unexpected my thoughts were. In the very moments before I was to expire, not for a second did I ponder the significance of my death. In the end, of course, I survived. You're all probably aware of this. But while I wouldn't say that I had any great revelation, at the very least this experience matured me. It was only after this that I understood what one would have to go through—the price one would have to pay—to become as calm and steady as someone like Old Cat.

So then, what actually happened? Why didn't I die? I waited for death within that mist for over ten minutes. After a while I began to feel something new. The cold had begun to seep into my body. As my pores violently contracted, all the heat was sucked out of me. At first I thought this was the harbinger of death, but as I became colder and colder, to the point where I began to sneeze, I realized that something was amiss. Opening my eyes, I discovered the dense mist had already mostly dispersed. Ma Zaihai was standing beside the door with the deputy squad leader slung over his back, his expression as puzzled as my own.

There was no poison? How ridiculous all this was. How could this have happened? Had we really just been warring with nothing but our own minds? The mist had become very thin, not to mention cold as hell. Ma Zaihai was all huddled in on himself. The doorway was colder than the room. He glanced over at me, then slowly opened the door all the way. The mist seethed and our flashlight beams lit upon nothing but the roiling mass.

The deputy squad leader must have fainted from sheer exhaustion. Of the three of us, he'd overexerted himself most severely—both physically and mentally—and he was injured. He'd just passed out. We put our equipment in order. Then, with Ma Zaihai carrying the deputy squad leader, we stepped out of the iron chamber.

On all sides of us, there was nothing but mist. It obscured everything. Our flashlights were unable to illuminate even a few feet ahead, but at this point they were barely working anyway. The majority of the mist accumulated below our knees, white and thick, swiftly rising up, then thinly falling back down. It rolled as soon as we touched it, as if we were walking through a cloud. The air was so cold, after a few seconds I could no longer feel my legs, and only when they moved could I be sure they were still there. Already this cold went far beyond the icy chill of the underground river. We huddled in on ourselves and, feeling rather terrified, surveyed our surroundings. The falling temperature very quickly restored my train of thought. This mist was not the heavy gray fog we'd seen earlier, but rather the kind of freezing-cold water vapor often seen in large-scale freezers. But the temperature here was far lower than that of any freezer. It was just too cold.

We took out our sleeping bags and draped them over our shoulders, but they barely helped. I stamped my foot. There was iron grating running beneath us, covered with a layer of ice. An echo resounded each time I stamped down. Evidently, this was a relatively wide-open space. Where were we? What was supposed to be at the bottom of a dam? Shouldn't the rotor for the main generator be sunk down here? How come it all resembled a gigantic icehouse?

We continued cautiously, the iron grating vibrating rhythmically beneath our feet. The farther we went, the thinner the mist became. Soon enough, I saw we were tromping along a walkway, like a ridge between two farm fields. On either side was a massive, square, concrete swimming pool–like depression riddled with cement ridges crisscrossing the frozen pools within. It resembled a work site for burning lime, only its construction appeared much more detailed. In the ice were a number of large black shadows, each the size of a small cow. I stepped carefully atop the ice to have a look at what was inside. It was frozen solid, the water at least six feet deep. I still couldn't make out anything distinct about the shadows.

We continued along the grating, the cold increasing with each step. After 150 feet I already wanted to go back. Ma Zaihai couldn't stop shivering. Then we saw a familiar iron wall, and, within this wall, a familiar airtight iron door. It was covered in a thick layer of ice and hung with long, daggerlike icicles. Broken shards of ice carpeted the ground, and a crowbar leaned against the door. Presumably, someone had recently used the crowbar to pry open the ice-sealed door. I let out a deep breath. Had Yuan Xile opened this door?

I picked up the crowbar and was about to stick it in the wheel lock and open the door when with a click, it suddenly turned, if only slightly. Ma Zaihai and I each took a quick step backward. We watched as the wheel slowly began to rotate. My instinct was to raise the iron bar in defense. Ma Zaihai planted himself against the wall beside the doorway. The door opened gradually. Just as I was guessing whether it was Chen Luohu or Yuan Xile, a swarthy face—big and flat as a pancake—emerged and blinked at us. All of us, including the owner of the big, flat face, froze in astonishment.

It took me a full minute before I recognized the dark face sticking out from behind the door as Wang Sichuan's. This wasn't slowness on my part. He was unrecognizable, like he'd just emerged from a slaughterhouse. His face was covered in crusted blood, the skin on his forehead all flared up, and there was something very unnatural about the blackness of his skin. A long time passed. Then at last he yelled out, "Old Wu, you're still fucking alive!"

I stepped over and hugged him at once, the tears immediately flowing. Then Ma Zaihai recognized him and he started to cry, too. Wang Sichuan cried out in pain. For Wang Sichuan to have survived was just too wonderful. It felt like winning the lottery. But we military men frown on crying, so I used my sleeve to wipe my eyes. I looked him over. His clothes were all scorched, and when I hugged him I could smell the stink of something burned. "What happened to you?" I asked.

He swore loudly. He'd stepped on an exposed power cable, he said, and was nearly cooked alive. He'd gotten to the dam more or less the same way we had, though he'd climbed atop a different section. There he'd found a three-story-tall cement tower topped by a searchlight, likely some kind of guard post. At the top of the tower was an iron bridge that led to a door in the side of the dam, inside of which was some kind of power distribution room. Countless huge and worn-out power cables crossed through the room, their insulation layers already frozen and cracked open. He never would have expected electricity might still be running through them after so many years, but the moment he stepped on one he found his expectations refuted. First he smelled burning flesh, then felt like he was floating. His body went numb from head to toe and he shot into the air like a bomb had gone off. Ordinarily, a fall like that would have been very painful, but all he could think about was the smell of roast meat. He was just too hungry.

Seeing the hand gesture Wang Sichuan made to describe the thickness of the power cable, I felt once more how incredibly strange this place was. This kind of temporary dam would need no more than a small electrical generating unit to satisfy whatever illumination or other needs might arise. Based on the size of that cable, this dam was generating far more power than I thought. What did they need all that electricity for? There was too much here beyond my comprehension, and I didn't have time to consider these questions.

After his shock, Wang Sichuan vomited from nausea and lay dazed for a long time. There was an ironwork wall beyond the power-distribution room. When he heard the sirens, he took refuge in the iron chamber to rest. There were some mishaps in the iron chamber, but he said they weren't worth relating. And now he'd opened the door and ran into us.

I patted him on the back and gave a deep sigh at his incredible fortune. How lucky it was that he was such a big guy. Had it been me, I would surely be burned black all over and long dead.

We each let out a deep breath. Seeing Wang Sichuan, I felt my whole being relax. Ma Zaihai was still young, and not only was the deputy squad leader injured, he was also, despite his obvious sense of responsibility, not readily able to adapt to changing situations and new obstacles. I had been the de facto leader of this team, and it weighed on me. Now Wang Sichuan could share some of this responsibility. All at once my mood improved.

Wang Sichuan asked about our experiences. I recounted them systematically and in full detail. Hearing what had happened with Yuan Xile and Chen Luohu, he stared blankly at us. Part of him couldn't really accept it. I didn't know how to say it any clearer. I was just as ignorant as he. So I said that, for now at least, our most important task was to figure out just where exactly we were.

The dam seemed to have a symmetrical structure. Both sides had a caisson freight elevator, so there had to be two underwater generator rooms. China was extremely backward at the time. The nation had almost no electric lights, and for a long time after liberation we continued to live in the Dark Ages. So even if there were just two generators per side—the main and the auxiliary—the electricity produced would have been enough to support a small town. Ma Zaihai added that on this kind of dam, construction was probably begun separately on each side with the middle built up afterward. That was the method the Soviets used.

Wang Sichuan looked puzzled. "What part of the dam are we on now?" he asked me.

The caisson can reach the very lowest levels, I thought to myself. We should be at the base of the dam, where the electrical machinery is bottled under poured concrete, but based on what we'd seen on the walk over here, the huge space outside seemed to be a massive icehouse.

Brothers who faced death with me, having written to this point, I feel I must say something: I had known Wang Sichuan and the rest for less than a month. We weren't really friends yet, but this was when our iron bond began to be forged. Now that I'm retired, when I think back, I've found that my life's greatest blessing is none other than these memories of youth and my comrades in arms, both alive and dead. So often do I lament that no matter how mighty one is while young, raging at the clouds and wind, when one is old there remains only some narrow room in which to type a few words, write a few stories. This is all that is left to me.

You could say that my reunion with Wang Sichuan was unexpected, but you could also say that it was inevitable. The dam's attached, two-sided design ensured that, sooner or later, we were bound to meet up. Unfortunately, Wang Sichuan really wasn't the savior I was hoping for. Although he did reduce the psychological pressure, he didn't change our physical situation. Nonetheless, having him there enabled me to compose myself and begin to ponder what we should do next.

Everyone was hurt or comatose or at least cold and hungry. If you'd replaced us with young people from this day and age, I can assure you they'd have fallen apart long before this point. All this hunger and exhaustion was bearable for people back then, but we still had no idea what was going to happen. Only the devil knew for sure whether our guesses and inferences were correct. Who could say whether this was even the bottom of the dam? Perhaps we were already in hell.

My first thought after I calmed down was that we needed to find some way out of here. The mist would have to disperse eventually, and given how close we'd been to the mouth of the cave when we ran into Yuan Xile, we should be able to make it back there as well—so long as we didn't lose our minds like she had. I figured that since the caisson could descend, it should be able to ascend as well. I asked Wang Sichuan how he'd started his up, but he couldn't say. Then I realized my oversight: How were these caissons operated? There was no switch in the bare interior of the iron chamber, but there was another possibility. The freight elevators in the large-scale, pre-1949 mines had a switch on the outside and a person specially responsible for its operation. At that time miners lacked any sort of human rights. To control these workers—or should I say these indentured laborers—it was essential to prevent them from operating the elevator on their own and thereby escaping. But who had pulled the master switch? Trails of cold sweat dripped down my back. Was someone else inside the dam? This was a truly terrifying thought. If there were such a person, then he'd been able to see us, but rather than make any sort of direct contact he'd waited until we entered the iron chamber, then secretly dropped us to the bottom of the dam. Why?

I wasn't going to accept this possibility until I had some proof to back it up. First we needed to figure out how to get back to the surface. I assume I needn't spell out what would become of us if we couldn't figure out a way back up. We hesitated in that iron chamber for a long time. In the end it was something Wang Sichuan said that got us going. The sole materialistic explanation for Yuan Xile's and Chen Luohu's disappearances, he said, was that they'd escaped into the vast icehouse. But they definitely hadn't entered this second iron chamber. They were still somewhere out there. No matter what, he declared, we couldn't leave them behind. Wang Sichuan's sense of responsibility was the most admirable moral characteristic I ever encountered. It was probably his inability to waver on such matters that made me feel so secure. I did not believe, however, that we needed to rescue Yuan Xile and Chen Luohu. It wasn't we who'd left them behind. It was they who'd left us.

But, Wang Sichuan said, Yuan Xile had surely been through a similar situation before. Her recent actions were very likely a duplication of the course of her previous escape. Should we be able to find her, she just might be able to lead us out of here. At once it was decided. The deputy squad leader was still comatose. In his condition he shouldn't be further exposed to the cold. Ma Zaihai would stay behind while Wang Sichuan and I looked for Yuan Xile and Chen Luohu. And with our numbers slightly lessened, our speed would increase. We hurriedly ate a bit of food, wrapped our sleeping bags tightly around us, gathered several flashlight batteries, and set out.

CHAPTER 40

The Freezer

I t was probably the layer of cold mist that made the open space beyond the chamber seem so large. Shivering, Wang Sichuan and I walked back along the elevated iron-grate walkway. Soon the door to the second iron chamber had vanished. This was Wang Sichuan's first time outside. All his attention was quickly drawn to the black shapes frozen in the pools. He kept stopping and shining his flashlight on them, hoping to discover what was inside. The ice was far from transparent, and thick clouds of mist blocked our view. At last he gave up.

I looked around as I walked, scanning my surroundings in much greater detail than I had before. What had the Japanese used this place for? I wondered. The temperature was surely lower than that of the underground river. To keep it this cold, there had to be a compression engine somewhere around here. Back then refrigeration compressors were used only in walk-in freezers. Indeed, this place resembled nothing so much as a freezer for fish or some other aquatic product.

After we'd reached a certain point, Wang Sichuan suggested we walk along one of the concrete ridges that ran through the pools. It appeared to continue far into the depths of the mist. Though it was so narrow that maintaining one's balance would be difficult, it was better than just walking across the ice. I agreed. Swaying as if we were on a tightrope, we made our way into the mist. As we left the regular iron-grate walkway I felt a twinge of timidity. It had been like a lifeline to us. The trek on the cement ridge was endless. Perhaps it was the severe cold or perhaps we were overcautious, but either way our progress was slow. Shaking from the cold and surrounded by a dense mist, neither of us had anything to say. By the end of it, I felt as if I were in a trance.

At last Wang Sichuan stopped. He called out from behind me. A line of large shadows, each about half as tall as a man, had appeared up ahead. Increasing our pace, a moment later we reached the edge of the open space. The shadows were a row of cryptic machines arrayed along the wall, their exteriors covered in icy frost. From them emerged a riot of pipes that snaked over to the concrete pools and plunged into the ice. Numerous placards were hung just overhead. Wang Sichuan knocked the frost off a few. They were serial numbers, with something like "Cold-03-A" written on each, all of them arranged in a specific order. The serial numbers on the pipes were much more complex, seeming to indicate that they were responsible for keeping the pools cold. These, I guessed, were the refrigeration compressors. The temperature dropped severely as we walked alongside them. My teeth began to chatter.

We soon came upon a huge doorway—approximately fifteen feet wide—cut into the concrete wall. The door itself was covered in frost and outfitted with a torque-operated door bar. Partially open, its iron body was astonishingly thick. Wang Sichuan kicked it several times, but it remained absolutely still. Something about it felt very familiar, as if I'd seen it before, though I couldn't recall where. It wasn't until Wang Sichuan snapped off several chunks of ice, revealing the characters written underneath, that I finally remembered. Written on the door, in very large script, was "Plan

53." It was nearly identical to the huge iron door we'd dug up from beneath the rock on the first part of the underground river. Could the space behind this door also be filled with explosive charges? It didn't seem too likely. The door was cracked open just wide enough to admit a single person. The hinges were frozen solid and the thing wouldn't budge.

I took a deep breath. Then Wang Sichuan and I filed in one after the other. The temperature inside was slightly warmer, and consequently the mist was especially thick, but after we took a few steps it began to disperse. We stared wide-eyed. Behind the door was an ironwork tunnel, very tall and as wide as the doorway. It seemed to be a passageway for transporting large-scale equipment. We walked farther in. The smell of rusted iron became stronger and stronger, the ground beneath our feet increasingly rough and uneven. Ahead of us was only darkness. I was hesitating about whether to continue on when Wang Sichuan tapped me on the shoulder. He pointed at the wall. It was covered in scales of bubbling rust. A long section had been rubbed off by someone's hand, and where the rust had spread to the floor, we distinctly saw footprints. Two pairs of them.

These marks had been made only recently. My spirits rose at once. It seemed we had located Yuan Xile's trail. Following the markings, we quickened our pace. Soon we were running down the pitch-black passageway, shining our flashlights all around us. In the time it takes to smoke half a cigarette we were out, only to find ourselves atop a high platform. The area below was vast and open, the ceiling tall and hung with steel crossbeams. As we shined our flashlights down, an astonishing scene appeared before us. Down below was a gigantic factory. Two huge iron rails ran along its floor like a pair of giant scars. A set of iron stairs led down from the platform. A few moments later, we were on the factory floor. From this vantage, the room looked even more vast.

Various machines were strewn all about. Old, dust-covered tar-paulins covered pile after pile of things unseen. A hook used for heavy lifting hung from overhead, its twenty years of disuse not immediately obvious. At the very least, the room didn't smell of rusted iron. A ventilation unit identical to that of the caisson ran along the baseboard. It must have remained in operation these past twenty years, for the air here was relatively clean and dry. We switched on our flashlights, though we didn't know what we were searching for. Few of the structures the Japanese left behind in the Northeast had been kept in such perfect condition. The vast majority had been destroyed prior to their departure. Had the Japanese really left in such a hurry?

I soon found myself standing before a long partition. At first glance, the mass of papers pasted across it looked similar to the posters proclaiming new production records during the Great Leap Forward. Looking closer, I discovered they were actually schedules, all of them written in Japanese, along with a series of structural blueprints I didn't understand. The blueprints were stained with mildew and had already turned soft and yellow. The moment I touched one, a whole stretch of them dropped to the floor. I dared not touch anything else. Shining my flashlight before me, I watched as war propaganda posters and black-and-white photos appeared now and again in the circular beam.

"This has to be where the Japs assembled the Shinzan," I said to Wang Sichuan. It had been broken down into its smallest com-ponents prior to being transported here. The job of reassembling it probably continued over the course of several months. Here the components would have been maintained and repaired if necessary, oiled, and then reassembled into larger parts.

"In that case," said Wang Sichuan, "moving this stuff out of here would definitely require some kind of gigantic freight elevator. We'd better look around for it. Maybe that's the way out."

We scanned our surroundings as we walked. Something on the wall caught my attention. Hanging there was a wooden board with black-and-white photos of all sizes pasted over every inch. Some were group shots, some just of one person. All of those photographed were wearing the kind of Japanese military uniforms you see on TV, disgraceful smiles on their faces. These had probably been shot during some holiday here. There was one photo that particularly drew my interest: Several Chinese workers, so thin their bones looked like firewood, were dragging some object out of the water. It was still half submerged and utterly black, like a mass of jellyfish. A Japanese soldier stood watching them. I couldn't tell what the thing was. The photo was too blurry. I was about to call Wang Sichuan over when I realized he was already yelling my name. He'd walked some distance away and was standing by one of the tarps. I hurried over just as he yanked the cover half off. There, beneath the tarp, was a deathly pale human hand.

Wang Sichuan pulled the tarp all the way off. Amid the cinder blocks and steel bars was a corpse, dressed in the uniform of the engineering corps. The body was squeezed into a pile of steel bars. We pulled it out. It was hard as a rock, probably due to the cold. This person had been dead for some time. We turned him over. The face was unfamiliar to us, its expression panic-stricken. His eyes were opened so wide they bulged in their sockets. He was a young man, but I couldn't tell whether he'd been among the four groups who entered with us. Considering how long he'd been dead, he'd probably been part of Yuan Xile's team. Counting him, we'd now come across three of its members: two were dead and one was crazy. Where was everyone else?

Knowing yet another person had died disturbed me, especially because this soldier was so young. I have always believed that making mere kids risk their lives like this—all before they have truly begun to enjoy life's pleasures—is just too unfair. Wang Sichuan was far from overly sentimental. He and other Mongolians possess a rather philosophical view regarding the passage of life. Though he would always claim to be a materialist, I firmly believe that inside he remained a purebred Mongolian, believing that to die is to be summoned by Tengri to return to the gray wolves, the white deer, and the grasslands. There is certainly nothing wrong with this kind of detachment, but I always used to say that the more detached a person is from death, the more cold-blooded he becomes. Your Genghis Khan was no softie, I would tell him. Perhaps in his heart he believed he was merely sending his foes back to heaven. Wang Sichuan refuted me at once. Qin Shihuang, the first Chinese emperor, showed no detachment when thinking about his own death, he said. That a person so scared of dying could nonetheless kill people like flies makes your argument just silly. Even the tiniest bit of detachment would be better than that.

A solid layer of blood covered almost half the body. This seemed unusual to Wang Sichuan, so we undid the corpse's stiff clothing. There were two bloody holes in his back, each as thick as a thumb. The skin around them was all flared up. As military men, we were all too familiar with injuries like these—they were bullet wounds.

Even Wang Sichuan's dark skin turned white. This made no sense. Had it been some sort of accidental death, we could have accepted it. Exploring an environment as complex and dangerous as this would make accidental deaths difficult to avoid, especially for wet-behind-the-ears new recruits. Murder changed the matter completely. Bullet holes meant someone had fired a gun, and that they had had a reason for doing so. Who would take a gun and murder his own comrade? Had the Japanese done this? It didn't seem too likely, but they'd been gone only twenty years. Supposing that the trainee-level reinforcements were stationed here in their teens, by the time we arrived they'd only be in their thirties. Still, this place hardly seemed habitable, and we had yet to see a single sign of life. In which case, could there really be an enemy spy among us?

My mind spun. Wang Sichuan abruptly began to stuff the corpse back in among the steel bars.

"What are you doing?" I asked him.

He said that by murdering someone the spy had revealed his existence. So he'd hidden the body beneath the tarp, hoping to keep anyone else from discovering it. We'd surely be next on his list if he found out we were on to him. Against his gun we were dead meat. We had no choice but to cover the body back up.

"This way," said Wang Sichuan, "he'll have no idea that we know what's going on and we can grab him when he's not paying attention."

After struggling for a bit, we managed to return the body to its original position. "We have to be much more careful now," said Wang Sichuan.

I nodded. My mind was in a flurry. I'm used to high-tension situations, but the sensation I had was very different from the nervousness I might feel when confronting some natural obstacle. The two of us sighed, turned around, and prepared to continue on. At once I was aware that something wasn't right. I shined my flashlight before me. Yelling out in fright, I stumbled backward to the floor. There was a man stretched out on the ground, his ghastly face craning up toward us. He stared at us with fixed eyes.

Yuan Xile had already given me this very sort of scare, but that didn't mean I was immune to it. This man had crawled up, practically right behind our backs, without making the slightest noise. Now he was flat on the ground, staring wide-eyed like some strange beast. Wang Sichuan and I both leaped in fright. I fell to the floor, my lower back knocking against the steel bars. The pain was so great it nearly knocked the wind out of me. Regaining myself, I hurriedly swept my flashlight before me. The moment I spotted him, he dodged out of the beam. Suddenly he was up on all fours. With lightning speed he scrambled into the dark recesses of the factory, his movements no different from an animal's.

"Grab him!" I yelled. By the time I stood up it would already be too late.

But Wang Sichuan had his own methods. "Shine the light on him!" he said. I swung the flashlight beam after the fleeing man. Wang Sichuan weighed the tube of his flashlight in his hand, then launched it at him.

I watched as the flashlight cut a magnificent arc, then smashed viciously down on the man's knee just as he was about to disappear into the darkness. He let out a muffled groan and toppled over. He tried to get up, but the moment he righted himself he fell back down. This was the first time I'd actually seen Wang Sichuan's skill with the *bulu*. While muddling along near the Chinese-Mongolian border, I'd heard miraculous descriptions of Mongolians throwing the *bulu*, but I never would have expected that, when truly used "on the hunt," the movement could actually be so beautiful. Wang Sichuan later told me this throwing style was known as the *jirugen bulu*. Had he wanted to throw hard, no way would I have been able to make out the flashlight's trajectory. I would have heard only the sound of it smashing down, but the man's knee would have shattered. Truly the best-looking *bulu* style, he said, was that used for knocking birds out of the sky. One of his *anda* (his sworn brothers) was a real ace, far more formidable than he.

By the time we ran over, the man was back on all fours. Limping, he thrust himself through a sheet of tarpaulin concealing some back area. Inside, tarp-covered piles of supplies extended in endless rows. In an instant, he was gone. Wang Sichuan and I continued after him. Many of the tarps were covered in taut rope netting secured to the floor on either end, making it easy to trip. Wang

Sichuan charged forward, tearing apart the piles. Beneath the tarps were canned goods and devices like corrugated sheets—seemingly a kind of filtration net—as well as a number of fuel tanks. The supplies were stacked in shallow, German-made frames, draped with a tarp and then tightly bound with a length of hemp rope or iron wire. These were packages for airdrops.

We were soon deep inside the dark warehouse. Nothing but close rows of supplies as far as the eye could see, the area vast and filled with shifting shadows, no different from a maze. This is bad, I thought. Wang Sichuan suddenly motioned for silence. His flashlight was on a tarp to our left, a section of which bulged and quivered. We tiptoed over and I leaned in close. Taking a deep breath, Wang Sichuan pulled off the tarp. A plume of dust was blown into the air. Out leaped a white shape, knocking me to the ground. There was so much dust my eyes wouldn't open. I coughed violently, unable to see a thing. I heard Wang Sichuan curse once and then give chase.

I swore to myself and waved away the dust. The two of them were gone. "Wang Sichuan!" I yelled. I was about to go after them when I saw something that stopped me in my tracks. At first I wasn't sure what it was, but after I brushed off the dust and pulled the tarp away, my eyes went wide. Underneath was a military sand table, complete with a crushed wooden model of the dam and a miniature Shinzan surrounded by cranes, mounts, and a number of tiny devices. It was all there.

I'm not sure if the readers have ever heard of a sand table before. Sand tables are small-scale models of terrain made using sediment, toy soldiers, and other materials. This one was probably used to simulate the final phase of the plane's assembly on the underground river. Putting together a bomber as large as this in an underground void would naturally be much more complex than building one in a factory. This sand table was the consummate combination of the meticulous and the crude. The topographical base was slapped together with dowels and other pieces of wood seemingly carved on a whim, acceptable as long as they had the general shape. The pieces that decorated this rough landscape, though, were truly astonishing. I don't remember all the structures, but what made the deepest impression on me was that already-broken dam, and the Shinzan behind it.

The sand table gave an approximate idea of the size and shape of the underground river. It had become astonishingly wide. Around the river were the variously sized shapes of a command station, a bunker, a crane, and a small railway. All the underwater obstacles on the way were distinctly marked. I could even see the area where Wang Sichuan said his way had been blocked by a pool of quicksand. The sand table showed that, using a great quantity of steel bars and concrete, the Japanese had built a foundational structure beneath the water and atop that erected a huge platform, supported on stilts. Beneath the platform was a filtration canal, allowing them to monitor the content of the underground river water. The most surprising structure on top of the platform was an elevated three-rail track, with a long slope up into the void, like a three-tubed antiaircraft gun aimed at some target in the emptiness. Beneath the track was a triangular structure that resembled an upside-down high-voltage tower. The Shinzan was stopped at the end of the track, positioned at the very tip of the three rails—the very tip of the gun, in other words. Just over half its length rose above the dam. Chills ran down my spine. I had thought as much this whole time, but only now did I know for sure: the Japs had wanted to fly the goddamn Shinzan into the void!

By World War II, the Japanese already had considerable experience flying planes from aircraft carriers. Although I myself didn't understand the mechanics of it, it was obvious they had believed it possible for the Shinzan to take off from here. As I thought of the Shinzan's wreckage sunk beneath the water, my mind filled with questions. Given everything the Japanese did here, had the Shinzan ultimately taken off or not? And why had so many buffer bags been piled underwater? And where was that three-track railway?

A bolt of lightning flashed through my mind. I felt a chill spread from my neck all the way down to my heels. Remembering the shape of the plane's wreckage, I distinctly recalled that the Shinzan's front end had been facing away from the dam. Not only had it taken off, it had already flown back out of the abyss!

CHAPTER 41

Out of the Abyss

B y no means am I familiar with the number of precise cal-
culations required to get a heavy-duty bomber to take off
within a cave, but if you're talking about flying a bomber
this massive back out of that abyss and then bringing it in for a
landing—well, I think I can imagine some degree of the difficulty
involved. You'd need to maneuver the plane in toward the mouth
of the river, a challenging task in itself, but then, to complete the
descent into such a small and narrow space—that's just too much
to ask. The length of the runway wouldn't be a problem—tow-
ropes could be used to slow the plane down—the main issue is that
the roof of the cave gives you no room for error. Mess up and you're
scrap metal. From the beginning the Japanese obviously hadn't
planned on a smooth landing. Those buffer bags had been in preparation for a crash, and that's just what happened. To think of that
fearful emptiness was terrifying. How daring those little devils had
been! And I wondered, just what had the pilot seen down there?

Then, from behind me, came the sound of Wang Sichuan's
voice. I turned. He was walking toward me, his face covered with
dirt and dust, dragging back our pale little animal man twisted into
an extremely uncomfortable position. Wang Sichuan's strength was

immense. You weren't breaking free once he seized you. The man had stopped resisting, and it looked like Wang Sichuan was dragging along a corpse.

I hurried over. Wang Sichuan pressed the man to the ground, swearing, "Goddamn, that wasn't easy. It's black as a crow's feather out there, and this son of a bitch runs faster than a rabbit. He almost got away. Lucky my eyesight's not bad."

I shined my flashlight over the man's face. I'd never seen him before. He was ghastly pale and soaked with sweat. Maybe it was from the chase, maybe he was always like this. He stared at me, his eyes bloodshot and his whole body quivering. His eyes stabbed at me with limitless hatred. Surprisingly, his uniform was different from Yuan Xile's and the corpsmen's we'd come across earlier. He was wearing a Lenin suit with a long jacket and a cloth belt. He didn't look like a soldier. This sort of attire was more like what Li Siguang and the rest from the Chinese Academy of Sciences had worn in their day. Maybe he was some kind of expert. We searched his pockets and found an employee identification card. His name was Su Zhenhua, and sure enough, he was from the Ministry of Geology.

"Seems they were a lot more choosy with the first group," said Wang Sichuan, an angry look on his face. "The standards were way higher."

Once the Soviets had left, Yuan Xile was one of the most important of the so-called Russian ass-wipers. She was on the same level as Wang Ming or Bo Gu during the Land Reforms—real high. The Ministry of Geology wasn't just about geology. Some people had their positions because they took orders directly from the old men at the very top. They were special emissaries, lapdogs like Li De, the foreigner sent by the Russian Communist Party to boss around the Chinese Communist Party. I hated anybody resembling a special emissary, but I could always sense their presence whenever anything important happened.

I called out "Su Zhenhua" several times, but he just stared at me, his eyes evincing deep hatred. I turned his face in my hands. It was just as with Yuan Xile. He'd gone mad. What the hell had happened to the first team? Anyone who wasn't dead was crazy.

Wang Sichuan was at a loss himself. "How are we supposed to take him with us?" he asked me. "This guy's stubborn as a bull. The moment I loosen my grip, he's gone for sure. Are we going to have to tie him up?"

I didn't know what to do either. Let's take him back to the second chamber, I thought. We can have Ma Zaihai look after him and then figure it out. Just as I was about to speak, Su Zhenhua squeezed a sentence through clenched teeth. His speech was garbled, the accent unplaceable. I hadn't the slightest clue what he was saying, but Wang Sichuan's expression changed at once.

"What did he say?" I asked.

"That was Mongolian," Wang Sichuan told me in a low voice. "He said, 'Beware of shadows, there are ghosts inside!'"

This was the only sentence Su Zhenhua ever spoke in our presence. Given his expression at the time, we didn't know whether it was a warning or a curse. From then on, he continued only to stare at us, the look in his eyes like he wanted to flay and swallow us alive. I had no idea what he meant. Ghosts in the shadows? If you were to say there were ghosts, this I could understand. With everyone who'd died in this underground base, it wouldn't be so strange to find some here. But ghosts in the shadows? Which shadows was he talking about? Could all these shadows, stretching one into the next under the flashlight beam, really have ghosts in them? Now that shadows had been mentioned, I suddenly recalled the dark shapes frozen into the pools back in the icehouse. Those things gave me a strange feeling. Were these the ghosts that Su Zhenhua was talking about? But we were materialists, no way could we believe in supernatural stuff like that.

Wang Sichuan and I talked it over for a moment. He too thought we should bring Su Zhenhua back to the second chamber and have Ma Zaihai look after him. We seemed to be on the right track, he said. We should also make a thorough search of all the supplies stored back here. We were running low. "If that's the case," I said, "I can go get Ma Zaihai and the deputy squad leader and bring them here. You see if there isn't something we can use to start a fire. We can boil some water and warm up when we get back." Indeed, this place was much preferable to the second chamber.

Wang Sichuan agreed. With all the fuel tanks lying around, starting a fire would be a piece of cake. I wrapped my clothes around me and told him to be careful. "There might be explosives here," I said. "Don't let me return to find the place already blown to smithereens."

Wang Sichuan laughed. "I was lighting campfires out on the grasslands while you were still sleeping on a kang," he said. "Don't talk such nonsense."

I jogged a short distance, passed through the iron passage, and after making my way back through the huge gate at the other end, headed for the second chamber. The sweat from our pursuit of Su Zhenhua froze to my skin. The only thing on my mind was getting to Ma Zaihai and the deputy squad leader as quickly as possible, bringing them back with me, and drinking hot water until I felt better. Not once did I think that something might go wrong over such a short distance. I ran back through the mist, relying on memory and never pausing, until I suddenly noticed that everything looked exactly the same no matter which way I turned. At first I wasn't aware of what had happened, but after running for another ten-plus minutes, the powdery mist continued to spread all about me and a limitless ice field stretched into the distance. We hadn't left a single goddamn marker on the way out. I was lost.

Losing my way turned out to be an important link in that whole chain of events. The area was vast and open, my field of vision drastically limited. Without some kind of sign, it was almost a certainty that I would soon find myself lost and directionless amid the mist. This was hardly the worst thing in the world, and I didn't let it bother me. Only for the first few minutes did I feel any annoyance. Still, given my exhaustion at the time, it was obvious that the longer I stayed here, the more precarious the situation would become. I chose a direction and continued on. At the time I assumed that, so long as I kept going forward, even if I didn't find the iron-grate walkway at the room's center, I would at least run into one of its walls. As expected, after walking for two or three minutes, the frost-bedecked face of a high cement wall appeared from out of the mist. I roughly oriented myself, then turned around, climbed a cement ridge running perpendicular to my previous direction, and began to follow the wall. The second chamber should be up ahead, I thought. With the cold already unbearable, I began to speed up.

The giant machines placed along the base of the wall, as well as their great masses of pipes and power cables plunging into the nearby ice, were caked beneath a layer of frost. The whole scene had become one huge, uneven, frost-covered heap. These disparately sized pipes all snaked across the walkway, making it much higher and more difficult to traverse than the one Wang Sichuan and I had crossed earlier. Frost thick and soft covered the pool that stretched beside me and made the ice much less slippery. It was easier to walk on the ice than to pick my way among the refrigeration pipes. On the ice I went faster and faster, not paying any attention to what was beneath my feet, certain that the ice was solid. I was wrong. I had walked about ten minutes when, all of a sudden, the ice beneath my feet gave way. The ground sloped down before me and I began to fall. I swung my body back around and squatted down heavily.

I wasn't sliding too fast and was able to hold myself steady. A giant black void with steep sides had appeared out of the cold mist in the space just in front of me. Someone had dug a deep pit in the ice.

Actually, the hole was not that big, about the size of a PLA truck. It was hardly necessary to use the word *giant*, but the pit really was deep, likely reaching all the way to the cement bottom. Inside was a vague cloud of mist. I couldn't tell what was down below. We'd all cut holes in ice before. It was necessary if you wanted to go fishing in the Greater Khingans during wintertime. Once the ice was a certain thickness, cutting a hole was no easy task. I could imagine the time and effort that must have gone into making this one. I doubt it was a one-person job. I rubbed the edge of the pit. Cracks spiderwebbed outward. It had been smashed open with no more than shovels and brute strength. Who had done this? Su Zhenhua and the others?

It seemed likely. I didn't know what accident befell them after making it here, but before it occurred they were certain to have explored the place. Having seen these strange ice pools and the shadows frozen underneath, someone would have suggested they dig one up and take a look. If our team hadn't encountered all we did and had arrived here intact, I'm sure I would have had the same idea. Just what exactly is down there, I thought to myself, and had they managed to dig it up?

I squatted back down and shined my flashlight into the pit. By disposition I'm fairly cautious. I was not even thinking of jumping down and taking a look. If Wang Sichuan were here, he'd probably already have been on the bottom. The bottom was jagged and uneven. After reaching a certain point, the excavation seemed to have stopped. I could see the indistinct shape of one of the shadows frozen in the ice, half of it already exposed. They must have stopped digging right after the thing appeared.

I became more and more curious. Why hadn't they continued? I wondered. Now I considered jumping down, but a six-foot drop into an ice pit would be quite dangerous. I'd have a rough time climbing back out and would risk freezing to death inside. There's a kind of pitfall in the Northeast constructed just like this. It's intentionally dug only a few feet deeper than the height of a bear, so when one falls in, it's unable to escape.

Just as I was hesitating about whether I should first go and find Ma Zaihai or just descend directly into the pit, I felt a slight breeze behind me. I was so cold I'd become sensitive to even the lightest wind. Shivering, I made to turn around and see where it was coming from, but before I could move, I was given a ferocious push from behind. I tried to squat back down, but couldn't keep my balance. I tumbled headlong into the pit.

CHAPTER 42

Plotted Against

I was falling headfirst. I quickly brought my hands up to protect my head. I'm a fairly resilient individual. Even after being knocked six feet down, with my head spinning, I could still tell which way was up and which was down. I looked up at once. Who's the bastard plotting against me? I said to myself.

Just as I lifted my head, a chunk of ice came hurtling toward me. It smashed into my face. I ducked back down to protect myself. Another chunk smacked against the back of my skull. Tiny pieces of ice dripped down my neck and into my clothing. Furious, I shook my head back and forth. Just as I'd flung most of it off, several more chunks came at me, much heavier and in far greater numbers than before. One piece smashed savagely into the nape of my neck, nearly knocking me out. My adversary was trying to bury me alive.

I was stunned. As a prospector I'd faced my share of dangerous situations, but never had anyone tried to kill me. Had the spy been lying low nearby, seen that I was exhausted and alone, then decided to take me out? I became enraged. You made a very serious mistake not using your gun, I said to myself. I may only be technical personnel now, but I served my time as a soldier. Would you have messed with me then? I too had to run five kilometers with a sandbag strapped to my back. With this thought spurring me on, I grabbed a chunk of ice from beside me and hurled it upward. Heedless of whether my aim was true, I immediately threw the next piece, then the next. The rate of ice coming back at me greatly lessened. Whoever was up there was clearly trying to dodge my throws.

I knew that I couldn't waste this opportunity. Stepping hard against the wall, I tried to climb. After I'd scrambled for a moment, my heart sank. There was nothing for my feet to grip. The moment they hit the wall, they slid right back down. Goddamn it, I swore, suddenly desperate. With a roar I leaped as high as I could. I made it halfway out of the pit, my arms clinging to the icy ground. Then a black shadow flashed before my eyes. A boot flew into my chin, and I was knocked all the way back down.

This fall was much heavier than the last, and my vision went black from the pain. I dropped my flashlight as I fell, but before doing so I managed to catch a split-second glimpse of my adversary's clothing. What kind of outfit is that? I wondered. I felt my heart clench up. It was a Japanese military uniform. A Japanese soldier? Could the person trying to bury me alive really be a Japanese soldier? This place had only been abandoned for twenty years. If there was enough food, the remaining Japanese soldiers could probably have survived, but nothing about the cave had suggested that anyone was still living here.

A pile of icy mush dropped from above, half burying me. He'd changed his strategy. Now he was dropping whole heaps of the stuff, hoping to bury me alive before he'd even knocked me out. The ice chunks from before had already frozen around me. Not good. He wasn't going to be able to knock me out, he knew that, but I also didn't have a chance in hell of climbing out amid all this chaos.

Perhaps it was the ice, perhaps the imminent danger, but my mind suddenly cleared. I realized that to continue like this was a very bad idea, and if I didn't get out of here soon I would be done for. I had to turn things around, and fast, or the outcome would not be pleasant. But what was there for me to do? Play dead? By now my flashlight was buried beneath the fallen ice. Using all my strength, I pulled my feet from the hole they were sunk in, then reached into the mush and groped blindly about. My hands found not my flashlight but some unknown, strange-feeling object. I grabbed on to it. My heart skipped a beat. My God, I thought.

I could no longer pay attention to my adversary above. Protecting my head with my left hand, I began to brush away the chunks of ice beneath my feet. I had a feeling I knew what this thing was, and if I was right, then we were in big trouble. The thing had felt conical—almost like an iron bell—and terrifically cold, the same temperature as the ice around it. No one else would have found anything strange about it, but I'm a special case. When I was still in school, I did fieldwork in Jiamusi. My field team once discovered this very sort of object frozen within a glacial cave. We'd been scared to death. Our whole team had nearly tried to climb back to the surface with their bare hands. I managed to fish out my flashlight. Using it as a kind of shovel, I continued to dig. Soon enough I'd reached the bottom of the pit. A pitch-black cone appeared before my eyes. I had long since realized what it was, but still I gasped as my suspicion was confirmed. It was a warhead.

Because only the tip of it protruded from the hard ice below, I couldn't judge the caliber, but it sure wasn't a howitzer shell. It was much too big. It had to be some large-bore shell used in heavy artillery. I suddenly understood why the previous team had dug out only a portion of it. I wouldn't have messed with the god-damn thing either. The cover to the shell's detonator had already been knocked off. If a shovel had come down on it one more time, everyone would have been blown to kingdom come. I gulped. And if all these shadows were artillery shells, then how many were there? Based on the size of the place, five thousand for sure. But why had the Japanese frozen them?

A great chunk of ice fell on my head, interrupting my reverie. The person up top had never paused in his assault, and I could consider the matter no further, but my heart was filled with worry. I hurriedly covered the warhead back up, telling myself that I had to escape as soon as possible and tell Wang Sichuan and the rest what I'd found. Even though I didn't know what kind of warhead this was, it served as clear evidence that the Japanese had made preparations to blow up the entire dam. This sort of gigantic, concrete-built, fortresslike dam would be extremely difficult to destroy. If you used ordinary, small-ordinance dynamite, it would barely damage the place. The Kuomintang had run into this very problem when they were preparing to blow up the Fengman Dam. To thoroughly destroy a dam, you need to place a great quantity of explosives beneath its base, just as they'd done here. We were waiting inside a giant powder keg. It was just a matter of time.

And given my current predicament, a worst-case scenario might not be so far off. I had no choice but to arch my body over the warhead and protect it from the falling ice. In the confusion, I could no longer even begin to think about freeing myself. A man could easily go mad in a situation like this. It was as if someone had you completely at their mercy, could hit you as much and as hard as they wanted, while you were unable to strike back. And yet despite it all, you couldn't give in. More than ten minutes passed. I was already frozen stiff and nearly buried beneath the ice. Finally, believing I really would die here, I took a deep breath, grabbed a hunk of ice, and flung it upward, shouting, "You goddamn son of a bitch, there's a bomb down here! You fucking throw one more thing and we're both going to die!"

The chunk of ice that came hurtling down served as his reply. I dropped my head and dodged out of the way, about to swear again. Then everything suddenly went calm. There wasn't a sound. Even the ice stopped sliding down the pit walls. I waited a moment, then cursed loudly at him once more. There was no response. At last I shined my flashlight upward. Nobody was there. Gone? Fear rose within me. Had he decided this was taking too long and gone to fetch a more lethal weapon? With some effort I managed to pull my legs out. The ground was covered in icy mush. With each step my whole body sank down, as if I were in a snowfield. I took two more steps before realizing how utterly exhausted I was. I could go no farther. Then two flashlight beams came shining down from above. I raised my head, but couldn't make out who was behind the light. Then I heard Ma Zaihai's voice yell out in surprise, "It's Engineer Wu!"

I relaxed, but then yelled up, "Look out! There's a Japanese soldier here!"

Ma Zaihai couldn't make out what I was saying. I heard the voice of the deputy squad leader. He'd understood, but didn't know what I meant. Ma Zaihai reached in and pulled me out. My whole body was stiff. "What's going on?" he asked me. It was windy up top and so cold I couldn't stop trembling. I quickly raised my flashlight and shined it all around. There was no trace of the man anywhere.

After coming to, the deputy squad leader had scolded Ma Zaihai. The reason that they, the engineering corpsmen, were with us prospectors was to ensure that we came to no harm. We were high-ranking state personnel, so when our group encountered danger, it should be the corpsmen who rushed to the front, otherwise they were no more than a burden. Now it was two prospectors who were scouting ahead, while the soldiers slept back in the nest? Who could bear to lose face like this? The deputy squad leader had forced Ma Zaihai to come along, and they'd set out to look for us.

I was moved by what he said, though such a standpoint was obviously too inflexible. Given the situation, though, I said nothing. I told them what had just happened, the pit, the warhead, the Japanese soldier. They agreed it was beyond belief. "If it really was the Japanese, then this situation has gotten much more complex," said Ma Zaihai. "We'd better be careful. The War of Resistance has been over for many years. To still be killed by the Japanese would be ridiculous."

We did a brief search, though not the slightest hint remained of the soldier's presence. "Something's not right here," said the deputy squad leader. "Our adversary is probably not alone. He must have taken off when he saw our lights, but he might be back in a moment with an accomplice. It's not safe for us to wait here. We'd better get going as soon as we can."

There was no longer any reason for me to return to the chamber, saving us a lot of time. I took a moment to orient myself, then Ma Zaihai put me on his back and we set off toward the iron door. Our journey was very smooth. By the time we reached the factory, I could already see the distant light of Wang Sichuan's fire. As soon as the word *fire* crossed my mind, a piercing pain shot through my body. The faster I could warm up, the better. The deputy squad leader and Ma Zaihai were unbearably cold themselves. They ran the whole way, Ma Zaihai shouting, "Engineer Wang! Engineer Wang!"

Then someone moved from beside the campfire. A moment later, ten people emerged from behind a canvas sheet. They were all dressed in Japanese military uniforms.

CHAPTER 43

Japanese Soldiers

The three of us froze. Up till then I'd been in a state of slight disbelief. Could the Japanese uniform I glimpsed have been no more than an illusion? How sure could I be about what I saw while I was being kicked from a ledge? Never would I have expected that, before long, I would actually see this many Japanese soldiers. It was like we'd passed through a tunnel in time: seeing those vile yellow uniforms made me feel as if we'd been transported back to the War of Resistance. But something wasn't right. Why did all these soldiers look so familiar? I looked again, and then I saw it. The Japanese officer raising his head was Old Cat!

As I stood there in shock, Pei Qing and Wang Sichuan walked over to greet us. Wang Sichuan circled around me, looking at the broken bits of ice coating my clothing. "What happened to him?" he asked the deputy squad leader. I was picked up and set down by the fire, my clothes removed. The fire was really something—huge and warm—and I began to tear up, though I had no idea why.

We were still clothed in rags, but Old Cat and the rest were all wearing neat and tidy Japanese military garb. The best was Old Cat in his dark-colored officer's uniform. With his inscrutable expression, it made him look just like a Japanese staff officer from the movies. After being wrapped in a sleeping bag, I found myself sitting directly across from him. At last both of us laughed. And with that, everyone around us began to laugh as well.

"What the hell is going on?" I asked them. "What are you helping those bastards for? At what point did you defect and become Japanese devils?"

"Don't wrong the innocent," said Pei Qing. "We're undercover behind enemy lines." We all cracked up again.

Pei Qing said the route they took was just too damn cold, though he still didn't know why. They'd discovered these uniforms in a storage area. At first no one dared wear them, but after the cold became unbearable, they all put them on. It was a complete set, meant for one of the Japanese brigades stationed in northeastern China. They too had laughed as they looked at one another.

Remembering the point where we'd split up, I asked how they'd gotten here. Had they ever located the source of the telegram? Several of their faces fell. Pei Qing sighed, nodded his head, and said they'd found it, but the people were already dead. He gestured wearily as he said this, then gave a basic retelling of what had happened.

Here I must once more put my memories in order. Pei Qing and the others gave us no more than a sketchy narration of their experiences. With all the years that have passed since then, I seem to have already forgotten many of the particulars. Or perhaps it was Pei Qing's story that wasn't especially detailed. In any case, those parts aren't important.

Following the power cable, they'd floated down the waterway. They called it "River 6," the name given to it by the Japanese. It turned out to be a tributary of "River 0," the main river, the one that flows into the dam. They'd drifted deeper and deeper into the cave. It was just as Old Tang had surmised: the power cables and underwater rails signified that the region had been a densely built-up, high-activity area. The terrain became smoother and flatter the farther they advanced. Not a single obstacle presented itself, and the signs of Japanese activity became increasingly numerous and varied. After they'd been drifting for about forty minutes, the river bottom began to trend upward. The water level became shallower and shallower. Before long a number of shoals appeared. The shoals increased in number, until at last they ran together as a continuous expanse. At first there was still some water atop the shoal and they'd had to wade, but soon the river came to a stop, replaced by a great rocky beach. At this beach River 6 began to branch off into smaller tributaries running back into the cavernous depths.

They marched up the rock beach. They could see a huge cavern up ahead. It was quite flat, though thrown into complete disorder. Stacks of supplies protected by water-resistant canvas sheets covered the cave floor. They lifted off the covers. There were loads of writing desks and correspondence equipment. All manner of power cables hung from the stalactites. Cables thick and thin snaked across the ground, the ceiling, and every place in between. There were also temporary beds and wooden trunks filled with supplies. It was from these that they'd taken their Japanese military uniforms.

At the end of the limestone cave were a number of branching paths, some piled with supplies, some so deep you couldn't see the end. A mass of power cables ran down them. Old Tang surmised that the end of River 6 was the communications center for the entire underground river. That meant it was also the wiring center for the telephone system. The power for this place was provided by the small-scale generator we'd come across in the sinkhole. From what Pei Qing and the others could see, the Japanese had neglected to burn their files, simply covering them up with canvas sheets instead. They must have been expecting to return. This ran contrary to all our experiences with abandoned Japanese installations.

Once more I found myself at a loss as to what exactly had happened when the Japanese left. Just what had they been ordered to do?

After taking a rushed look around, Pei Qing and the others continued to follow the power cables, searching for the source of the telegram. Old Cat thought the survivors from the earlier exploration team would have waited here to be rescued. He whistled to alert them of our presence. This lonely whistle received not a single sound in response. In the end it was Old Tang and the former communications soldier who, after examining the countless electrical connections, located the telephone wire. It extended into a passage in the far recesses of the cavern. Old Tang led the way. About sixty feet into the tunnel, they began to smell an odor of decay. Then they saw the telegraph room. The automatic transmitter was inside. Next to it a canvas sheet covered something. Pei Qing lifted it off. Three corpses were underneath.

There were two men, one of them old, and a woman. All three were draped with khaki-yellow Japanese overcoats. Underneath, they wore PLA uniforms no different than ours. They had already begun to rot. Pei Qing didn't recognize them, but they had to be the survivors Old Cat was looking for. Well, not survivors, really. They'd been dead for some time.

The search team was extremely disheartened. They picked up the corpses and carried them out of the communication room. Pei Qing switched off the telegraph. It was still in the middle of an automatic transmission. Checking for cause of death, they discovered a black line along their gums, just like the corpse in the sinkhole. They seemed to have been poisoned to death. Old Tang had said he believed they'd been hit with some slow-acting toxin. Their deaths were far from sudden, giving them time to send the telegram. Old Cat had shaken his head and said no, that was impossible. If it was as Old Tang said, then why was there a survivor left to cover the three of them with a canvas sheet?

Usually a prospecting team will consist of no more than five to ten people. Counting these three, as well as the still-living Yuan Xile, the survivor Old Cat had guessed at, the dead soldier in the warehouse, the corpse in the sinkhole, and the madman Su Zhenhua—there might still be one or two more people we had yet to encounter.

Old Cat had ordered a group to continue searching the cavern while he and Old Tang discussed their next move. Pei Qing couldn't get close enough to hear what they were saying. The system of tunnels and passageways was complex. Searching was far from easy. The majority of the corpsmen Old Cat had brought along were new recruits, and Old Tang was a bit of a softie. When it came to technical skill, everyone looked to him, and he was an able fighter to boot, but when difficulties arose, he lacked either the force or the charm to spur others into taking the necessary risks. The soldiers were on the verge of giving up. Even the inscrutable Old Cat could see no way out. They could swear all they wanted—and indeed some of them did—but it was of no use. For the time being, they had no choice but to stop and take some R&R. While all this was happening, I had already led the headstrong deputy squad leader and the fearless Wang Sichuan into the sinkhole and on to the gigantic underground "River 1." At the time I had no special experience when it came to commanding soldiers, but I knew the sort of person it took to lead a squad well. A true officer should be like the deputy squad leader, obstinate in his need to carry out orders, brave and fierce like Wang Sichuan, and sly as Old Cat. Unfortunately, this sort of person was rare as could be.

As Pei Qing related their experiences to us, part of it seemed somehow illogical. Of course, Pei Qing spoke with a heavily accented form of Mandarin. I don't know how many years Mandarin education had already been popularized, but the effects of the campaign had yet to appear. He also spoke very rapidly, and

I didn't have the energy to focus on every little detail. Still, though, it felt like something didn't add up. In the end, Pei Qing said, it was Old Tang, a leaves-no-stone-unturned kind of guy, who figured out something was amiss. It was the telegraph room.

During the War of Resistance, wireless telegrams were used for long-distance correspondence, but the transmitter had to be located at a high point. Mountains got in the way of the signal. Transmissions were generally only made across regions of flatland. So why install a transmitter in a limestone cave at the end of an underground river? This telegraph room had certainly been in heavy use. There was a Japanese codebook and a great deal of telegraphic data lying all about. The transmission antenna, though, didn't seem to be nearby. It was likely back on the earth's surface, they surmised, where it could be used to contact other bases.

If this telegraph was for communicating with bases above the surface, then was it purely by chance that the signal was transferred onto the phone line? Could it be that whoever sent the message had meant to transmit the signal all the way to the surface? One therefore had to ask: Had the signal been received? Had the 723 Project headquarters known all along there was something dangerous in this cave?

It was Pei Qing who raised this question. He asked Old Cat whether, before coming after us, he'd been told a whole slew of previously concealed information. From today's perspective, his question might seem overly direct, but given the way people dealt with each other back then, it really was the norm. Old Cat paid him not the least bit of mind. Who knows, he said. If the transmission antenna really does run all the way to the surface, then the wind and rain probably wrecked it a long time ago. This was rather intentionally missing the point. As they argued about it, Old Tang and the communications soldier went on fiddling with the automatic transmitter. Just as Pei Qing was preparing to lay into Old

Cat again, Old Tang stopped them. He removed the headphones he'd been wearing and told them to listen. In addition to sending messages, the automatic transmitter could receive them as well. To verify what Old Cat had said about the surface-level antenna being broken, Old Tang had started up the machine's receiving function. The moment he did so, an urgent string of telegraphic code immediately piped through the headphones.

I was astounded. Although intercepting cables was not difficult, especially as this was the age of telegraphic code—prior, in other words, to the introduction of frequency-hopping transmitters—still, to do so often required a lengthy process of scanning frequencies. To receive a telegram the moment you switched on the receiver meant both this transmitter and its opposite were set to the same frequency. The chances of that happening accidentally were extremely minute. Listening to the transmission, the communications soldier said something was wrong with the coding method. It seemed to be pure gibberish. Old Tang and the soldier checked the Japanese codebook. The code sounding in their headphones was actually a Japanese military cipher. So where was the antenna and where was this message coming from?

Well, first, the cable couldn't have originated underground. That would have contravened physical laws. Second, in 1962, it would have been impossible for an antenna to receive a telegram from within Japan itself, much less one that was still using a military codebook from 1942. This cipher must have originated from someplace abandoned twenty years prior, probably some decrepit secret base nearby, left behind in the wilderness of Inner Mongolia.

None of them understood Japanese. So even with a codebook, they were unable to figure out what the cable meant. After the communications soldier listened to it for a considerable length of time, he realized that the content of the message continuously repeated. Its counterpart—wherever it was—must also be an automatic transmitter. Old Cat relaxed. Even though no one had been rescued, having found the source of the cable and this much data meant he could report the mission a success. They took detailed notes of the code being transmitted, dismantled the telegraph, packed it up along with the codebooks and deciphering equipment, and carried them out. Old Cat planned to return to the surface and let the professionals decode the message—see just what exactly the thing was saying—before deciding what to do next.

While packing everything up, Old Cat and the others had another pleasant surprise. One of the privates was going through a stack of data books when he discovered several engineering blueprints, one of which proved especially crucial. Only half the drawing could be made out, but in that legible section was a meticulous depiction of the area around the dam, the plane's takeoff structure, and all the underground river's various tributaries. Relying on this blueprint, they made their way through the branching paths of the limestone cavern. They entered a sinkhole and, following a group of power cables, navigated the tunnel system underneath for over ten hours until they finally reached one side of the dam. There were a couple minor adventures after that, and then they bumped into us.

Old Cat, Pei Qing, and the rest of them had obviously had it much easier than I. This made me rather resentful. We'd entered the sinkhole on the basis of a note. If it was one of them who'd given it to me, then some irresponsible person had pushed us into a situation of considerable danger. Of course, falling into that enormous underground river had been mostly our fault. Had that not happened, who knows how things might have gone?

Wang Sichuan had long since related our experiences to those present, even going so far as to tell them that, most likely, there was an enemy spy on the team. Old Cat's expression showed considerable displeasure. The list of dead was getting too long.

Telegraph room: three dead.

The generator in the sinkhole: one dead.

Workshop and warehouse: one dead and Su Zhenhua crazy.

Adding to this the madwoman Yuan Xile, then we'd already found seven of the first team, five of them dead—their deaths all abnormal—while those who'd survived had both gone crazy.

I told Old Cat that by now there were probably some things he should tell us. At the very least, I said, we need to know just how many people were on the first team. Pei Qing chimed in as soon as I said this, as did Wang Sichuan, Ma Zaihai, and the deputy squad leader. Pei Qing was quite agitated. His argument with Old Cat had gotten serious, and now he couldn't hold himself back.

Old Cat and Old Tang were both silent. For a moment, both sides were deadlocked, no one saying a word. At last Old Cat abruptly relaxed, sighed, and then spoke. "All right. But I can only tell you this one thing and you must not ask me again. There is no benefit in you knowing too much—not for me, nor for all of you either."

Go on and say it, I thought to myself. We understand. After we leave this place, no one will bring it up again.

Old Cat gave a rather strange laugh and said, "The first team entered here half a month ago. Nine people in total—four experts, four corpsmen, one specially appointed supervisor."

"Nine people?" Ma Zaihai gulped. "Then there are still two people we haven't found yet?"

Old Cat shook his head. "No," he said, "just one."

Ma Zaihai counted it out on his fingers, then counted again. Something was wrong.

"There was one person," said Old Cat, "who came out alive."

We stared at him in surprise. "Who was it?" asked Ma Zaihai.

Narrowing his eyes, Old Cat pointed at himself. "Me."

CHAPTER 44

Old Cat

I t was a long time before I could finally react. The others were no different. At last Wang Sichuan asked, "You mean to say you've already been here?"

Old Cat fished out a cigarette, lit it, then nodded.

Everything had been turned upside down. Quite a few people's faces had gone white. We looked at each other in blank dismay. My mind remained in chaos, but then, as I thought about it once more, I wanted to laugh. It all made sense, I realized. Back when we first arrived, Old Cat had known the colonel and the rest of that gang had already long since discovered this cave. I thought this was the slyness of Old Cat reading the military, but if he'd already been down here, well, of course he would have known. And when the underground river rose, he was able to both appear just in the nick of time and know that the way forward was at the very top of the cavern. At the time, I had once more believed this was merely due to his wealth of experience. How had we been so naive?

For a short while everyone was silent. Pei Qing was the first to respond. "Mao Wuyue," he said coldly, "I've known something was up with you for a long time, but I didn't think you were involved this deeply. What exactly is going on here? Tell us, or don't blame us if there's no love lost."

Old Cat leisurely shook his head. "I just told you that was all I could say. Our superiors have their own considerations. Anyway, it's better for you all that I not say anything."

"Goddamn it," yelled Wang Sichuan. "What the fuck kind of leader are you supposed to be?" Jumping to his feet, he charged at Old Cat. Old Tang rushed in between them, grabbed Wang Sichuan, and twisted him into a pretzel. Old Tang was very agile, and the hulking Wang Sichuan was subdued in a moment. He wasn't about to give up, though. As soon as Old Tang turned his back, Wang Sichuan seized him and flipped him onto the ground. The two of them twisted together. Pei Qing rushed over. My heart leaped in fear. Was this about to turn into a free-for-all? But Pei Qing meant only to mediate. He pulled the two of them apart.

Pointing at Wang Sichuan, Old Tang swore, "Are you a soldier or what? You think you're some kind of intellectual, don't you? Didn't Old Cat just say he's under orders? You're a goddamn nobody. Are we supposed to listen to you or to headquarters?"

This might seem like no more than angry bluster, but Old Tang had raised two important points: First, it's not that they weren't saying it, it's that they couldn't say it. And second, the orders came from headquarters. This was a hint for us to ask no further. I knew Old Cat would die before he said anything he was sworn to conceal, even if it was as simple as the new location of the engineering brigade headquarters. Wang Sichuan was the kind of guy brave enough to hit a political commissar if his blood rose. I was afraid that if he did anything else he'd give someone reason to call him a counterrevolutionary, and then he'd really be done for. I ran over, grabbed him tight, and made him shut up.

Seeing how tense the atmosphere was, Ma Zaihai attempted to change the subject. "Leaders," he said, "let's not waste any more time. If there's only one person left, could this be the same individual who just tried to kill Engineer Wu?"

The others hadn't heard this part yet. A surprised look flashed across Old Cat's face. "What do you mean, tried to kill him?" he asked. I told them how, just now, I was nearly buried alive in an ice pit.

Old Cat's brows wrinkled as I finished my story. "Should we send someone to go look?" asked Old Tang.

Old Cat immediately waved his hand. "No need," he said. "This thing's not right!"

"What do you mean?" I asked. Old Cat replied that the first prospecting team had nine people in total, three of them women. The remaining survivor should be a woman, but based on my description, my attacker had been a powerful man.

"When you were attacked," asked Wang Sichuan, "could you tell if it was a man or a woman?" I thought about it, then firmly stated how big he was. Back when I was a kid, I used to fight all the time in my village. Whenever I was hit I could always tell whether it was a boy or girl who was throwing the punches. If the person who attacked me was a man, then he wasn't part of the first exploration team. Who was he? Why had another man appeared? Was it possible there really were Japanese soldiers down here?

Everyone began to talk at once. We went over it again and again, but couldn't think of another possibility. Then Pei Qing quieted everyone down with a click of his tongue. With a dark look on his face he said, "Could it be Chen Luohu? He's the only one missing."

Wang Sichuan shook his head. "Impossible," he said. "Chen Luohu's too much of a coward to ever hit anyone."

"You can't just go by appearances," Pei Qing said. "The more unimpressive someone looks, the more likely it's just an act. I think he seemed a little over the top."

What a mess, I thought. Old Tang waved his hand, quieting everyone down. He said the deputy squad leader and I were both injured, and he and the others were all exhausted from the journey here. For the time being, we should stop thinking about this and get some rest. He would arrange for some of his men to make a quick search of the area. When our energy had returned, we could discuss our next move.

It was true. I was exhausted. After Old Tang said this, we all calmed down. We split up and at once the atmosphere relaxed. They had already boiled some water and cooked the condensed vegetable paste. Now a few corpsmen ladled out a bowl for me. Seeing that I was cold, Old Tang gave me some of the chili sauce he'd brought along. One bite and my whole body began to sweat. But I remained tired as ever. As I ate my eyelids drooped down and I nearly fell asleep.

I was once told that ancient warriors could sleep even while on horseback. In all my years of toiling for different prospecting teams across China, riding not only horses but every other domesticated animal besides dogs, never once had I been able to sleep on the back of some animal. Now I believed the stories. My sleepiness was so extreme that nothing else mattered. I just wanted all the world to go away. If someone wanted to kill me, then let it happen. I wanted only to sleep.

But I could not. Looking back toward the bonfire, I noticed that Old Cat and some others had unrolled a number of blueprints and were poring over their contents. These were the structural drawings they'd found near the telegraph room. I was sure of it. I climbed to my feet, walked over, and asked Old Cat if I could take a look as well. Old Tang told me I'd better rest, but I said I was fine and that I wanted to see what was really going on down here. Old Cat passed me one of the drawings. The thing was rather timeworn. It felt soft and limp in my hand. I spread it out on the ground.

Wang Sichuan also came over. At a glance I could tell he was full of energy. Those goddamn nomads really are much stronger than us rice eaters, I thought. I forced myself to focus on the blueprint before me. It was the entire underground river system. In an instant I had found the markings for both the dam and the enormous River 0. The meticulousness with which the Japanese had designed these blueprints was astonishing. Both the large and small tributaries were rendered with incomparable clarity. The opening through which we entered the cave was distinctly marked. There seemed to be three more such entrances, all of them leading to other tributaries. The underground river system was truly immense. We gradually pressed closer, forming a tight circle around the map.

The underground river had seven tributaries in total. Numbers 3, 4, 5, and 6 all diverged from River 2, the river we began on. All four of these tributaries off River 2 eventually seeped out through cracks in the rock. This was why none had formed into a mature river, nor did any ultimately empty into a subterranean reservoir. The communications center at the end of River 6 was the only military installation at the end of any of these four tributaries. Were this river system compared to a large tree, River 2 would be the trunk and Rivers 3, 4, 5 and 6 would all be branches. Two other tributaries also formed a stand-alone system. After merging in the upper reaches of the cave, River 1 and River 7 became River 0, which flowed into the dam. Surprisingly, the area between the eight rivers was far from solid. Each of the rivers was connected to the others by a great mass of still-forming limestone tunnels, all of them distinctly depicted by the Japanese. By traversing these complex, mazelike caverns, they would have been able to smoothly shuttle from one river to the next. There were also a number of markings designating provisional generators like the small one we discovered on the sinkhole platform, as well as several symbols that we found unrecognizable. A question occurred to me as I looked at the drawing. I asked Old Cat what they were planning to do now. Why had they decided to keep going till they got all the way down here? Was it to rescue that final woman?

Old Cat shook his head and pointed at a section of the blue-print. "For this," he said.

I looked where he was pointing. It was a spot just to the side of the dam. At first I thought he meant the Shinzan, but then I realized he was indicating the great void beyond. I didn't understand. When I had looked upon that boundless darkness with my own eyes, my blood froze and my body shook, but on this drawing it was merely a blank expanse. Why was Old Cat interested in all that emptiness?

But Old Cat said nothing, just continued to smoke his cigarette. Old Tang then jumped in. He pointed to a long line of alternating long and short dashes. He motioned for quiet and in a low voice said, "First look at this line, then I'll explain it to you." I nodded and he continued: "The symbols used by the Japanese are different from ours, but we can guess what they mean. There are different kinds of lines all over the blueprint. Look. Solid lines represent electrical cables. They're everywhere, like vines, all of them emerging from power stations. Now look at these dotted lines. They all end at telephone marks, so they must be telephone lines. But on the whole blueprint there's only one line of long and short dashes. What is it supposed to represent?" He moved his hand along the dashes. "Look at the ends of the line. Do you see where this is?"

I followed his finger and looked. It was the telegraph room at the end of River 6. "Aha!" said Wang Sichuan beside me. "The telegraph room. In which case this line—"

"That's right. This is the line that connects the telegraph room to its transmitting antenna. We were wrong. The antenna wasn't on the surface. It was right here." He pointed at the outer edge of the dam. Here the dashed line stopped and became an asterisk.

My hair stood on end. Goddamn! The transmission antenna was on the side of the dam, pointing out toward the void. The 1942-standard cipher they'd received didn't originate on the surface. It came from the abyss itself. Twenty years ago, the Japanese had not only flown in, they'd sent a message back out!

CHAPTER 45

The Message

Old Tang's voice was very calm as he spoke, but hearing him we all felt unspeakable terror. "Twenty years ago," he said, "a Japanese Shinzan bomber took off from a river thirty-six hundred feet below the earth's surface. It soared over an underground dam and glided into the immense void just beyond, disappearing into the limitless darkness. None of us knows what the Shinzan encountered out there, or what the pilots saw."

By itself this was crazy. Now we'd discovered a mysterious transmission had somehow come out of the darkness? Then I recalled the huge number of airdrop-ready supplies. It was obvious. This entire base had been set up to airdrop people into that abyss. Arriving some twenty years earlier, the Japanese must have asked themselves the moment they looked into the void: What is this place, what's inside, and how do we get down there? It was evident that not only had they solved this final question, they'd also sent back a message from within.

After discovering this place, the Japanese proceeded to build a vast infrastructure, then successfully used a long-range bomber to airdrop people and supplies into the abyss. And the crashed Shinzan was certainly not the first plane flown into the abyss. The small night fighter whose wreckage we discovered earlier had surely been used in some sort of trial run. Even though, in the end, the bomber crashed, the entire course of events could still be described as "magnificently insane."

I asked Old Tang what he intended to do now.

Corpsmen are different from us prospectors. Corpsmen must be rigorous, testing and verifying everything to ensure their reports are always 100 percent correct. This was the work standard promulgated by Chairman Mao. The engineering corps is forever at the forefront of the military, paving roads through mountains and building bridges across rivers. The least mistake could lead to failure and military disaster. Sure enough, Old Tang told us that they had to make completely certain that the signal was emerging from the abyss. Such a verdict could not be made without verification. That's why they'd come all the way down to the dam. Now they needed to find a way to the abyss side of the dam to look for the antenna. It was this search that had originally led them down to the warehouse level. The search-and-rescue mission had to continue as well. The situation outside the dam was unknown, so making any too-specific plans would be pointless. The corpsmen would finish the search of the dam while we prospectors stayed behind. Our job was already complete.

It's been complete for a long time, I thought to myself. There wasn't going to be some humongous oil lake at the bottom of the void. It was evident the Japanese activity here had little to do with resource prospecting. Our assignment had already been finished before we'd even entered the cave.

No one spoke in opposition to Old Tang. Old Cat said nothing, just silently drank his tea and listened to us. Looking at his expression, he seemed to feel that what we were discussing was ridiculous. At the time I couldn't have cared less what he thought. Never would I have expected that, soon enough, I would feel the same way.

With reality feeling as surreal as a nightmare, I drifted into sleep and long, vivid dreams. The vast abyss had become a tremendous mouth. I was standing atop the dam, facing into the gale-force winds and watching the abyss expand toward me. All around me the rock walls slowly corroded into the darkness. Then I was sitting in a plane, aimlessly flying through the void. There was nothing around, the flight unending.

Despite my terror, I didn't wake up. I slept for ten hours straight. At last, when it was time to eat, Wang Sichuan awoke me. Old Tang had already left with some of the others. Old Cat was gone as well. He was leading a group of corpsmen investigating the factory and warehouse. There had to be a heavy-duty freight elevator somewhere nearby. I was sure Old Cat was more than just a simple prospector, otherwise he could never have convinced Rong Aiguo to dispatch the rescue team. My intuition said this affair went far beyond my understanding. I didn't want to think about any of it anymore.

As I ate, I listened to Pei Qing and Wang Sichuan discussing the dam. They were attempting to infer what the icehouse had been used for. We had only a vague idea of the layout of the average dam, and this one was far from ordinary. The purpose of most of its installations—icehouse included—was a mystery to us. All we knew for sure was that on both sides of the dam were identical caissons, capable of transporting supplies underwater. Beneath the dam's water level was a huge icehouse filled with countless frozen bombs. Beyond that was a factory and warehouse piled high with supplies.

With his mouth full of mashed vegetables, Wang Sichuan spoke: "The way I see it, we're already at the lowest level of the dam. If they really were planning on blowing it up, then it wouldn't make sense to place the bombs anywhere but the very bottom."

But why did they freeze all the warheads? Such measures were only required for nitroglycerin, but that stuff could never be used in an artillery shell. The heat produced when the chemical was released would cause the inner warhead to explode much quicker than the outer shell, and the danger in transporting the stuff would have been too great. There was one other thing that required low-temperature preservation: biological weapons.

While it's a fact that the Japanese conducted biological warfare throughout China, most civilians have only heard of the atrocities of Unit 731—the inhuman Japanese biological research center. Having trekked through China's forests and explored her caves, we prospectors know Unit 731 was only the tip of the iceberg. In my dozens of years on the job, I've come across innumerable cement structures located deep in the forests of the Northeast. All had been built by the Japanese during their invasion of China, and every last one was basically demolished. Nonetheless, evidence of dungeons and dissecting rooms could still be discerned. A comrade in arms told me that, in addition to these research labs, the scale of germ warfare in China was far greater still.

These bombs were probably not biological weapons. What purpose would they have served? The Japanese objective in the area was clear. Why line the base of the dam with weapons like that? I returned to my original question: What had the Japanese planned to do with all those bombs? A thought then occurred to me. What would happen if the refrigeration compressors stopped working? Even though the temperature here was very low, the ice would eventually begin to melt. And then what would become of the warheads?

The icehouse didn't seem as large as I'd thought. I could hear the sounds of loud movement from that direction. Every now and then soldiers would return. These new recruit tenderfoots were so cold the mucus streamed from their nostrils. They really were just kids. The wait was very dull. We chatted for a bit, but Wang Sichuan couldn't keep still. Soon he cried out that we should go see what they were up to. We wrapped overcoats tightly around ourselves, then walked back up the stairs, through the pitch-black tunnel, and into the icehouse. We headed toward the sounds. We'd taken no more than twenty steps when I realized something was different. It seemed to have grown colder. Frost had already formed across my eyebrows. That had never happened before. It felt as if we'd been caught in a blizzard in the Greater Khingan range. Before long I could see the shape of someone up ahead. It was Old Tang stamping his feet and smashing something into the ground. They were breaking a hole in the ice.

Several privates were wielding simple tools, sparing no effort as they smashed them down. They didn't seem to be having much effect. They'd produced only a thin layer of powdery ice. Still, what they were doing was dangerous. There were bombs below.

I walked over to Old Tang. "You'd better be careful," I told him. "What is the purpose of all this?"

Shivering, his lips purple from the cold, he told me to look at what was underneath the ice. Beneath our feet I saw a large black shadow, but because the top layer had already been smashed rough and uneven, I couldn't tell what I was looking at. It certainly wasn't a bomb. This thing was huge. I took a lap around it. The shadow was shaped like a giant paper clip. All along its length were numerous U-shaped protrusions. I gasped. It was a large-scale radio antenna. We knew one of these had to be around here somewhere, but what was it doing frozen beneath the ice?

On closer inspection I realized that the antenna wasn't the only thing down there. There was a second shadow, also giant, although comparatively dim. It must have been buried in a deeper layer of ice. This shadow was three times as large as the antenna and appeared to be a massive strainerlike disc.

"What the hell is that?" I asked Old Tang, shivering and pointing at the monster paper clip. "Is it the antenna you're looking for? What's it doing in the ice?"

"It's not the antenna," he replied. "This thing's got a nickname. It's called the 'Würzburg Giant.'"

"What? What giant?"

Putting it simply, he said, the Würzburg Giant is a kind of tracking radar the Japanese imported from Germany. Its main function was to automatically control searchlights during night-time air defense. While in China, the Japanese hadn't needed such advanced nighttime tracking technology, so you don't see too many of them. Most were set up on the Inner Mongolian and Pacific Ocean fronts. China later unsuccessfully attempted to copy the device's design. The technology eventually died out, but during the war it was the most advanced tracking equipment around. Old Tang said that he too had been shocked to come across a shadow this large, but the thing itself was probably not as big as it looked. Different thicknesses at different layers of the ice distorted the images below. The device would have been used for guided navigation, though this one might be just a spare. Precision guidance would have been a necessity for flying a plane down here.

Wang Sichuan asked Old Tang what they planned to do with the thing once they dug it up. Could this have something to do with the telegram?

"It's more than just that," said Old Tang. He pulled a piece of paper out of his pocket. On it were several rough pencil sketches. Old Tang's group had been searching the icehouse, looking for the caisson controls and attempting to gain a preliminary under-standing of the place. The sketches were representations of the ice-house's layout. The compression engines and electrical circuits that surrounded the room were all marked. The shadows beneath the ice had also been clearly noted. Old Tang pointed to several spots with his pencil. "The shells that you mentioned are vast in number and spread all around the icehouse, forming a ring. In the center is the Würzburg Giant. Look at these lines here. These ladderlike shadows are the tracks used to transport the device. We also found four black shapes alongside the Würzburg Giant, each the size of a PLA truck. Those are probably the two groups of searchlights that accompany it." I nodded and he continued. "This doesn't seem extremely odd to you? Placing a guided navigation radar device at the center of a ring of bombs? What's the point of it?"

I was already much too cold to think. Wang Sichuan sneezed and said, "Could it be a trap?"

I understood what he meant. After engineering corpsmen lay land mines on the battlefield, they set up some phony target to get the enemy to approach. If the fuse covers on all these bombs had in fact been removed—meaning they were poised and ready to explode—then Wang Sichuan's suggestion did seem fairly reasonable. But a radar device in the middle—what kind of bait was that? Who were they hoping to attract? Then again, maybe they'd wanted to guide the plane to smash into the dam, destroying everything.

This didn't make any sense, but I lacked the strength to consider it any further. The icehouse was too cold. I could endure it no longer. Old Tang told us to go back to the warehouse, saying that if we really wanted to help, we could go assist Old Cat. After returning to camp, we drank several cups of hot water and didn't want to go anywhere. Something didn't seem right. I began to feel increasingly uneasy.

Then it occurred to me: perhaps the reason the Japanese abandoned this place wasn't as simple as we had thought. Nowhere in this entire system of rivers and caves had we seen any evidence suggesting the Japanese had tried to destroy the base. Everything had been left in good order. A great quantity of supplies remained neatly stacked and essentially unblemished. Even the various files and documents were left intact. We'd found a pilot's corpse within the Shinzan, but where were the other members of the flight crew?

Why had the corpse been left in the pilothouse? I don't know whether the cold from outside had penetrated the warehouse or if my thoughts were just that unsettling, but I began to shiver uncontrollably. I still remember that feeling. It wasn't fear, just the shock piled on shock of limitless discoveries coming to light one after the other. A thought flashed across my mind. What if this base had already been abandoned by the time the Shinzan flew back?

There must have been something strange about my expression, because both Wang Sichuan and Pei Qing were looking at me oddly. Wang Sichuan asked whether it wouldn't be best for me to sleep a little longer. When one's body is in revolt, he said, it isn't wise to push it.

I shook my ahead. "What do you guys think?" I asked them. "How long did that Shinzan fly around the abyss before it returned?"

"What do you mean?" asked Wang Sichuan.

"Is it possible," I continued, "that after the Shinzan flew into the abyss there was some kind of emergency up here and everyone was forced to leave, so that when it flew back out there was already no one left? With no guidance from the ground, the pilot would definitely crash. His corpse was then left behind in the wreckage of the plane, while those still living among the flight crew disappeared to who knows where."

The problem was that I had no idea how long a Shinzan could stay aloft. Later, I checked. Flying at full speed, it could cruise for ten to fourteen hours. Given that this base spanned the entire cave system, evacuating it would take at least one hundred hours. But Wang Sichuan wasn't one for details. He agreed that it seemed reasonable enough. Pei Qing wasn't so sure. "Based on the way the place looks," he said, "it hardly seems as if there was an emergency. They didn't dismantle the transmitter. Even the codebook was left behind. Even with an army on their doorstep, they wouldn't have behaved so carelessly."

It felt not like they'd evacuated, but as if everyone on the base had suddenly disappeared. Old Tang had said something like this as well. It seemed like the Japanese had planned on returning, he'd said. It was as if they were only handing the base over temporarily, but then they'd never come back. Something beyond our imaginations had happened here. The state of this base in its final dozen or so hours remained absolutely unfathomable. And it seemed highly likely that whatever had happened, it didn't begin until after the Shinzan flew into the abyss.

The more I thought about it, the less I understood. After standing back up, I went to look at the sand table, hoping to draw some clue from it. Then Wang Sichuan suddenly let out a quizzical "Huh?" He raised his head and began to look around. I did the same, only to discover that he wasn't looking, he was listening. From someplace far overhead, the air-defense warning rang out once more. It was a deep sound and very faint. If you didn't listen closely, it was easy to mix up with the noise from the exhaust fan.

Pei Qing looked at his watch. The alarm continued to ring for a long time, then all of a sudden it stopped. He relaxed. "It rang for three minutes. This means the state of warning has been canceled."

I breathed a sigh of relief. Buddha preserve us, I said to myself. Things up top are finally getting better. Before I could finish my thought, there came a great noise of machinery springing to life. The sound was all around us, now rising, now falling, seeming to resound from every corner of the dam. Several young soldiers rushed animatedly from the recesses of the warehouse. Good news, they told us. The dam had finished releasing the floodwater. Now, they believed, the mist would soon retreat below the warning line.

Wang Sichuan was about to ask how they knew this when there was a commotion over by the entrance to the icehouse. Several of Old Tang's soldiers appeared, carrying some object. They called out for us to help. The thing was terribly heavy. Even with four of them carrying it, they were barely doing more than dragging it along the ground. We hustled toward them. It was a great chunk of ice, the size of a coffin. Wang Sichuan shouted for me to hurry up. Gritting his teeth, he put his hands underneath it and together they lifted it off the ground. Pei Qing and I tried to help, but the privates told us they were OK. More were coming, they said. Another group of soldiers hefting a second slab appeared only a moment later. I called some of the others over and, giving it all we had, we lifted it up. It felt uncommonly heavy. Then I saw something was frozen inside.

We brought the ice block over to camp and set it down. The force of the fall smashed several inches off the bottom. I asked what they'd dug up. The soldiers rolled the block over so I could see. A corpse was frozen inside.

"It's one of the goddamn invaders," said a soldier. "We just found him, frozen to death in the ice."

The corpse had its arms wrapped around itself, its appearance haggard. The irregular surface of the ice distorted the figure within, but I could tell he was draped with an overcoat, his body small and frail. He looked no different than a child.

CHAPTER 46

The Dead Woman

I n the later stages of the war, the Japanese had been hard-pressed for troops. The final batches of soldiers sent to Inner Mongolia were all very young. The Japanese also have small builds in general, otherwise we wouldn't call them "Little Devils." So the height of the corpse was perhaps rather normal.

"There are a bunch more down there," said one of the privates, "all of them hanging off the radar device. Goddamn, we were digging and digging and then from out of the ice appeared this black face. Scared the hell out of me, and I smacked myself in the head with my pickax."

We all cracked up, but the deputy squad leader berated the soldier. "Look at your pitiful expression. How can you bear to act like such a fool? Why aren't you getting back to work?"

This soldier was probably one of the deputy squad leader's. At once he stopped laughing, straightened the block out, and ran back. I wanted to help out as well, but the deputy squad leader said there was no need. It was too cold out there, and they could barely endure it. Once they'd brought in all the corpses, they were coming back. They'd been forced to give up.

Very soon Old Tang returned as well. He shook the frost from his hair, whole swaths falling to the ground, then went straight to the fire, hoping to warm up. His face was cracked from the cold. Two or three more blocks of ice were carried in, then everyone filed back through the door. I could feel the temperature rise once the icehouse door was shut. "There are still several more corpses," said Old Tang, "but we're not going to dig them out. We'll freeze to death if we try."

The temperature in the icehouse must have continued to fall, although I didn't know why. We drew close to the fire and its heat helped us regain some of our spirit. The group of young corpsmen drank cup after cup of warm tea. Some of the others crowded around the frozen corpses, looking them over with curiosity. Pei Qing was especially interested, turning over block after block. He seemed unwilling to stop until every last one of their faces was revealed. He was so tired he began raspily gasping for breath. I wondered what he was looking for. After turning one over, his face suddenly went white. At once he stopped what he was doing and squatted down.

Carrying my cup of tea over, I asked what he'd discovered. He appeared to be in disbelief. "A woman," he said.

The young soldiers had been yakking away, but as soon as he said this, they went silent and snapped their heads in our direction. I could feel something strange in the air, a shiver of excitement that felt out of place. We looked over at them and they back at us. There was something odd and too eager about their expressions. One of them stood up and came over. Then the rest followed, until they'd all crowded around the frozen corpse.

At the time it felt rather awkward, but I later realized this was all perfectly normal. The corpsmen were young and full of vigor. They spent the whole year trekking through remote and thickly forested mountains, laying roads and building bridges. It was an arduous job, nearly impossible for women, and so any opportunity to see one was, as they say, a joy to the eyes and pleasing to the mind. Not to mention that for those of us from that generation, any female Japanese soldier was inevitably associated with Yoshiko Kawashima, the Japanese spy. The name was practically synonymous with seduction and lust. These were young guys, so even though it was only a corpse, it was still enough to make their cheeks blush and their ears turn red.

I looked over the corpse. With the warehouse still quite cold, the ice block was basically unmelted. All of the corpses were clad in similar attire, though this one was much more petite. With one glance you could tell it was a woman. Her hair was the giveaway, worn in a bun. In China, female soldiers always cut their hair short, but for Japanese female soldiers, this seemed to be the only hairstyle that existed. That was all I could make out. After looking at her for a few minutes, the engineering soldiers realized she was completely different from the image of Yoshiko Kawashima they had in their minds. Dejected, they slunk back to the fireside. Only Pei Qing continued to stare at her. I called his name. He looked up. The trace of an odd, nearly imperceptible expression flashed across his face, but then it was gone. A moment later he sighed and said, "It's just a little girl. Those devils had no qualms at all about making her a soldier."

"Women are never free from blame in wartime," said Wang Sichuan, nearby. "Know how many Chinese she's killed? What's there to take pity on?"

Pei Qing's face twisted, but he forced a smile. Then suddenly he turned to me. "Old Wu, help me boil some water. Let's melt her out. I want to see what she's got on her."

"Huh?" I said. "What are you thinking now?"

He explained that in the Japanese military, women were generally either assigned to special units or they worked as secretaries for officers. And though they could be quite young, their military posts were often very high. He wanted to see where this woman had come from and whether she might have any documents on her that could provide us some clues.

"Boiling water isn't going to work," said Old Tang. "The ice is too cold." It would only cause the ice to crack, he said, ripping apart the body inside. By the time the ice melted, the ground would be nothing but bloody water. There were too many examples of this during the Korean War. The frozen remains of many volunteer soldiers were dug out of the snowy ground and had to be melted out little by little using heated towels. I had heard about this cracking phenomenon while stationed in the Greater Khingan range. A local villager told me if you pissed on the ice during cold weather, it would split apart.

Pei Qing was forced to abandon his idea, but the factory was far from warm. Who knew how long it would be before the ice melted on its own? He asked me to help push the slab closer to the fire. I had no interest in this, but it seemed impolite to argue. As soon as I pushed, the whole thing rolled over. "Be more careful," said Pei Qing angrily. He hastily started to turn it back over.

I frowned and felt utterly exasperated. It's a pity at the time I didn't give it more thought, but a moment later my attention was drawn to the figure in the ice. The girl was carrying a very large, extremely odd-looking steel backpack. It was circular and half as big as her body. My first thought was it was a metal snail shell. What sort of geological instrument is this? I wondered. Or is it some kind of land mine? I called Old Tang over to take a look.

"It's not a land mine," he said. "Land mines have a fuse." He too had never seen a geological apparatus like it. The thing looked just like an iron shell. I was sure there was something odd about it. It was as if I'd seen it before. That was only a vague feeling, though, and I couldn't recall in the slightest where or when I might have run into it.

The young soldiers were full of energy and crowded around once more, wanting to see what was going on. Letting them look, I asked to hear their ideas on what it might be. What sort of case is circular, I asked, and what would someone place inside? "Cookies?" said one of the soldiers. The deputy squad leader scolded him at once, but Old Tang turned on the deputy squad leader. "Didn't Engineer Wu just ask to hear their opinions? If that's the example you set, who would dare suggest anything?"

Pressed by his superior, the deputy squad leader had nothing to say. Still, he didn't seem all that pained by it. He's just too pragmatic, I thought. He was also headstrong and closed-minded about everything, and thus hadn't moved up in rank. Patting him on the back, I told him not to worry about it and to stop looking at me like I was his officer.

"It resembles a telephone wiring pack," said Ma Zaihai. "Look at the holes in the middle. Bearings would have been screwed in there. Then you'd wrap the telephone wire around these and you could string it along as you walked. This case is definitely some sort of wiring box."

"No way," said another of the soldiers. "A length of machine-gun ammo could also be rolled up into that shape. This thing is too big to be a telephone wiring case. The wire would get all tangled."

I knew Ma Zaihai was right, something was definitely rolled up in there, but I was also sure it wasn't telephone wire or machine-gun ammunition. Both were much too heavy. Since none of the other corpses were carrying anything this big, it had to be fairly light. Otherwise, why give it to the sole woman to carry?

Wang Sichuan clicked his tongue in disapproval. "You pedantic young masters ought to stay in the research institute and do scholarship," he said as he walked over. "Why are you being so polite to the Japanese devil woman? If you really want to know what it is, let's smash the thing to pieces and take a look." He pulled out a hammer.

Pei Qing stepped in front of him. "Wang Sichuan," he intoned coldly, "have you any discipline left?"

Within the team Pei Qing had always kept fairly aloof, but he was neither overly unsociable nor eccentric. If he had a problem with something, he would say it directly. Wang Sichuan was therefore puzzled to see him behave this way. But Wang Sichuan was also never slow to anger, and Pei Qing's high-and-mighty tone was the thing he loathed most. Wang Sichuan stared at him, his bullish eyes huge as copper bells. "What is it? Did someone step on your tail? Say it. What rule have I broken?"

Pei Qing didn't drop his gaze for an instant. "First, you're profaning the dead. Second, it's unclear what exactly is frozen in there. Supposing there's something dangerous inside, are you going to take full responsibility for it?"

For a moment Wang Sichuan was stunned. Then he laughed. "Profaning the dead? Bullshit. Is she your mom or your wife or something? What are you, Japanese?"

Wang Sichuan is known for having a loose tongue, but this was over the top. When we joke, we generally know where to stop. Wang Sichuan was by far the most crass, but he was just as well educated as the rest of us and I'd never heard him say anything too excessive. This insult went beyond the realm of joking. I have no idea how he thought it would be all right.

Sure enough, Pei Qing's face immediately clouded over. As he leaped forward, he uttered three words: "Fuck your mother." What came next was his foot, but he was no match for Wang Sichuan. With one slap he was knocked to the ground. He climbed back up, grabbing an iron club used for ice breaking. As soon as I saw this, I ran over and restrained Pei Qing. Old Tang then came between them and began to berate them both.

I pulled Pei Qing over to the side. Gradually he calmed down and tossed the club away. He threw me off and walked deeper into the warehouse. Wang Sichuan's face had turned even darker than usual, his eyes bloodshot. With a firm voice, Old Tang yelled at him to give it a rest. I looked back at Old Tang. I wanted to say the hell with everyone and everything, but he gave me a glance that meant: "Go keep an eye on Pei Qing. Don't let him get lost out there."

I had no choice but to go. I followed him for a long way, until at last I watched him walk in between two rows of supplies and sit down. I wanted to let him cool off for a bit, so I didn't walk over. Instead, I found a place some distance off where I could keep an eye on him. As I watched, he buried his head between his knees and began to sob, his entire body shaking. Seeing Pei Qing like this gave me goose bumps. Perhaps he had some awful childhood memory of the Japanese. Probably it was also just the oppressive nature of the place. It had surely been affecting our psyches for some time. The pressure had built up and now it had exploded. This wasn't the time to ask about such things, nor was it appropriate for me to console him. I could only stand there, filled with a deep discomfort at the sight of this grown man crying.

With difficulty he managed to relax. I watched as, expressionlessly, he stood up and walked back to camp. I followed him as he walked into the firelight. The atmosphere turned awkward. Not one of the several people there spoke. Picking up his belongings, Pei Qing moved them to a different part of the camp. He'd originally been sleeping very close to Wang Sichuan. When the other man saw what he was doing, he opened his mouth to shout something, but I gave him a kick. "Leave it," I said. "While your colleague is around, it would be best to just watch what you say."

Wang Sichuan swallowed his words, turned around, and went off to bed. In a moment he was snoring soundly, and the tension began to ease at last.

Then I remembered something: Why hadn't Old Cat come back yet? I recalled the two soldiers who'd returned to tell us the floodwater discharge was over. Turning around, I looked all about for them. I was perplexed. I hadn't seen anyone leave. Could they have returned for just a moment and then left again to find Old Cat? I pulled each man aside and asked if they'd seen any of Old Cat's soldiers. They all shook their heads. They'd all been with Old Tang and none could recall having recently run into anyone from Old Cat's group. Something was wrong here. I shook Wang Sichuan awake and told him what was going on. Rolling over, he scanned the faces of the young soldiers. Could we have made some mistake? All the corpsmen were wearing Japanese uniforms. What if the missing two had actually been Old Tang's? I asked all those present if any of them had notified us that the dam was no longer releasing floodwater. They shook their heads.

"What is it?" Old Tang asked. We related what seemed to have happened. All those present agreed there was something peculiar about it. For us to say two corpsmen had both suddenly appeared and then soundlessly vanished couldn't help but seem somehow wrong.

"Then let's go look for them," said the deputy squad leader. "Maybe when all the commotion started they went back to wherever Old Cat is. With all the people and the noise, it would have been easy to miss them."

I nodded. "As a matter of fact, we've had no news at all from Old Cat. No matter what, he should've returned by now. Should we go see what he's up to?"

Once I put it like that, everyone agreed something wasn't right. Old Tang nodded at the deputy squad leader and ordered several men to head deeper into the warehouse. The breadth and depth of the warehouse were both considerable, every inch of it piled high with supplies. Looking into the darkness, I felt a stab of apprehension. Soon after he'd walked off, we heard the deputy squad leader yell out Old Cat's name. He continued to shout it, the sound getting farther and farther away. There was no reply.

We'd all begun to feel a bit nervous. Old Tang gave me one of his Iron Eagles. "It's nothing," he said. "Everything bad that could happen already has. There's not going be anything else. They just walked too far away, that's all." Iron Eagle is an old cigarette brand, the first to begin production in the early days of liberation. I took a long look at the pack. Man, I thought to myself, even in these times there are still people who can get their hands on these. I took a puff. The flavor was impure, but invigorating. I turned again to look off into the warehouse. Now even the sound of the deputy squad leader's voice was gone.

We still didn't know how big the warehouse was. Thinking back on it now, a simple recitation of its size in square feet would never do justice to its complexity or its odd shape. The ceiling was quite high, with stacks of goods on suspended multilevel walkways and iron tracks for hauling supplies. The floor was covered with towering piles of materials. The devils must have thoroughly researched the form and structure of a dam, then utilized this space to the greatest extent possible.

Ten minutes passed without any communication from the deputy squad leader. Old Tang made us keep waiting. "He's carrying a gun," he said. "If something really happened, he would have fired a warning shot."

I felt rather anxious. Not wanting my mood to affect anyone else, I got up and walked over to look at the corpse. Pei Qing was sitting off to one side of it. He stared, dazed, at the ice block, as if looking to see how much it had melted. I handed him a cigarette, but he refused. I could feel the questions bubbling up inside me. Making sure that none of the corpsmen were paying us any attention, I asked him what was going on. He ignored me. He gave me no more than a quick glance before turning back to the ice. I tried several times to give him a friendly nudge, but he just slapped my hand away.

There was nothing I could do. I walked back over to Wang Sichuan, but he was asleep, or at least pretending to be. Though I pushed him, he didn't budge. I was at my wit's end. The old saying is true: The eunuchs are anxious while the emperor is carefree. Attempting to calm my nerves, I told myself that Old Tang was an experienced soldier with a good understanding of the deputy squad leader and the rest of the men he'd sent. If he said there was no problem, then there wasn't any problem. Anyway, we hadn't heard the sound of gunfire. Perhaps they'd made some huge discovery and couldn't come back immediately. That was possible. I wandered back to the fire and lay down. Looking up at the disorder of wires and ropes hanging from the ceiling, I considered our situation. The shadows of the cables trembled ceaselessly in the firelight. In a moment I had fallen asleep. I slept for six hours. When I awoke the deputy squad leader still hadn't returned. Old Tang was now gone as well. The only people left were Pei Qing, Ma Zaihai, Wang Sichuan, and a few corpsmen I didn't know. Only Ma Zaihai and the corpsmen were awake.

Where was everyone? I asked Ma Zaihai. He said Old Tang had eventually decided to take a group of men and go after the deputy squad leader. Two hours had passed since then, and there had been no sound of movement. Ma Zaihai also wanted to see what the matter was. He'd just been considering what to do.

Is this warehouse swallowing people or what? I thought to myself. My heart began to thump. After shaking Wang Sichuan awake, I told him and Ma Zaihai to collect their things. There was something we had to do. Wang Sichuan was still dazed when he awoke, but he quickly understood what was happening. Puffing on a cigarette, he said he feared things had already gone to hell. Old

Tang was always so capable. If there'd been some delay, he definitely would have sent someone back. It's certain that something has gone wrong, he said.

"That's all obvious," I replied. "The real question is, what do we do now?"

Wang Sichuan scratched his head. "Why not go look for them?" he said. "Or we could just sit here and wait, but that's a pretty passive way of doing things."

I didn't hesitate for an instant. Pei Qing was sleeping some distance away, and there were three corpsmen left in camp. Ma Zaihai was clever and could handle himself, so I told him to follow us. The three of us switched on our flashlights and headed deeper into the warehouse.

I never would have expected the warehouse to be so big. I'd thought that behind the darkness were walls, but I soon came to appreciate the size of the base of the dam and the huge number of things it contained. Holding the iron ice breaker, Wang Sichuan knocked it against the supply piles we passed in hopes the sound would draw the others' attention. Soon we could no longer see the firelight behind us. The temperature dropped precipitously. Ice crystals had formed across the floor, making it perilously slick. We could see signs on the ground that others had come through here. Then, after turning several corners, we gasped. In front of us was a great concrete wall, some indecipherable slogan painted across it. We'd reached the end.

CHAPTER 47

The End of the Warehouse

Whatever message the slogan was trying to convey was lost on me—probably it was "Safety in Production" or something along those lines. I couldn't believe the warehouse had actually come to an end. It wasn't as big as I'd imagined. More importantly, if the warehouse really did end right here, then where had Old Cat and the rest of them disappeared to? There was nowhere else to go. It wouldn't take ten hours to search something like this. The concrete wall was quite long. We walked along it till we hit another wall. Still there was nothing to find, nor were there traces of any activity. The others seemed to have disappeared.

Ma Zaihai began to worry, but as usual Wang Sichuan refused to give up. He walked back along the wall, saying, "Impossible. These people are alive. They haven't conjured themselves away or vanished into thin air."

I was sure that something fishy was going on. Then I spied the tarp-covered piles of goods. Could there be another exit hidden beneath one of these? I wondered. I walked back the way we'd come, looking for any materials that appeared to have been disturbed. Sure enough, a net fixed atop a length of supplies had been pulled apart and the rivets holding down the sheets of tarpaulin underneath loosened. We began turning over the tarps one after another, when suddenly Ma Zaihai cried out. Built into the concrete floor beneath one of them was an iron double door, similar to the one we'd seen back in the cave, though much smaller. This door was not welded down. On it was printed some strange symbol, the color already faded.

Wang Sichuan wanted to open it up, but Ma Zaihai blocked his way. "Engineer Wang, Engineer Wu," he said, "I should go first. That symbol means high voltage. The whole level is probably filled with power cables. I'd guess the wires for the entire place run through it." He had us back up and wrapped his hands in the tarp. The door was almost two feet thick. After lifting one of the doors halfway, he nearly collapsed. The two of us hurriedly helped him push the door until it rested on the concrete floor. Opening half the double door made an opening wide enough for us to enter. We jumped down to the platform below and shined our flashlights inside. The ground was covered in power cables, each with the circumference of a rice bowl. The temperature was extremely low, the cables all encased in a thick shell of ice. A ladder led down. We could see someone had already knocked the ice from its sides.

"They really went down there," said Ma Zaihai, his eyes wide.

"Where does this place connect to?" I asked.

"A recess like this connects anywhere that needs electricity," said Ma Zaihai. "It makes maintenance much more convenient. These recesses are generally only found in permanent fortifications where they can be hidden in the base's structure. If you set one up in some temporary base on the front and someone throws a grenade down the tunnel, there goes all the power. This doesn't look temporary at all and they obviously took measures to conceal it. When the devils built this dam, they clearly assumed it would be in use for more than twenty years."

I nodded. The Japanese had never expected the Soviets to be so fierce. Even less could they have anticipated the atomic bomb. Without these two factors the war would have continued for another ten years.

So this was where Old Cat and the others had gone. Wang Sichuan called down several times, but there was only an echo. "What if, down there amid all those power cables, they got lost?" I asked.

"It's hard to say for sure," said Ma Zaihai, "but the structure down there shouldn't be too complex, and the path should be marked fairly clearly."

"Then let's go take a look," said Wang Sichuan as he stepped down onto the ladder.

One after another we climbed down. To avoid getting lost, we smashed the ice along the wall with our hammers. The going was rough. The ceiling was tall enough that we didn't have to worry about knocking our heads, but the floor was strewn with power cables, each of them dangerously slick. Worst of all was the cold. This place clearly connected to the icehouse. The temperature had dropped below any bearable limit, and from somewhere an exhaust fan blew cold air at us. Shivering uncontrollably, we wrapped our overcoats tightly around ourselves. The wind rushed straight down my collar and into every opening in my clothing.

"Just what exactly is that icehouse for?" asked Wang Sichuan. "And how come this windy tunnel seems just like a cooling duct?"

"That's probably what it is," said Ma Zaihai, but he was only a private. These were matters for specialists. His job was to take things apart and put them back together.

"What kind of thing needs such a fucking cold cooling device?" said Wang Sichuan, speaking his thoughts aloud. A muffled bang suddenly rang out behind us, as if the iron door had been dropped back into place.

Wang Sichuan and I glanced at one another. Shit, I said to myself. I turned and ran like mad back the way we had come. I scrambled wildly up the ladder and climbed onto the platform where we'd first dropped in. Sure enough, the door overhead was shut. Wang Sichuan pushed with all his might, but the door wouldn't budge. He looked at me, his face furious and panic-stricken, then swore violently. Whoever was outside had not only shut the door, he'd locked it as well. I was dumbfounded. The spy! He existed and was trying to get us!

I could have slapped myself. How the hell had I been so careless? If Old Cat and the rest had come this way, then why was the iron door still hidden beneath the tarpaulin? Because someone else hadn't wanted us to discover it! Everyone can get muddle-headed sometimes, but I've always felt myself to be a generally bright individual. Ma Zaihai had already lifted the tarp from the door when I first saw it, but how could I have failed to consider what it meant? There was far too much on my mind at the time.

Wang Sichuan grabbed the gun and made to fire it upward. At once Ma Zaihai and I snatched it back from him. This iron door was two feet thick and probably lined with some blastproof material that not even a grenade would penetrate, much less a gun. The bullet would just bounce off it and slice right through us.

Again we tried to force it upward. We cried out. I understood at last what had befallen Old Cat and the others. We were being plotted against. The door being blastproof meant it was basically soundproof as well. We could ruin our larynxes and still no one would hear. Unwilling to give up, Wang Sichuan twice bashed his shoulder into the door, very nearly wrenching his waist. The door was too heavy. Smashing against it wasn't going to do the least bit of damage to the bolt.

Wang Sichuan let fly with a string of Mongolian curses. A burst of cold wind blew through, causing my teeth to chatter. If we didn't find a way out of here quick, we'd freeze to death. Old Cat and the others had been trapped for at least ten hours. Who knew if they'd ever managed to find a way out? Another burst of wind came blowing through, so fierce it took my breath away. Having no choice, the three of us set out with our backs to the wind, Wang Sichuan calling out for Old Cat and Old Tang.

In today's cities these electrical canals are everywhere, often filled with stagnant water and fiber-optic telecommunications cables as well as electricity. At each intersection in the tunnel, there's a manhole leading up to the surface. For a while we encountered no such intersection. As we walked, we pondered whether we'd gone the wrong way. Should we turn around and face into the wind? Perhaps it would lead to the icehouse. But unlike inside that giant freezer, at least here the temperature was endurable. The farther we went in that direction, the more the temperature would drop and the wind increase. Something bad was sure to happen, and not one of us was willing to find out what. Avoiding cold and seeking warmth are bodily instincts, impossible to defy. Now that I think about it, people were in excellent physical shape back then. Despite the harshness of that environment, even someone like me was able to carry on.

After walking through that icy channel for about half an hour, we came upon the first intersection. A shaft led upward. Wang Sichuan pushed several times on the iron door overhead. It didn't move an inch. It too was locked.

"For fear that the enemy will take advantage of these tunnels," said Ma Zaihai, "regulations generally stipulate that all openings be locked up."

Wang Sichuan cursed. "And if they're all locked, then what?"

I patted him on the back. "Relax, there's always a way out."

But in my heart I was unsure. Choosing a direction, we smashed several marks in the ice and continued on. I prayed, whether to Buddha or Tengri it didn't matter, to bless us and ensure our Japanese adversary had forgotten to lock just one or even half of an iron door.

The tunnels were hardly complex, but they were very long. It seemed as if all the wires for the entire dam ran through here. It took at least half an hour between each intersection. After three hours we'd found only four doors, each locked more securely than the last. The path ahead was pitch-black. Our eyebrows were covered in a layer of ice. Crystals had spread throughout our hair. Our hands and feet had gone numb. We were in a whole lot deeper than we'd imagined. That's not idle talk. Wang Sichuan's iron club had frozen to his hand without his noticing. As he switched it to his left hand, he tore off a layer of skin. Old Cat and the rest had surely found themselves in a predicament just like this. I hoped they'd already found a way out. If they hadn't, then things didn't look good for us. We were running out of options. All we could do was keep going.

Then, after we'd walked for a few more hours, a number of circular holes appeared in the concrete wall, each half as tall as a man. Not one of the power cables passed through them.

"Air vents," said Ma Zaihai. We looked inside. There was light at the end.

CHAPTER 48

The Outer Edge

T he light was very dim, probably emanating from one of
the emergency lights we'd seen earlier. Who knew what
was on the other side? But this was our last and only hope.
Even if it ran through a tiger's den or a dragon's lair, so long
as it led out of here, we'd have to charge ahead. There was no
need to deliberate over which tunnel to take. The three openings
clearly led to the same place. We wriggled into the middle one
and crawled thirty or forty feet to the end. A frozen iron grate was
fastened over the opening. Ice covered the space between the bars
and a faint light shined through, but it was impossible to make
out what was on the other side. Ma Zaihai removed the bullets
from his rifle, then smashed the butt of it against the four corners
of the grate. The space was extremely cramped. He couldn't use
much force. After working at it for some time, the grate finally
opened and a powerful wind rushed in, stealing the breath from
my lungs. I ducked my head at once and gasped for air. Covering
my mouth with my overcoat, I looked out. It was utter blackness.
Nothing was out there.

The three of us looked at each other. Beyond this tunnel wasn't
some room, it was the endless abyss. Looking out, we saw a stretch

of nothingness. There was only the crazed wind pouring dizzyingly into the tunnel. The mist really had dispersed. Even our flashlight beams picked up nothing. Ma Zaihai yelled that he was going to stick his head out to look. We grabbed the hem of his coat. A gust of wind came from behind us as soon as his shoulders were outside, ballooning his clothes. He floated outward as if he were being pulled. His face turned pale with fright, but we held fast and he didn't fall. "Quickly now," said Wang Sichuan. "Take a look around and see what's out there."

He lay flat and shimmied his torso out. He shined his flashlight all about. Then we pulled him back in. "This is the bottom of the dam," he said. "There's a cliff about thirty feet below us. Beside the opening is a ladder leading down to it."

"Is there any sign of Old Cat and the others?" I asked him.

"How am I supposed to make them out?" he replied. He could see the searchlight up above, but it was far away. This really was the very bottom of the dam, with only crisscrossing layers of cement and rock all around. The flashlight beam stretched only a short distance and nothing could be seen clearly.

"Does the ladder go up as well?" asked Wang Sichuan.

"It's a little unreliable," he replied. "The wind is too great, stronger even than it was atop the dam, and the ladder is already decayed. If we were to climb halfway up and it snapped, well...I don't think I need to say what would happen."

I felt this was a risk we could take. It was just too cold in here. Even the fierce wind rushing in from outside felt comparatively warm. If we continued to search the electrical canal, we wouldn't be able to last much longer. Here at least we had a slim chance of survival. The bars on the ladder were thick as a thumb and very sturdy. What happened earlier with the deputy squad leader was likely a freak accident. As long as we took care while climbing up, we should be fine. The three of us talked it over. "Let's not decide yet," said Wang Sichuan. "We'll check it out and if it's not all right, we'll just head back."

With that, Ma Zaihai rubbed his hands, reached one arm out, grabbed on to the ladder, and swung over to it, his coat flying open in the wind. Trying as best he could to stick close to the wall, he yelled out to us, but even from such a short distance we couldn't make out what he was saying. He could only signal that it was all right. Then he climbed up.

I was next. I felt a stab of terror the moment I leaned out. It was like leaning into outer space. There was nothing beyond. Below me was the abyss. If I fell, who knew if I'd ever hit bottom? All I could feel was the gale-force wind. Grabbing tightly to the ladder, I swung over. For an instant I began to fly, but I adapted, adjusted my movements, and stuck myself to the wall of the dam. I climbed up enough for Wang Sichuan to come out. Shining my flashlight down, I watched him climb on. He was much heavier than us and therefore much more stable.

With a solid grip on the ladder, I began to observe my surroundings. Before me was the dam. My flashlight beam illuminated a long, narrow strip of its concrete wall. Only a section of it was visible, the more distant areas merging gradually into the blackness. Its surface was extremely rough and covered in a layer of some dark substance, similar in color to the mist. The substance was on the ladder as well. I looked at my hands. They were coated in a thin layer of the stuff, like liquid but also like dust. I immediately wiped them on my coat and covered them with my sleeves for protection. The devil only knows if this stuff's poisonous, I thought.

As for the space behind me, what was there to say? Nothing was out there. I felt like we were holding on to the very edge of the world. I began to regret my decision. Who knew how far we'd have to climb? It was impossible to say. Even now my heart clenches as I think back on it. As I shined my flashlight about, I saw this wasn't the only ladder. More appeared in the distance, a number of them in fact, each spaced a long ways apart. Between them jutted parallel rows of steel bars like the ones that had saved me earlier, each curved into a hook one could hold on to. They had evidently been placed to allow workers to travel from one ladder to another, stepping on the bars below, grabbing on to those above. They must have been used during construction and maintenance. Then something occurred to me: Here, at the bottom of the dam, what was there for them to inspect or repair?

Having seen Wang Sichuan firmly on the ladder, Ma Zaihai put his flashlight between his teeth and began to climb. The two of us followed his lead. It was impossible to think amid the blasts of wind. Just to breathe required all of my focus. I had no concept of how many rungs I climbed or how far we'd come. In a situation like that, you're neither calm nor agitated. Your state of mind becomes very unusual. As I looked back at the interminable blackness behind me, I realized this was probably the feeling of awakening. My body and soul seemed to comprehend some message, one that had arrived from somewhere miraculous. Had I continued to feel this way, I doubtlessly would have been converted straightaway to Buddhism or some other religion, but this mood was cut short by Ma Zaihai's boots.

I looked up. He had stopped, and my head had smacked right into his boots. I looked around. At once I saw it: Off to the right, about sixty feet from us, was some colossal thing of concrete and steel bars, like a great, spiny hedgehog perched on the wall. Its massive round body was made of concrete, and the bars were its spines. The whole thing was enormous, roughly the size of a three-story house. From this distance it appeared to be nothing less than some monstrous creature.

Ma Zaihai gazed at it for a moment. Then, climbing onto one of the steel bars next to us, he began making his way across. My principle has always been "Don't look for trouble." The moment I saw him step out I felt anxious. I climbed a little higher and yelled over, "What are you doing?"

He turned around, the sound of his voice drifting in and out as he called back. "That's the antenna!"

"Why are you worrying about that now?" I shouted. "Our first priority is getting out of here!"

Some idea seemed to have taken hold of him. "Wait right there," he told me. "I'm going to check it out."

Wang Sichuan tapped me on the leg from below. He asked what was going on. I didn't know. This private was too capricious, too undisciplined, but the more I thought about it, the more I felt bewitched into following him across. I climbed onto the steel path. The wind was much more powerful as I made my way along the wall. Even keeping upright was a struggle. I was still only halfway across when, forcing my head up, I watched Ma Zaihai prepare to step over the final gap. Suddenly a great gust of wind rushed forth, pressing me against the side of the dam. I closed my eyes and held on tight. When I opened them, Ma Zaihai was gone.

My heart skipped a beat. Had he fallen? In a flash I saw him. He was hanging on to a steel bar some twenty feet down the face of that convex structure. He must have lost his grip when the wind came blasting through. I signaled down to him, asking if he was hurt, but he had no free hand to respond with. Kicking against the wall, he tried with all his might to pull himself up, but he seemed to be injured. After climbing for only a moment, he could exert himself no more and hung back down.

Not wasting a moment, I climbed toward the antenna and yelled for him to hold on. As I reached the final gap, I realized why he'd fallen. From here, the distance to one of the steel spines was considerable. My fingertips only brushed the bar. I brought my arm back and adjusted my position. I needed to swing over. I cursed the Japs for their corner cutting. A distance like this, and still they wouldn't place just one more bar?

Wang Sichuan was right behind me, his nerves as frayed as mine. Leaning back, I took a deep breath and swung out. In an instant the bar was in my right hand and my left was behind me, still hanging in midair. The rush of it covered my body in a cold sweat. Had there been another burst of wind just now, I would have been a goner. I lifted my feet up onto a nearby steel bar, stabilized myself, and climbed down. I leaned over and grabbed hold of Ma Zaihai. "You goddamn idiot," I yelled at him, "what the hell were you thinking, climbing over here?"

Holding my hand, he used all his strength to pull himself back up. He turned to me, panting. "The antenna. The antenna is here."

I looked at the steel bars all around us. As a matter of fact, they were different from the ones that had led us over here. Not only were they thinner, they were without a trace of rust. I was rather startled. This thing was so big and its steel forks so numerous, its reception strength had to be immense. But by no means was that why he'd climbed across.

I continued to scold him. "So it's an antenna. That's still no reason for you to take such a risk."

He laughed at me and scratched his head. I assumed he was embarrassed, but he reached behind him and brought his rifle around. He pulled back the bolt and leveled it at me. "I'm sorry, Engineer Wu," he said, "but I'm going to have to inconvenience you for a moment."

CHAPTER 49

Control Room

We'd all been through boot camp. We'd all been told countless times before target practice never to point our guns at anyone else. How many stories had we heard of someone dying when a weapon accidentally went off? Even an empty gun could eject a firing pin fast enough to kill a man. So I found looking into the black hole of the gun muzzle stupendously irritating. At once I brought my hand up, yelling, "What are you doing? Put the weapon down. You want it to go off and kill me?"

He didn't seem concerned in the slightest. "It's fine," he said. "I unloaded all the bullets and the safety is on." He handed it to me.

I grabbed the rifle and looked it over. The bullet magazine really was gone. I was amazed. When had he taken it out? Then I remembered that he'd taken all the bullets out before he knocked out the iron grate with the butt of the rifle. "You need my help for what?" I asked him. "What is it you really want to do? Did you stop caring about your life when you saw the antenna? This thing isn't going to lead us out of here."

He undid his Sam Browne belt and tied one end to the rifle strap. "Company Commander Tang said the whole reason they came down here was to find this antenna. If they took the same route we did, then they too would have come across it and would surely have climbed over to check it out. If they went a different way, I still want to take a quick look at it. Then, once we find them, we can all leave straightaway and won't have to come back down here.

"And you should let me go," he continued, "because I'm an engineering corpsman. Although you two are, of course, much more learned than I, there are nonetheless some details that only I will understand. Let me take a look at the antenna. I might be able to figure out where Company Commander Tang is right now."

He said this so sincerely, so solemnly, that I couldn't help but trust him. Wang Sichuan jumped over, landing just beside me. "What's going on?" he asked. "Looking for trouble again, are you? What's this place got to do with anything?"

By the time I explained it, Ma Zaihai had already tied the other end of the Sam Browne belt to the belt around his waist. Then, having me hold tight to his gun, he began to climb down toward the underside of the antenna's bowl-like concrete base. The nearer he climbed to the bottom half of the bowl, the steeper it began to slope toward the wall. Footholds became increasingly few, until at last he could do no more than hang on with his arms as the lower half of his body dangled helplessly in midair. Fortunately Ma Zaihai was both strong and agile. There were only a few places where I had to steady the gun in my arms and help him swing across. Soon enough he'd disappeared from view. A few moments later, he yelled back. Then the sound of some object striking the antenna rang out. After several more such knocks, he called out to us to climb down after him. I pulled on the line. He seemed to have fixed the other end to something, so I wedged the gun into a section of the antenna and began climbing down the attached lengths of rifle strap and Sam Browne belt. Wang Sichuan followed closely behind.

After descending about thirty feet, I saw a damp hole in the rock, so water-washed it appeared covered in wax. I had no time to take a closer look, for just then, at the spot where the base of the round antenna met the wall of the dam, I noticed a square window, about three feet high and wide. Power cables ran down the concrete bowl and into this opening. It was around one of these cables that the Sam Browne belt was tied. Ma Zaihai was kneeling inside the small window. "Behind here is the telegraph room," he said.

"I thought the telegraph room was in the cavern Old Tang found," said Wang Sichuan.

"I saw the transmitter he brought back," said Ma Zaihai. "It was too small, definitely not the transmitter of a primary telegraph room. And no way would the main transmitter and the antenna have been placed so far apart. If they were attacked, the cables might be cut, so the primary telegraph room would be near the antenna. Underground bunkers are designed with the main transmitter in the primary telegraph room. All others are merely small-scale transmitters built into temporary command posts. If the dam were overrun, right here would be the hardest place to cut off from the antenna."

"You son of a gun, how come you didn't say this before?" asked Wang Sichuan.

"To tell you the truth, when Company Commander Tang said we should find the antenna, I figured what he really wanted was to find this primary telegraph room. He's much more experienced than I, so I didn't think it my place to say anything." Ma Zaihai scooted deeper into the tunnel, giving me space to climb in.

"We've already located a telegraph room," I said, "and verified that telegrams were sent from the transmitter there, so what's the point of finding this place?"

"While I can't guarantee it," he said, "ordinarily the main telegraph room is also the general headquarters. There's probably going to be something important back here."

By now I had already squeezed myself into the small window. Actually, the window wasn't as small as it looked, it's just that there were so many power cables. They stretched chaotically down the long and narrow space, taking up most of the room. Twisted together and each as thick as a wrist, they resembled the tentacles of some monstrous beast. From outside Wang Sichuan shouted for us to be careful not to get shocked.

After crawling about twenty feet, we reached the tunnel's end. The power cables ran through a hole cut into the wall, which had then been tightly resealed. "This is the external maintenance passage," said Ma Zaihai. "The internal maintenance passage is beyond. That they sealed off the tunnel suggests that something is wrong with the air outside."

"This isn't engineering class," I groaned. "Doesn't the wall just mean we're stuck out here?"

Ma Zaihai didn't reply. Grabbing his water canteen, he began striking it against the wall. A moment later a crack had opened up. "So that maintenance is convenient, this sort of separation wall is generally made of lime," he said. "It might look sturdy, but you could break it open with your fingernails. At most, there will be a layer of iron netting inside, but we can just cut through it." As he said this he struck the wall once more and a wide gap opened up. "No netting even," he said. "I guess there are not any mice in this fortification."

We spent the next ten-plus minutes making the hole big enough to fit through, then we continued on. Following the same pattern as before, we broke through two more isolation walls. Between them was an air-dispersal ventilation shaft, used to prevent the buildup of poisonous gas. It was just like the one we'd seen in the caisson and thus far too narrow for a person to enter. At last we reached the end of the cables. Each connected to an electrical box, emerging from the other end as thin wires that ran through the panels below us and down into the room underneath. Ma Zaihai pointed at one of the panels. Grabbing hold of the cables threading into it, he wedged his legs against the wall across from him and pulled with all his might until the panel burst open.

The space below was pitch-black. Sweeping my flashlight about, I saw we were in the ceiling of some room. Chairs surrounded several tables stacked with papers. Ma Zaihai jumped down and scanned the room with his flashlight but found nothing of note. Wang Sichuan and I jumped down as well and looked around. This room was different from any we had seen so far. The space was square and about the size of a basketball court. Equipment was arranged all around us. I saw a row of great iron boxes, each of them taller than a person and covered in a multicolored array of indicator lights and electrical switches. Huge and heavy, they'd been placed one after another along the room's four walls. Numerous rust spots had formed across their outer sheeting, but compared to the other machinery we'd seen, much of it so rusted as to be dropping whole flakes of the stuff, the damage here was minor. These iron boxes had clearly gone through some rust-prevention process. A great sheet of iron hung from one of the walls. Upon this were engraved lines of every color, forming a sectional map of the entire dam, albeit a simple one. Numerous indicator lights were fixed along the lines. The iron box that stood beneath it was covered with far more buttons than any of the others. It was some kind of console. Four long writing desks were lined up in the center of the room. Telephones and numerous piles of documents were neatly arranged atop them. Everything was covered in a thick layer of dust. The reason this room felt so different was all the precision instruments. Up till now we'd seen only huge machinery and crude concrete structures. We'd been in refrigerated storage, a warehouse, and an electrical canal. Here, at last, was a place fit for technical personnel.

"What's all this used for?" I asked Ma Zaihai. One by one he explained the purpose of each piece. Everything was in Japanese, so he couldn't be exactly sure what controlled what, but he knew their general uses. He said the large iron boxlike instruments must control the dam's equipment. There were mechanisms for inspecting and regulating the dam's pressure and water level, electrical circuits that operated the large sluice gates, and controls for all the generators. The sectional blueprint had to be a map of the pipelines running through the dam's interior. The lighted diodes indicated whether the pipelines were currently open or shut. This, he said, was definitely the dam's control room—or at the very least, one of the dam's control rooms.

We didn't see the transmitter we'd been anticipating, nor did we see any door that might lead to one. The room appeared to be sealed off. Shining his flashlight upward, Ma Zaihai observed the progression of the electrical wires. He tracked them along the ceiling, down the wall, and onto the floor. At last he pointed at four iron plates. They were locked with bolts thick as doorknobs. Undoing the locks, he pulled the iron plates open. A trapdoor. A ladder hung down into the darkness. There was another room below.

"A hidden trapdoor," said Ma Zaihai. "Even if this place was captured, it would still be a long time before this control room was found. Japanese military structures were all built this way."

At first glance there seemed nothing worrisome about the room below. Still I remembered with concern other times, other rooms. I steeled myself and was about to descend when Wang Sichuan grabbed hold of me.

"Wait a second," he said. "I just thought of something."

"What is it?" I asked.

He pointed at the dam's sectional map. "There are two extra-large indicator lights sticking up on both sides of the dam. Don't you think they represent the caissons?"

Ma Zaihai looked where he was pointing. The two lights were bigger than all the others, their colors different. He took a breath and nodded. "Yeah, I think they are."

"Then doesn't that mean their operational controls should be right here?"

I gave a start. I knew what he was thinking. Wang Sichuan walked over to the control box and shined his flashlight along the densely packed buttons. Beneath each button was a label, written in Japanese, but he wasn't trying to read the buttons. He leaned in closer, then beckoned me over. Dust had been rubbed from a few of the buttons. The machine had been used only recently.

"Interesting," said Wang Sichuan. "Perhaps there really is a Japanese soldier here."

Who'd started up those caissons after we entered and dropped us to the bottom of the dam? I didn't believe it was some "left behind" Japanese soldier. The whole way in, we hadn't seen a single sign of life. And this place was covered in dust. Clearly this room didn't see a lot of activity. I looked at the floor. There'd probably been footprints here, but now that we'd walked all around the room, they were no longer distinguishable.

"So then who was it?" Wang Sichuan asked. "The spy must have been here before us. Could it be the final woman from the first team, the one we haven't found yet?"

"For now we can only assume it was her," I said. "I really can't think of any other possibility."

"No," said Ma Zaihai, "it had to be someone who knew the layout of the dam. To get in here from the outside, we had to smash through the isolation walls. The only other way in would be through the trapdoor. It's pretty unlikely that someone here for their first time would just happen upon a place this concealed by luck. He or she had to already know the layout of the dam."

He was right. And after making it here, she realized immediately that the apparatus beneath the sectional map was the control box. She wiped the dust and read the labels until she found the switch controlling the caissons. She knew what she was looking for and so left the other machines untouched. "Regardless of who it is specifically," I said, "there's definitely something strange going on. Maybe it really is a Japanese spy. It was probably this person who murdered the young soldier in the warehouse. The ruination of the first team and their ultimate failure to complete the mission was also likely the work of this agent."

The two of them nodded.

"We don't know where this woman is," said Wang Sichuan, "but maybe she's still nearby. We might be about to run into her."

"Should we head back and grab the rifle so we can defend ourselves?" I asked.

"We still don't know for certain that we can get out through the lower room," said Ma Zaihai. "If we can't, then we'll have to come back the way we came. If we take down the gun, it'll be very difficult to climb out of here."

"Then we'd better be extra careful," said Wang Sichuan.

Ma Zaihai was the first down the ladder. After he reached the bottom and confirmed no one was there, the two of us climbed down. This room was nearly twice the size of the one above it. Six transmitters were arrayed along the wall nearest the dam's exterior. Stacks of telegrams were strewn messily atop them. Ironwork desks piled with dust-covered documents took up the rest of the space. This has to be the dam's command center, I thought. A huge blueprint of the underground base hung on one wall, identical to the one Old Tang had found but much larger. Wang Sichuan spied a microphone sitting atop one of the long tables against the wall. "This has to be where they read the emperor's letter of surrender before they withdrew," he said. He tried to convince Ma Zaihai to switch on the mike, but after he'd fussed with it for some time, the power light remained off. It appeared completely ruined.

I told them to stop walking around. I scanned the room with my flashlight. Sure enough, there were two sets of footprints heading in two directions: one to an ironwork double door, the other to a dark green wooden door. The ironwork doors were clearly blastproof, probably with some corridor beyond. What was behind the wooden one? A bathroom? We walked over and opened the green door. It was an office.

Dust filled the room. The furnishings and decor were very simple, though traces from where decorations had hung could be seen on the walls. Japanese swords, most likely. A dust-covered military uniform of some unknown rank hung in the corner. All over the room was evidence of dust disturbed. We followed a trail of handprints but found only a large stack of documents. We didn't speak Japanese, nor were we historians, so the papers were useless, but apparently somebody was very interested in something they thought was in this room, though they didn't seem to know exactly where it was.

We left the room and followed the other trail, toward the iron double doors. It was as I'd expected. After pushing them open, we were greeted by a long, pitch-black hallway. I shined my flashlight down it. Some footprints ran down the corridor, others into the room behind us. There had to be an exit ahead. We took off without a second thought, following the footprints into the darkness. Before long the corridor branched in three directions. The footprints ran down each one. Unable to determine which was the right path, we had no choice but to investigate them one by one. Our first selection ended in a power distribution room. Switches filled every inch of it.

"Why not try and flip a few?" said Wang Sichuan.

"Absolutely not," I said. "If they turn off some important mechanism, the compression engines in the icehouse for example, then the devil only knows what the consequences will be."

We returned to the fork and took the second corridor. We were soon standing before an iron door, triple-proofed, just like the others, and terribly thick. In a battle, every space in here would become a very-difficult-to-capture bunker. The big guy pushed the door open. Inside was a great hall. We swept our flashlight beams across the room.

I'm taking such pains to relate our search for the right path because it really was so critical. Later, while giving a summary of the incident, we felt some residual "fear after the fact." Had we not checked all the corridors, had we found the exit on the first try, then the true, hidden face of this sprawling underground bunker would have remained forever concealed. So often one's choice can change so much.

Past the door we saw a strange room. It looked so familiar, as if I'd seen it only recently. We walked inside. On the wall directly across from us hung a square curtain, fifteen feet in both length and width. Numerous low seats filled the room, and at its rear rested some strange apparatus. I walked straight over to the front of the machine. It was a miniature film projector. I hadn't known film projectors this small existed until I watched the Zero Film back on the surface. Could this be the underground base's movie theater? Was this where their superiors strengthened the soldiers' brainwashing and savagery? Looking back at it now, it was probably where the Japanese soldiers came to relax and have fun. In those days, though, our concept of the Japanese didn't allow for them taking part in recreational activities.

I was extremely curious about the little projector. Taking a closer look, I discovered it had been wiped clean of dust. Whoever was here before us must have been interested in it as well. I checked it all over. Sprouting from the back was a very familiar-looking shape. It was a circle with a spool in the middle, like you could hang something off it. This was uncanny. This feeling of familiarity was different from the sense of having seen this room before. It was a kind of anxiety, as if there were two electrically charged pieces in my mind about to touch and they were sending sparks back and forth. I needed to remember where I'd seen the thing. It was terribly crucial. I could feel it.

I called Wang Sichuan over and he motioned to Ma Zaihai. The three of us put our heads together. It came to Ma Zaihai at once. "The iron case! The shell-like iron case the female corpse was carrying. Maybe it attaches onto the projector."

No way, I thought. The iron case had looked like a snail shell. That case could be attached onto some component of the projector? Suddenly I realized what was wrong. The case wasn't a part of the projector. No, by God, but within that iron case was none other than a roll of film!

CHAPTER 50

The Film Canister

T he three of us looked at one another, unsure what to make of our discovery. I sat down and forced myself to think things over. Now that we understood what the iron case was, a number of clues began to fit together. We knew how it all started: the only reason the Japanese established this base and transported the bomber down here was the void. How they'd discovered the place, we didn't know. Perhaps while prospecting for oil or coal deposits they'd simply happened upon it. The original motive was unimportant. For in any case, upon finding the abyss, they'd obviously become consumed with the desire to know what was hidden in the outer-space-like darkness beneath this mountain.

They then used the Shinzan bomber to explore the abyss. Naturally, they would never have relied on the naked eye for the results of this survey, so aerial recording equipment must have been affixed to the Shinzan. For some reason the base was suddenly abandoned after the plane took off. Lacking guided navigation, the Shinzan crashed into the underground river. Buffer bags stuffed with Chinese corpses had been sunk along the watery runway, so the plane was not completely destroyed. While others might have sustained injuries, there was only a single fatality—the twisted corpse of the pilot we discovered in the wreckage.

We had discovered the film canister on the body of a corpse encased in ice, so were those frozen corpses the missing members of the flight team? They survived the crash and grabbed the film, but then why had they frozen to death in the icehouse? Had they discovered something that made them, instead of leaving, go to the lowest level of the dam and pile warheads all around the radar device? And then there'd been an accident and they'd gotten stuck there? The arrangement of the radar and the warheads really did look like Wang Sichuan had said, like a lure and a trap, but why do all this? Was it because of something they'd seen in the abyss? Or rather, had they believed that, because of the Shinzan, something was actually being drawn back from the abyss?

The next part was simple: After the members of the flight team had been dead and frozen for twenty or so years, the first prospecting team discovered this void. We didn't know what happened to the first team. Supposing their ruin had been the work of an enemy agent, this person must have come from Japan, known everything that was down here, and that the Chinese had discovered this place. This person then infiltrated the first team, killed some of its members, and sabotaged the mission.

Based on the marks we'd found, the spy was searching for something, most likely the film canister. The spy was unaware that the canister had actually been frozen beneath the ice, so, when we arrived a month later, "he" still hadn't found it. To buy himself some time, he'd dropped us down to the icehouse, hoping we'd freeze to death. What he didn't realize was that someone from the first team had survived long enough to use the automatic transmitter, causing Old Tang and the rest to discover a structural plan of the base and thereby locate the icehouse. Later this person tried to bury me alive and locked us in the electrical canal.

"If this really is the case," said Wang Sichuan, "then whatever the spy's really after, he's pretty damn clever. He's had us in the palm of his hand this whole time. But since the person missing from the first prospecting team is a woman, why did you think your attacker was a man?"

I bit my lower lip in thought. "There are two possibilities," I said. "The first is that I was mistaken. The second is that the woman from the first team was actually a man in disguise. The Japanese aren't that big, so it isn't impossible. Actually there's one more. He could have been mixed in with our team when we came in." I remembered the two notes I'd been given.

"How about you?" I asked Wang Sichuan. "Who do you think it is?"

He shook his head. All of the engineering corpsmen were new faces. Honestly, it could be anyone. "If I had to guess," he said, "then it would either be Chen Luohu or Pei Qing. Those two are the most suspicious. But I'd say it's Pei Qing."

Wang Sichuan was biased in this respect, but by now I had some doubts about Pei Qing as well. Still, I didn't want to say them aloud.

For a moment we were silent. Then Ma Zaihai asked, "So what do we do now? The enemy is unknown and we're still out in the open."

"I've never done counterespionage work before," I said, "but since we three were all trapped together, it's obvious that each of us is innocent. If we keep circling around the issue like this—with the enemy hidden and attacking us at every step—we're dead meat. Since we already know he's after the film, we'd better grab it first and get out of here. Once we're back on the surface, we can let our superiors decide the next step." This suggestion was not only in our own best interest, but in the best interest of the military and even the nation as well. We agreed at once.

"But if it really is as we suspect," said Wang Sichuan, "then with so few people left in the warehouse, that son of a bitch has probably already got the film."

"That's possible," I said, "but we have to get back and see." Besides, it was certain that Old Tang and the others were also trying to find their way back there. We had a duty to leave them a message regarding our whereabouts and what we'd learned about the spy. Otherwise they'd probably keep looking for us, sending out teams in all directions. Any deaths that resulted would fall on our shoulders. It made the most sense for one of us to stay behind and wait for Old Tang while the other two grabbed the film and headed for the surface. Who would stay and who would go was a delicate question. For the time being, I decided not to raise it.

The warehouse was our first stop. We had to get there before the spy. For two full hours we passed through the core region of the dam—the workers' dormitory, cafeteria, and armory, as well as countless control rooms, small-scale workrooms, and bathrooms— winding our way around innumerable corners until, at last, we came upon a staircase. It was an emergency stairwell, extremely narrow and cramped, probably used for evacuation when the caissons weren't working. After walking up twenty levels, we could hear the sound of wind. We walked another ten and pushed open a thin iron door. We were back atop the dam.

A strong wind rushed into my nose and mouth. The solitary searchlight was still there, the nothingness beyond quiet and profound. After all we'd experienced, it felt strange to see it again. On the other side, the river had already dropped to its lowest point. Everything that had been submerged beneath the floodwater was revealed. We saw a pile of corpse bags the size of a small hill, the giant Shinzan broken between them. The trail it had cut as it crashed down was distinctly visible. Many structures had emerged and a number of lights could be seen shining in the dark. In powering up the searchlight, Ma Zaihai had probably switched these on as well. The river had not dried up completely. Although the water level was extremely low, I could still hear the sound of the current. The dam's sluice gates were shut, and water retention had begun. Soon it would rise once more.

Ma Zaihai pointed toward a section of the darkness. "The filtration gate is over there. That's where I left our raft. I tied it real tight, so it should still be there."

"If we can take that raft to the surface, then consider your wish of becoming a deputy squad leader granted," I said. And what if the raft is gone? I said to myself. Then we'll just wade right out of here, even if it means courting death.

There wasn't much time to think about it. We discussed for a moment how best to reach the warehouse. We decided we should find a ladder and climb down the outer wall. Just as we were about to set out, Ma Zaihai suddenly hissed, "Look over there!"

He hurried over to the river side of the dam. "What is it?" I asked.

"Someone's there!"

I looked where he was pointing. A flashlight beam was moving swiftly through the darkness. Someone was hurrying across the plank-and-wire walkway.

"Who is it?" asked Wang Sichuan.

Ma Zaihai looked out anxiously. "I don't know, but he's heading for the raft."

"Shit!" We all knew this was bad. One flashlight. One person all on his own. Was it the spy? Had he gotten what he wanted and was he now preparing to make a stealthy exit? There was no time to assess the situation. We had to catch him, regardless of whether he was a friend or an enemy. Before I could say anything, Ma Zaihai and Wang Sichuan had already rushed off and begun climbing down a riverside ladder.

This side of the dam had neither a strong wind nor a bottomless abyss. We flew down the rungs. At the bottom of the dam, the walkway extended in all directions. We couldn't see where he'd gone. Just as we were hesitating, sharp-eyed Wang Sichuan saw a flashlight beam up ahead, about fifteen hundred feet away.

"After him!" I cried, but he pulled me back.

"We have no weapons. If it is the spy and he's carrying an automatic rifle, then, head to head, we're no match for him."

"So what do we do?" I hurriedly asked.

"We have to take him out in one blow." Wang Sichuan was very calm as he spoke. "Listen, this isn't a joke. Our adversary is a spy, a cold-blooded killer. You're a technical specialist, and Little Ma is an engineering corpsman. Neither of you have real battle experience. This is no time to be rash."

I was enraged. "What battle have you been in?"

"I may have never been to war, but by five I was riding horses with my dad. By fifteen, my friends and I were heading into the mountains to hunt wolves. When we Mongolians were kids, our games were all life-and-death. You're just not going to be as strong as us." He paused to look out at the flashlight beam, then continued: "This is a hunt, and our sole advantage is that it's three of us against one of him. We'll have to divide the responsibilities: one person will divert his attention, one will knock his rifle away, and the last will subdue him. Old Wu, being the smallest, will distract him, I'll take care of knocking his gun away, and then, in that instant, you, Little Ma, will make a surprise attack."

"But you don't have a gun," I said. "How are you going to knock his away?"

Wang Sichuan looked around for something to throw, but there was nothing atop the walkway. He reached into the water and hauled up a thighbone from within one of the submerged gunnysacks. "The Mongolian grasslands are just as empty as here," he said, "but so long as one's skills are great, anything can become a weapon."

Seeing his stance as he hefted the thighbone, I knew he was preparing to throw the *bulu*. "Why not just smack him across the head with it and knock him over?" I asked.

"Not possible," he said. "See for yourself."

Looking over at the swinging beam, I understood what he meant. There wasn't enough light. All we could see of the person was the area just around his flashlight.

"That's why you have to make him open fire—so that I know where his gun is."

I ordinarily had a lot of confidence in his skill, but this was all or nothing. "No way," I said. "We're just gambling on your *bulu* toss. What happens if you miss?"

"Don't speak such nonsense," said Wang Sichuan. "Keep hesitating and that son of a bitch will get away. You want to be trapped here forever?"

I looked up. The light beam had stopped moving. I knew we had no choice but to roll the dice. I nodded.

The three of us turned off our flashlights and continued cautiously, taking cover wherever we could find it. We quickly drew close to the source of the flashlight beam, and our quarry came into view. He was less than thirty feet away, wearing a Japanese military uniform, and moving things into the oxskin raft. The man appeared on alert. He kept looking all around. Then we saw the film canister. It was already in the raft. I crouched behind several gunnysacks, revealing only the top half of my head as I watched. He was wearing a gas mask. I swore. Even now he still wouldn't reveal his identity.

Wang Sichuan gave me a glance and motioned noiselessly. You draw his attention, he was saying, while Ma Zaihai dives underwater. I nodded. He prepared to hurl the *bulu*. Then, just as Wang

Sichuan was about to signal, the man suddenly stopped what he was doing and looked around in alarm, as if he'd noticed something. Wang Sichuan and I ducked back down at once. This guy's alert as hell, I said to myself. He really is a professional spy. We waited a long time, then looked back out. His movements had sped up. Clearly he was afraid.

Wang Sichuan made no more movements and gave us only a glance. Ma Zaihai immediately dove underwater. Straining my eyes, I watched as he swam under the raft. He was ready. Wang Sichuan nodded to me. Taking a deep breath, I muttered a mental "Buddha preserve us," then ran out, roaring madly, "Don't move!"

Immediately the flashlight beam was on me. I made it two steps before he opened fire, the bullet whizzing past my head. That's not good, I thought. That bullet was way too close, and he probably couldn't even see me yet. This son of a bitch really knows his way around a gun. Instinctively, I rolled to the ground. Two streaks of flame flew past where I had just been standing. One second later and I would have been toast. Luckily Wang Sichuan was no slouch himself. A moment after I hit the dirt, I heard the characteristic hollow smash of the *bulu*. This had to be his most powerful throwing style—the one he said was used to take down wild oxen. Then came a series of noises followed by a splash. I knew we'd done it. Leaping to my feet, I sprinted toward the noise.

Water splashed in all directions. Wang Sichuan must have already jumped in. I was about to do the same when I saw the black iron film canister. It was sitting magnificently on the floor of the raft. I stepped into the raft and grabbed it, then picked up the burning-hot rifle and aimed it at the water. It was two against one and Wang Sichuan was there. They wouldn't need me. Safeguarding the data seemed more important.

The water roiled for some time. Ma Zaihai's head was first to emerge, but then he went back under. With everyone twisted together, there was no way I could determine who was who. I didn't dare fire. After tossing and turning for who knows how long, the water suddenly went still. With a thump Ma Zaihai climbed into the raft, his mouth wide and gasping for breath. I very nearly smashed him with the butt of the rifle before I saw who it was. "What happened?" I asked him, but he couldn't say a thing, just panted so hard it seemed he might die. When I went to help him up, he didn't have the strength to even take my hand.

After several seconds Wang Sichuan popped out of the water as well. With his great big lungs, he was barely panting. Paddling in every direction, he looked around. The water was calm. I shined my flashlight across it. There was nothing to see.

"Goddamn it," Wang Sichuan swore. "He got away! Do you have the goods?"

I raised the iron canister. Shaking his head, he climbed into the raft and pulled Ma Zaihai to his feet. "If only we hadn't eased up in the end, a merit citation would have been ours for sure."

I stared down at the pitch-black surface of the water. Somewhere, I knew, there was a pair of eyes staring right back at us. Looking over at Ma Zaihai, I could tell from his expression how much he wanted to get out of here. "What now?" he asked. "Should we just set out directly?"

To tell you the truth, upon seeing the raft, my only desire was to leave at once. I could barely consider anything else. I nodded. "Screw it," I said. "For the safety of the film, I think we should head back right away."

Ma Zaihai was overjoyed and began hauling in the anchor. I looked over at Wang Sichuan. He remained stock-still. My heart thumped and I looked straight at him. "What is it?" I asked. Did he still want to wait for Old Tang and the others? The situation had changed. Our plans had to as well. I knew leaving them like this was an irresponsible move, but with such a great excuse in my hands, I couldn't bring myself to worry too much about it. Wang Sichuan's sense of justice was too strong. Did we always have to do the heroic thing?

His expression was a little odd. He hesitated for a moment, then spoke. "I was just thinking about whether we should first head back to the projection hall."

"The projection hall?" said Ma Zaihai in amazement. "What do you want to go back there for?"

Wang Sichuan tipped his head toward the iron canister. "If we just hand this thing off to our superiors, we'll probably never in our whole lives know what's on it."

We looked at one another. And then I understood. "What you're saying is that thirty or forty years from now, might we not regret heading back straight away? That just maybe, in only a couple of hours, we could be privy to the most incredible thing in human history."

EPILOGUE

I nodded in response to Wang Sichuan's idea.

We reached the projection room two hours later and started up the projector. The film began to roll. To this day I still don't know whether we made the right decision, but I do know that whenever I think of what I saw in that room, my blood runs cold.

ABOUT THE AUTHOR

 With over a million subscribers to his microblog and five million books sold, Xu Lei is one of China's most popular and highest-grossing novelists. Born in 1982, he was inspired by his parents' travel stories to write fanciful tales about tomb raiders, which he then posted online. The series became Secrets of a Grave Robber, which now boasts eight volumes in print, three of which have been published in English. *Search for the Buried Bomber*, the first book in the Dark Prospects series, was hailed as China's most spectacular suspense novel of 2010. Xu Lei currently lives in Hangzhou, China.

Printed in Great Britain
by Amazon.co.uk, Ltd.,
Marston Gate.